THE CLASSIC WESTERN NOVELS OF ALAN LeMAY . . .

By Dim and Flaring Lamps

Missouri was a lawless place during The War Between the States. But Shep Daniels had a war of his own to fight . . .

"Again LeMay proves himself a master."
—*Houston Chronicle*

The Unforgiven

Survival was always a struggle in the Texas Panhandle. But now the Zachary family is fighting for its life against an unexpected enemy . . .

"This is how it must have been . . . this is the book about Indians and whites to read!"
—*Jessamyn West*

The Searchers

Mart Pauley had watched the Comanches destroy his home as a child. But this time he's a man—and he intends to get even . . .

"Charged with emotion and the feel of the land!"
—*New York Times*

D0424084

BY DIM AND FLARING LAMPS

ALAN Le MAY

BERKLEY BOOKS, NEW YORK

BY DIM AND FLARING LAMPS

A Berkley Book/published by arrangement with
HarperCollins Publishers, Inc.

PRINTING HISTORY
Harper & Row edition/May 1962
Popular Library edition/April 1963
Berkley edition/June 1994

All rights reserved.
Copyright © 1962 by Alan LeMay.
This book may not be reproduced in whole or in part, by mimeograph or any other means, without permission.
For information address: HarperCollins Publishers, 10 E. 53rd St., New York, New York 10022.

ISBN: 0-425-14254-X

BERKLEY®
Berkley Books are published by
The Berkley Publishing Group, 200 Madison Avenue, New York, New York 10016.
BERKLEY and the "B" design are trademarks of Berkley Publishing Corporation.

PRINTED IN THE UNITED STATES OF AMERICA

10 9 8 7 6 5 4 3 2 1

BY DIM AND
FLARING
LAMPS

★ 1 ★

During the afternoon the bone-chilling February rain let up, and the sky broke into drifting scud, with patches of clean blue showing through. For the first time since the morning melt the air cleared of its everlasting mizzle, and Missouri's lowland wilderness took on the colors of different kinds of smoke. In the flooded swamp tangles, where bobcats and the last of the Missouri black bears usually found shelter, the baldy cypress, ash, tupelo, and thorny water locust were the shineless black of wet soot, close by, or the blue of blown smoke far off. And between the swamps, on the rich dirt of scattered clearings, last year's unharvested cotton crop stood in shallow floodwater, ragged, rain-beaten, like dirty brown smoke unable to rise.

Often a lonely chimney stood among a small wreckage of charred timbers beside these fields; and sometimes, faintly seen above distant woods, real smoke rose lazily and floated for a while, where yet another farmstead smoldered. Abolitionist Jayhawkers from Bloody Kansas did that, secessionists said, on their murderous raids. No, rebel night riders did it, killing off Union sympathizers in the name of slavery, said the North. Neither view made sense. These remote plantings were inaccessible to Jayhawkers, for Kansas was far away; and there never had been enough Unionists among these pro-slavery farmers to serve as victims for all the burning and killing there had been.

In those early days of 1861 much had already happened. Seven Southern states had seceded; Missouri herself was about to elect delegates to a secession convention intended to

1

take Missouri out of the Union and put her unequivocally on the side of slavery. Yet, in spite of all, nobody really believed that there was going to be anything like a full-out war. In Missouri, at least, they didn't really need it, the way Missourians were tearing each other apart.

Shep Daniels, a long-boned young mule drover from Kentucky, kept turning in his saddle to look back. The wretched trace they were following wound and twisted through woods that shut off all view of what might be behind. Only the sky could have anything to tell him; and he was well satisfied to find even this empty of meaning for him, as he studied it now.

He was tailing a band of mixed draft stock, forty-odd head that he and his younger brother, Trapper Daniels, were trying to push to the shores of the Mississippi—out from among the deadly Missouri bushwhackers, out of a country where violence without restraint had made a shambles of the law. Far up ahead an eight-mule hitch pulled a work-sprained calf wagon, in which rode a bunch of mule foals too young to keep up. The harness mules, big but very tired, plodded steadily, heads swinging low, small hoofs finding no bottom in the muck, yet lifting half-bushels of gumbo with every step. The wagon was out of Shep's sight most of the time, but he could hear Trapper's characteristic mule-driving yell— "H-a-a-a! H-a-a-a!"—and the musket crash of his blacksnake whip, beyond the woods.

Behind the wagon, strung out for a winding furlong, trailed some twenty head of big brood mares, fine broad-backed stock of great power, but mostly heavy with foal. They would begin losing their foals pretty soon, now, as they neared total exhaustion. Behind the mares straggled a passel of yearling colts, big strapping youngsters, but untoughened; they were moving shakily, their long legs quivering. Some of these would not be able to follow much longer.

On chain-lead behind the wagon was one animal more—an enormous red-gold jack of fantastic height and bone, and not much substance else, so that he appeared to be built of pipe. This was the Jack of Diamonds, a young jack, but already proved as a sire of huge mules, and worth more, in the eyes of a muleman, than all the rest of the stuff here put together. He went stilting along, in strides of such great length they looked leisurely—the only brute in the whole cavalcade that was not in trouble.

At regular intervals, with a monotony of rhythm that was not his own, but controlled by the movement of the animals, Shep Daniels let his sixteen-foot blacksnake drift out, to close up the rearmost stragglers. It whispered, cracked, or popped like a pistol; sometimes the lash touched a stumbling yearling, with a stroke as gentle as the lick of a cat, but it never bit. Daniels was patiently, carefully trying to get the most out of their remaining strength, wasting no ounce of it by any needlessly quick move.

He had a hard time keeping his belly muscles from knotting up in an effort to lift them along by force of will. At the age of twenty-two Shep Daniels laid claim to fifteen years of experience in the handling of his father's mules—sometimes he called it twenty years' experience—and he had never seen heavier going in his life. No roads anywhere were more than barely passable, that rough, mean February of '61, and the mired track they were following through these inundated jungles could not be called a road at all. Every day it rained, maintaining a hub-deep stickum that could drag the very guts out of a team in a matter of rods. Every night it froze, turning puddles to glass, and churned mud to broken glass; and this footing was even worse than the mud, because it could lame a shoulder, bow a tendon, or quarter-crack a hoof. In the five days since they had plunged into the trace through this morass they had traveled a meager twenty-five miles of windings through the swamps much less than that as a crow would fly. All their built-in skill with horse and mule flesh had gone into the careful pacing of their livestock, to come this little way; yet half their animals were favoring lame and almost all near the limit of endurance.

Had they chosen to fork off to the north they could have got onto the Cape Girardeau plank road. Its planking was slippery and splintered with neglect, yet still so much better than what they were on that they should have reached the river in a day. Or they could have turned south, by longer but easier ways, and tried for Belmont, which was just across the river from Kentucky soil. But they had chosen the swamp traces between the two, a way so difficult that even the tough predatory bushwhackers might be expected to avoid it—or so they had hoped.

They knew now they had been wrong. Since yesterday afternoon they had been aware that somebody was behind them on the trace, and closing upon them by the hour. They had supposed this was Pap Daniels, fetching along a string of horses he had split off from them to pick up. He had expected to overtake them on the trail, and should have been with them before now. But early today, before the frost-cleared distances fogged up with rain, Shep had lagged a long way back to see how Pap was coming along; and he had found out it was not Pap and his horses in the trail behind.

From the top of a pin oak he had managed to get a fair look at the riders following them, where they straggled past a gap in the trees at something like a quarter of a mile. Shep counted fourteen riders; more might have passed the gap before he climbed to his lookout in the oak. Even at this distance he could see that they were heavily but unevenly armed; some of their weapons were carried crosswise of the saddlebows, as though too long-barreled for saddleboots. The horses were low-headed, and apparently laboring, pushed at the fastest plod they could be expected to maintain. That was almost all he could make out, but it was enough. Pretty plainly, what they had here was one of the many bands of marauders now ravaging the undefended land. They were the sort of people he had above all hoped to evade by taking to this flooded wilderness.

Yet, up to this point, a note of uncertainty remained. These freebooters liked to specialize in the easy pickoffs; the tenacity of this horse-killing swamp chase was not like them. Shep Daniels supposed they must have fooled themselves into expecting an easy capture, and now hung on out of stubbornness, having come so far on the way. For a moment Shep nursed a hope that they might still give up; they were gaining so slowly, inch by labored inch, they might not be able to close the few remaining miles before nightfall ended the short February day.

Then one more rider appeared, keeping the disordered straggle closed up to the rear. He sat straight and trim on a fine well-conditioned horse; and Shep would have recognized him from a long way farther off than he was. He knew then that this pursuit would not give up, or turn back, or fail to close while daylight lasted. And, though he would never have admitted it in words, he knew, as well as he would ever know it, that he was licked.

This isn't happening to me now, he told himself. *It happened to me a long time ago. . . .*

The start of it had been in the summer of 1860. Could that have been only a year ago? It was even less than that. June of 1860 was only nine months back.

★ 2 ★

On Tuesday, June 21, 1860, Shep Daniels stood on the St. Louis levee, at the stage plank of the little sidewheeler *Tealwing*, supervising the loading of five horses and forty-four huge young mules; and it seemed to Shep that he had never seen a prettier first day of summer in his life. All the long cobbled slope of the landing was aswarm with rousters, loading the close-ranked steamboats, and the riverport world was a world of sound. Bull-moan of boat whistles, clangor of bells, boom of barrels rolled down the stones, wheeze of steam. Rattle of a stage plank as the rousters went down its great springy length in the bouncing lope they called the coonjine. Big baritone voices in an improvised work song— "Swing them bunks o'black-eye peas—load me down, load me down!" Faster chatter of a white-wooled sing-boss, calling rhythm for a gang moving railroad iron—"Now go back an' git the other—you got the wrong one then! Now all pick it up, doo dah, doo dee, and you walk, walk, doo dee, doo dah, and you set it down, doo dee!" Crash went the iron and "Hiya-a-a-ay" rang the work chorus. . . .

Nothing anywhere on a mile of levee made a more heartening big-drum sound than Shep Daniels' whopping young mules, sent a few at a time up the plank to the pens on the *Tealwing*'s cargo deck. He had watched the same thing a hundred times before, but this loading was different, and so was this day and this year. Since the age of twelve he had traveled with his father and their livestock, always as stable hand, often as chief drover; many times—first when he was fourteen—he had handled whole trips by himself—a big

6

swing to pick up mules where they were, another big swing
to deliver them where they weren't. But this was his first trip
in charge of all their operations on the Missouri River, from
the Mississippi to St. Joe. He had his own stable hands to do
the work, he was free to make his own deals and trades—
though his father still owned the stock; and he had his new
clothes. Something close to exultation lifted him every time
his stiff collar gouged his sunburned neck, reminding him
that he was virtually his own man.

At twenty-one Shep was sometimes aware that he was
pretty rough around the edges. He didn't know how to wear
clothes, because he had seldom had any very good ones, and
his shock of hay-colored hair was rebellious to the comb.
When he wasn't thinking about it he was inclined to walk
with an awkward, slinging lurch, chiefly suitable for making
good time over rough ground. His formal education had been
obtained in a one-room schoolhouse, where a single school-
master taught all grades at once; and even this, since the age
of twelve, had been limited to those winter months when road
conditions made the movement of livestock impractical. In
general he was a whole lot more at home on the cargo deck
of a steamboat than on the upper decks where the quality
rode.

Still . . . he was better than six feet tall, all lean bone, and
stood as straight as a board, so that properly cut clothes hung
on him well enough, when he let them. He knew a great deal
that was not to be found in books about the horse and mule
trade, as carried on over most of Kentucky, Missouri, southern Indiana and Illinois, and parts of Arkansas and Tennessee.
He had a stockpen acquaintance with hundreds of mule users,
including a number of the great planters who were the power
and the glory of the Mississippi basin. A defensive mimicry
gave him a certain protective coloration among these latter,
and such basic manners as his mother had taught him made
him considerably more presentable than he himself would
have supposed.

He kept his sixteen-foot mule whip coiled in his hand, but
his boots were polished; he wore a well-made black suit, a
buckskin-colored vest, and a boiled shirt. His father, who

stood slightly in the background, trying hard to swallow all the advice that came to his mind, wore about the same kind of things, but looked rumpled, and faintly rusty, by comparison.

Pap Daniels was even bonier than Shep, but not nearly as tall. He seemed skimpily put together out of rawhide string and hickory slats, much warped and weathered. But there was an authority about him that lifted mules into the collar with half the lung power his sons required. When he angered, such fire jumped in his eyes that both men and critters got out of his way; and when he was in a hurry, any ordinary man could have been killed off by no more than trying to hang onto the tails of Pap's coat.

"I wish your ma had lived to see you," Pap said, almost plaintively. "You look slicker than a nickel's worth of hog jowl. And that's a solemn fact."

Actually, Pap would never wholly approve his son's present cultivated appearance. If he had had to visit a back-country customer in a fresh new rig like that, Pap would have worn the boiled shirt collarless, the band fastened with a brass collar button, imprinting a green spot on his sun-creased neck; and probably would have ridden a few miles with the pants under his saddle, to give himself at least a respectable fragrance of mules. And yet, at the same time, his wish that Shep's mother could have seen her son all curry-combed and flowered-out was sincere.

Shep's mother had come from Rosedale, Mississippi; her people down there claimed a distant, poor-relation connection with a distinguished Mississippi family named Shepardson, for whom Shep had been christened. The relationship had become more distant with each generation, and not even a remote contact with affluence had survived Ma's marriage to Pap Daniels. Yet, in a shabby-genteel sort of way, Ma had clung to her early dreams; to her, the mule had always been a species of brute that a gentleman might appraise, or purchase, but should never be seen actually handling.

With all his heart, Pap had wanted to give Ma a good life, the best anybody in the Mississippi Valley knew. He would have got it done, too, in some degree if he had not kept raising his sights to higher stakes. Plowing back every cent he could scrape into more mares—always for just one year more, and one year more—Pap had kept them about as mulepoor as anybody could possibly be. The Danielses were bigscale breeders now, rather than merely traders. Their little farm behind Paducah wasn't big enough for more than a holding yard, but Pap had developed a farm-out system; they had hundreds of brood mares, hundreds of mule colts, and scores of the biggest jacks the Mississippi Valley had ever seen, sprangled out all over parts of seven states. But he had tried too hard, for too much. Ma had not lived to see his plans bear fruit, so all his labors had come to nothing in the end.

Sad old man . . . pitiful old man, perhaps, if he had known it. He kept on now, going through the motions he had always made, telling himself that Ma would have wanted him to make real his dream, for the sake of Shep, and Trapper, the younger brother. . . .

"I believe, if I was doing it," Pap said now, "I'd carry the whole bunch right on to Ash Landing, and give Tyler Ashland his pick. Keeping holt of Tyler Ashland is the whole difference between profit and loss, on the Missouri River." He stopped himself. "But you're in charge. All that is up to you."

Pap Daniels was not sharing his son's exalted mood. He looked uncommonly grim, Shep thought, and he had an absent, distracted look that wasn't like him. Shep knew what he was worrying about, or thought he did. All hell was to pay in the back country of southern Missouri, where strong bands of night riders had for some time outpowered the law. The Danielses had a lot of livestock down there, strung out across a whole belt of counties they seldom visited more than once a year; most of it was well in range of the worst disorders. Reports of losses in some counties fitted in with an ominous silence from others. A lot of their mule raisers seemed to have disappeared off the face of the earth.

Shep said uneasily, "Pap, you sure you won't need me?"

"Trapper's going to met me with the horses, down at the end of the steam-car spur. He can ride up to the river and cut you off, if you're wanted." *He'll play hell,* Shep thought, but didn't argue. He dropped the possibility out of his mind.

Missouri's troubles went back some six years, to 1854, when neighboring Kansas voted on whether it was to be slave or free. Pro-Southern Missouri watched with deep concern, convinced that if abolition could expand and slavery could not, the Southern way of life would soon stand at bay. Then, at the eleventh hour, the outcome was predecided by a butt-in from far away. Into Kansas poured a sudden flood of abolitionist settlers, armed and sent west by the hastily formed Massachusetts Emigrant Aid Society. To Missourians, this brazen strong-arming of a free election seemed an open act of war. Such respected Unionists as Tyler Ashland himself were among the partisans who galloped into Kansas, sworn to run the Damnyankees home if they could or exterminate them if they had to. Over and over Missouri raiders rode the Kansas prairies, shooting and burning. . . . Yet the Kansas settlers stood fast.

Inevitably, perhaps, the violent measures frustrated in Kansas turned inward upon Missouri itself. Pro-Southern hotheads took the saddle to clear their own state of the minority who opposed them. Proslavery secessionists and proslavery Unionists turned on each other; feudists took saddle to avenge the victims. Finally, outlaws of no principles at all, like the James boys and the Younger brothers, rode unprosecuted, killing and plundering in the name of any Cause that came handy. Nobody was safe any more, no matter what his politics might be.

Politically, the Danielses carried no special torch for any faction. Their self-interest was with the mule, a critter unaware of any line between slave and free. And Pap was an honest trader; he backed every deal they made, at whatever loss, so that all over Missouri a scattering of people could be found to swear that the Danielses were all right. Up to here they had seemed immune to bushwhacker depredations.

Evidently they were not immune any more. "Don't see how to handle such a damn thing," Pap complained, sounding fretful. "How do you take a man's work team away—his crop in the ground, and all—on the theory he might get robbed, sometime?"

"Don't worry so much," Shep said. "We can do without that whole God-forsaken wilderness if we have to."

His father looked him over sidelong, with a cold and weary eye. The Danielses never did carry any substantial reserve of uncommitted funds. They had pyramided an enormous potential for producing draft teams, but it was a kind of thing hard to raise quick money on. If the southern counties were in as bad a shambles as rumor made out, the wrong brick might very easily be pulled out of the whole far-flung structure Pap had built. He had to go in there and see. But—

"Maybe" was all he said now.

Something in the sound of that one word awoke Shep's occupational wariness, as if an alarm bell had been softly tapped; so softly he wasn't sure he had heard it at all. Now that he noticed it, there was a peculiar look in Pap's eyes, one he had almost never seen there before. Not an expression, exactly; more of an emptiness of expression, a somber lightlessness that even seemed to make his shoulders sag when they did not.

"You feel all right?" Shep asked. "Maybe two teaspoons of soda in a cup of hot water—"

"Oh, no, no—I'm fine." The remedy was one the old man sometimes took for a number of ills he lumped together as the bellyache, but his failure to get mad at his son for suggesting it was a bad sign.

"There's something you're not telling me," Shep said.

Pap drew a deep breath and seemed about to answer, but there was an interruption. The last three mules were at the top of the stage plank, hesitating over setting foot to the forecastle deck. Up in the pilothouse Captain Jim Sam Delorme had been watching the loading; and now, for no reason whatever, he reached for the whistle cord, his big bearded face impassive, and let go with such a blast as should have shattered the cobbles. The three mules whirled, as the old scoundrel must have known they would do, to bolt down the plank for the shore.

Shep's long whip licked out—one, two, three—and each

mule in turn stopped short as the snapperlash exploded louder than a forty-four, inches in front of his nose. Three times more it cracked, just to one side of each nose, this time. The mules turned back and went aboard.

A scatter of passengers along the rail of the boiler deck promenade broke into spontaneous applause. Astonished, Shep looked up, and at once saw Julie Delorme, looking very trim, and made eye-catching before all others by the expensive plainness of her traveling outfit. He had seen her often, for she was much aboard her father's steamboats, and though they had never spoken, he had known who she was for a long time. She smiled at him, as their eyes met, and patted her white gloves together in a silent pantomime of applause. Taken off balance, he made no acknowledgment, until Pap raised his hat; when Shep gave his hatbrim an impersonal tug, without looking up there any more.

Pap grumbled something into his mustache about not knowing *she* was going to be aboard. "There's Jim Sam's girl up there," he said.

"Never noticed," Shep shrugged it off.

"Well, she notices you. There's one I wouldn't fool around with much, boy."

Pap gave little heed to what Shep was up to on his own time, but one thing he would not stand for was any messing around with the womenfolk of business connections, of whatever kind or status. Shep said crossly, "You know me better than that! I never so much as stood on the same deck with her in my life!"

"You will now," Pap told him. Then, with a strange gentleness: "I didn't mean it like you think. It's only—if you was to bust blind headlong into something . . . like a June buzzle bashing into a torch basket . . . I believe I'd feel it was my fault more'n it was yourn. We're still working on our first million, son."

"You started to tell me something," Shep insisted.

"Forget it. It wasn't anything." Pap shook himself into action. "Hup, now!" he ordered, as to a mule. "Good luck, and keep your powder dry!"

He banged his hard old paw on Shep's back with a power

that started him bodily up the plank and pretty well dispelled any question as to the state of Pap's health. Then he turned and went up the levee with his reaching, clodhopper stride, never glancing back. And Shep went aboard, to his mules.

There's something else, he was thinking. *Something's bothering him he wouldn't tell me.* It made him uneasy, Pap had always been so all-fired near impossible to scare.

★ 3 ★

Shep Daniels' new clothes changed his way of life with great suddenness, and far beyond anything he had expected of them; and he began finding it out in his first ten minutes aboard. He went straight to the main deck stockpens, meaning to change into the butternuts he always wore around the livestock, but his new canvas "telescope" suitcase wasn't in his tack pile. He had to go hunting for it on the upper deck, feeling most God-awful conspicuous as he tried to walk naturally among the first-class passengers. He seemed to stick out of his new rig too far, here and there, as it fitted in some positions but not in others. He knew everybody was staring, yet he couldn't catch anybody so much as glancing at him; he couldn't see how they did it. And presently he found out, with a shock, that he had been installed in a first-class stateroom, about as expensive as there was on the boat.

Pap hadn't raised him to even consider the possibility of such a waste of money. Like the time Shep had wanted to buy a cheap watch. Pap had a watch, a gold hunting-case affair, fat as a beaten biscuit; he had won it in a trotting race, once. Shep, as eldest son, would inherit it, when Pap passed on. Pap said stiffly that a man must be insane to buy a watch when he had a good one coming anyway, sometime. What was wrong with the sun? Even on the cloudiest days a man who couldn't read the sun couldn't tell time at all. "What'll I do on cloudy nights?" Shep objected. "Go to bed," Pap recommended.

A stubborn campaign to get his baggage transferred to the cargo got him no place. "Cap'n say" was all he could get out

14

of the chief steward. It finally turned out that Jim Sam Delorme was deadheading him. Something about the mules going to Tyler Ashland . . .

And next thing he learned was that he was also expected to eat with the passengers. Always before, in the days he had slept on the cargo, he had climbed the after-ladder to the galley, where they had handed him a tin basin heaped with side meat, greens, and black-eyed peas, the same as the rousters. But now, if he applied at the galley in his butternut dungarees, he was told they wasn't let to eat him there, he'd have to git et up fo'ard with the other gemmens. This forced him to a good many scrub-ups, but it was worth it. A whole new world opened up, and it happened to be Julie Delorme's world—or the outer fringe of it.

Up to here Shep Daniels had always looked forward to winter, which was their off-season; they never tried to move much livestock then. He could often get away to go trapping, or wild-hog hunting, or anything he felt like, for weeks at a time. He got as cold and wet in these pursuits as if he had been at work, but he had been out in every kind of weather so much of his life that he never thought about that. To him, summer had always been a time when a man toiled endlessly under damp heat, while dawns came early and darkness late. Even then, of course, the job of stableboy was a lot more fun on the rivers than on the roads or at home; but what with the stockpens mostly being set up next to the boilers, which somehow not only radiated hell's own heat but cut off all the breeze, and the chaff that kept sifting down your neck to cling to your streaming hide, Shep had never realized what life aboard the packets could be like.

Ashore the muggy heat of mid-country dog days might be abuzz with mosquitoes by night and flies by day, but a cool breeze almost always stirred on the rivers, or if it didn't, the travel of the steamboat made a breeze of its own. So there were no flies to speak of and no mosquitoes in the long twilights, when the fireflies lighted up the lowland woods along the inlets. Even on nights when people in the little towns sat rocking and slapping on their front sidewalks until after midnight, rather than smother under netting in their clapboard ovens, the lace-trimmed upper decks were pleasant with cool airs. He hadn't known what river travel was while he lived with the mules.

And there was Julie Delorme . . .

He was afraid of her at first, though he wasn't shy of girls as such; hadn't been since he had begun running Pap's river errands on his own, at the age of fourteen. The river towns had a good many women who took the air on the sloping, cobbled landings as dusk came on, and they were of a kind whose sex and its uses were no more embarrassing to a farmboy than the standing of a jack to a mare. But here there were other factors.

Pap's remark about their first million hadn't been needed. Only a little while ago, within the memory of living men, this rich river basin had been a deadly wilderness and men had been rated by their ability to survive. But the wilderness was overcome, and now great sudden fortunes were being made. Money was the new scoreboard, the scale for measuring both power and success. Senators and governors spoke courteously to it; small men stood twisting their greasy old hats in front of it. Even Southern pride of blood had to lean on it, for it made the difference between an aristocratic planter and his sharecropping first cousin, to whom he never spoke. Shep was acutely aware that Julie Delorme was the daughter of great wealth. The *Tealwing* was almost the least of the twelve or fifteen steamboats Jim Sam owned, which included some of the finest packets in the Mississippi trade; along with an unknown amount of property ashore.

And there was something else. Julie was not only rich, but the daughter of an overpowering legend besides. Captain Jim Sam Delorme came from well-to-do St. Louis people, well-connected in New Orleans, but he had run off up the wild Missouri in his early teens. His family thought he would get enough of the river in a hurry, but he did not. He was a pilot on the dangerous Upper River at nineteen and a "lightning" pilot in 1831—the year Pierre Chouteau reached a new head of navigation at Fort Union.

Jim Sam Delorme's people, originally an offshoot of old Louisiana Creole stock, had appeared in St. Louis more than three-quarters of a century before, in a condition of extreme indigence, which they swiftly remedied.

St. Louis had been a wild scramble of a town when they first came, overrun by adventurers among whom the Delormes proved well able to hold their own. They got into fur handling in a small way, then in a big way, later spreading out into warehousing, waterfront properties, merchandising, and banking; their initial indigence was long since forgotten. The Delormes had had their duelists, their rakes, and their freeplunging gamblers in the early years. It was as they rose to wealth that they became sedate, conservative, and cherishing of their position, until now the old wild days were not referred to in the family any more. Jim Sam's childhood was spent in an atmosphere of courtly dignity, patterned after that of the older New Orleans aristocracy.

He proved to have a natural gift for handling steamboats, as shown in his uncommon talent for "flanking"—a matter of drifting crosswise on a fast current to negotiate otherwise impossible turns.

The mountain boats took over a monopoly of the rich Northwest fur trade, and Jim Sam was swept along as the river came into its great days. The steamboats stacked up on shifting sandbars, they burned, they snag-ripped and went down. But the turbulent Missouri trade was not only opening a million miles of the Northwest, it was supplying the great overland trails to a newly building nation upon the Pacific. The high returns drew a savage competition, in which the toughest rivermen on earth struggled with a thousand miles of treacherous waters, hordes of hostile Sioux, and each other. The men who fought their way to command of such a trade were bound to become great legendary figures—and Jim Sam was one.

In legend Jim Sam was shaggy, cobble-fisted, and moved like the front end of a horse, but he wasn't like that now. He was courtly of manner, well-combed, and in the hands of downriver tailors. He almost never went to the head of navigation any more. Only when he sometimes seized the wheel in a vicious crossing could still be seen resemblances to the fire-eyed and bellowing king of ruffians he was supposed to have been. Sometimes Shep wondered if Jim Sam had really been more remarkable than many others, who had not ended as legends but merely as seedy old men whom nobody wanted to hear anything from or about. Hundreds of other bullyboys as reckless and hard-fighting must have hunted fortune on the Upper Missouri, with this difference: Jim Sam had found it, and Julie glowed in its light.

And on top of everything else, Delorme had to be the brother-in-law of Tyler Ashland, the one customer above all others who must never be ruffled or unfavorably impressed.

⋆ 4 ⋆

JULIE SPOKE TO SHEP ON HIS FIRST DAY ABOARD. "WHEN ARE you going to teach me to crack a whip like you can?" she asked him.

Now, what would *she* want to crack a whip for? "Beg pardon, mam?"

"Don't you want to teach me?"

He decided it must be an obscure pleasantry, signifying nothing. Couldn't be anything else. "It will be a pleasure, mam," he said, with grave courtesy; and never thought of it again. His whole intention was to remain respectfully aloof, satisfied to admire her from a distance, as a creature upon another plane. And doubtless he would have been allowed to do exactly that, had Julie been of typical raising, in some Southern plantation's Great House.

Julie had been born in a Great House—one of two at Ash Landing; but she had been left motherless at two or three and her father never remarried. After the loss of his wife, Felicity, Jim Sam couldn't stand the Great House any more. He still maintained it, in pretense that it was his residence; but he lived mostly aboard his boats, keeping his daughter with him, in the charge of a most singular slave woman called Caleese. Winters Julie went to school, still in the charge of Caleese, in the time-honored Ursuline Convent, at New Orleans. But all summer long they rode the rivers; and whether Julie knew it or not, a child with virtually the run of a great floating palace, forever opening up a new world around every bend, was probably the luckiest child on earth.

By the time Julie could walk, Felicity was keeping mostly

to her bed. Here Julie was brought at dutiful intervals, to be briefly shown; but mother and daughter had no meaning for each other. As for Jim Sam, he sometimes patted his daughter's cheek, with what he imagined was a proper fatherliness, but without actually seeing her. Then, when Julie was two and a half, a small pointless occurrence led Jim Sam to notice her for the first time. And though it didn't amount to anything as an event, in the upshot it changed the shape of Julie's life, and Jim Sam's as well; and in the long run even worked out to raise hell with Shep.

Once, deep in a black night through which he had kept the wheel, Jim Sam had tried to tell what had happened, and to explain the profound effect it had had upon him. He couldn't do it. The whole thing somehow eluded him, turning into such drivel when he talked about it that he never mentioned it again.

This thing he tried to tell, and could not, had happened as he was tying up at home, after a trip of evil exasperations. The green crew had somehow managed an unlikely fouling of the mooring lines, suitable for carrying away either paddle wheel or a rudder. Have your choice, or hold out for both. Jim Sam threw up a window in the texas, with intent to holler them all dead in a heap, but the presence of ladies on the landing balked him. He started down to admonish the blunderers by hand.

He had not seen Caleese carry Julie aboard; but as he whirled from the window, a little face appeared around the doorjamb, and said, "Pee-eek!"

At this point, that one time he tried to tell it, Jim Sam suddenly felt helplessly silly; but he blundered on. . . . His mindless reaction, damned well fit to be tied like he was, had come out in such a yell of fury as shook the timbers. "WHAT—" He never remembered what he had started to holler. Terror transformed the baby face—he saw that plain enough—and that was the instant that knocked the wind out of Jim Sam, leaving him in a jelly. Then the child fled, too scared to squall.

Julie was in the wide-eyed stage of innocence in which almost any infant animal is appealing. "Like a little pig. Like a new-hatched egg. I mean chickling. I mean chick, damn it. . . . Like a baby filly," he groped to explain it. In an absurd gesture, he bent to indicate something about a foot off the deck. "There was this little punkin-faced smile—only about so high—"

Something he could not even try to convey was the glow of happy excitement he had seen in the little face. Or rather, he saw it afterward, in retrospect, somehow imprinted in memory, without having seen it at all in the moment it was there.

He went after her, and picked her up, trying to comfort her; and soon Julie was crying, but her face buried in his beard, and her arms around his neck. Caleese appeared and tried to take her, but Jim Sam carried his baby around the boat for an hour. "It's a wonder I didn't bust out bawling myself," he lamely trailed off. "I don't reckon I'll ever get it out of my damned head. That little face . . ." He shut up, feeling ridiculous. Worst mushhead carryings-on he ever heard tell. No way to explain such a damn thing, apparently, without you lived it yourself. But one thing, there, was true. Even after he heard how foolish it sounded, as he told it, it stuck forever in his mind. It made a rebuff to his child impossible, though she glued onto him at every opportunity, worshiping him as if he were God.

She was now eighteen, two years beyond the marriageable age for Southern belles, and why she wasn't married by this time was a mystery to Shep, until he knew Jim Sam better. Probably no father ever sees a young man good enough to marry his daughter, and Jim Sam Delorme was in a better position than most to put off losing his daughter to a nincompoop. But his days of resistance were numbered—he could see it himself; and this year he had retreated to the smaller, slower, less luxurious boats of his Missouri River Line for a possible last stand. These carried more freight than passengers, and the callow squirts (as Jim Sam saw them) of the Delta aristocracy never rode them at all. Most of the time Shep Daniels was the only young bachelor aboard.

He stayed clear of Julie the rest of that first day, and part of another, but from there on he could find no way to manage it without seeming openly rude. Julie did not know he was acting under instructions—she would have laughed at the whole idea if she had. She supposed him to be absurdly shy. After all those summers on the packets she knew how to put even a Kentucky muleboy at his ease; and now she went to work on him.

"I don't believe you remember me at all," she began.

"Mam?"

"A long time ago—I must have been only about twelve years old—you used to make this run once in a while with your father. Only, you stayed down in the stockpens the whole while. Slept in the bedding straw, apparently. I used to come down and try to talk to you, but you paid me no mind. You don't remember that, do you?"

"Well—kind of—I guess."

"I used to think you were wonderful. It took Caleese half the winter to break me of walking just like you did."

"Aw, now, wait a minute!"

"Here—I'll show you. This is exactly the way you walked then." She took a turn on the deck in front of him, taking great wide-lurching, oopsy-daisy strides, arms swinging stiff from the shoulders except when she stopped, bent-kneed and with a stupid look, to cock her head and scratch it. Shep stared blank-faced for a moment before he decided it was all right for him to laugh.

"Before that," Julie said, "Caleese had to break me of walking like my father. Like this—" She stuck out both her stomach and her jaw, folded her hands behind her, and stamped along the deck high-kneed, like a hackney. "Now do you believe me?"

"I believe every word you say," he promised her.

"See you remember that."

Captain Delorme watched Shep sharply for a few days, but apparently decided he was harmless, at least under the stony eyes of the strange, tall, gaunt Caleese. Shep was always puzzled by Caleese, for he had never seen any other slave woman anything like her. The Delormes probably knew where she came from, but nobody else seemed to know what her past had been. She must have been a quadroon, or perhaps an octoroon, for she was almost straight-haired and no darker than a new saddle. She spoke, besides English, French, Spanish and Gullah; but only in the ominous-sounding Gullah, which is full of African fragments, could Shep hear anything of the Negro in her speech. Being assigned to Julie, she ordinarily would have been called Mammy, but her high-bridged nose, without prominence of chin, gave her a hawk-like, forbidding look, and this, along with something baleful in her green-gray eyes, made the term preposterous. She preferred to be called Tia Caleese, tia meaning aunt in Spanish, and sometimes identified herself as Julie's duenna. The rest of the slaves were afraid of her.

Caleese was in the background, silent but forever lurking, wherever Julie might be, and for a while Shep was bothered by this faintly spooky, black-garbed presence. But not Julie; she wasn't inhibited by it in the least.

"You're much improved," she told Shep. "How come I was so invisible when you were a muleboy? You seem to see me all right, now."

"Well, shucks, heck, you're a girl, now."

"What did you think I was before, a small boy?"

"Well—about the same thing, virtually."

"No difference at all between a girl and a small boy, huh?"

"Well . . . to all purposes . . . and speakin' in reference to the top-minnow stage . . . is there?"

"I only know what you tell me about these things," she said. "And now I come to think of it, I have some questions to ask."

Oh, no, you don't. Not again. He had been watching Caleese out of the corner of his eye, to see if she would interfere with this drift, but she seemed to brood upon distances. "Thought I heard a mule bust loose, down below," he said. He had already found out that Julie loved to upset him with remarks that would not have bothered him if any other girl had made them but that shocked and scandalized him coming from her. He started for the main deck stairs, in shameless retreat.

Julie giggled. "You come back here! I'll be good, now.

You're exactly the color of a ripe strawberry—you know that, don't you? It's very becoming."

"What was the question?" he demanded.

"Well ... I know young ladies aren't supposed to ask things like this. But—What makes a duck float?"

Jackassed again, by God. I don't know how she does it. "I ought to paddle you!" he told her.

"I know."

Sometimes, when he wasn't with Julie, he worried about his father, and the stickery thing there was that he couldn't figure out why. Looking back, it sifted down to nothing but a look in the old man's yes. *If Pap's going to leave me on the hook, he at least might give me something to get my teeth into,* he thought unreasonably. *Never saw that look before, short of a death in the family. We lose mules all the time. Most years come out bad in one place, good in another. This year it happens to be Missouri, that's all. By God, if something's happened to Trapper, and he's keeping it from me, I'm going to murder him, so help me. Hell, nothing ever happens to Trapper. Trapper happens to other people, I'm just fidgety. . . .*

She stood close in front of him, and lightly touched his cheeks with the fingers of both hands. "Why don't you grow a nice big beard? Like my father's?"

"How'd you know us apart?"

"I'd know."

The position in which she stood made it inevitable that his hands go around her waist, but she squirmed away.

"Let go. Go put your grimy hands on Caleese—she'll be here any sec." He was surprised into sneaking a quick look at his hands, to see if they actually were grimy—they had so often been so. She smiled at that, but made her next words sound innocent.

"I don't have any corsets on," she explained.

Corsets! Mentioned to a *man*? The word alone would have brought a shriek of horror from the Old Ladies' Deckchair Brigade, which would have considered her to be discussing the exploration of her anatomy. And the devil of it was, that was about it. The absence of her customary whalebone armor had made her seem to his hands as if she had nothing on at all. "What kind of iron man do you think I am?"

"That's just what I can't make out."

And there he stood, knocked speechless again, by a bit of nonsense that could not have ruffled him in the slightest coming from any other girl on earth.

I wonder where Pap is. The telegraph runs down as far as Rolla. Wouldn't you think he'd let me know what's happening down there? No. Why should he? Never did before. Doesn't matter a damn where he is; nothing I can do about it from up here, anyway. I sure don't know what keeps fretting me like this. . . .

Lazily, the *Tealwing* paddled up the current, taking two weeks to make Jefferson City, the little tree-shaded, country-town capital of Missouri, which most of the fast Delorme packets would have made from St. Louis in three days. Shep had time to get used to the haunting shadow of Caleese. She seemed to serve chiefly as a reassurance to Jim Sam, rather than any sort of barrier, and thus was a necessary element in the circumstance that Shep and Julie were now much together, at a time when he could never have tracked manure across the Delormes' pillared portico at all. He got used to his new clothes except for the sleeves, which continued to seem too long when he stood up and too short when he sat down.

And he got used to Julie, who knew how to keep him at ease when she felt like it, which was most of the time. If she had caught him picking his nose, she would probably have been game to pick her own, to cover up for him. Flustering him was so easy for her that the temptation to turn him strawberry-colored, at virtually the snap of her fingers, was sometimes irresistible; but even these sorties had the advantage of giving their relationship a frisky sense of intimacy, unjustified by length of acquaintance. And presently it began to dawn on Shep how sorry he would be when this trip was done.

Then, at Jefferson City, Shep's brother appeared on the landing, all unexpected, and rode aboard; and he brought with him more puzzlement in one hunk than Shep had tripped over before in his life.

✶ 5 ✶

TRAPPER DANIELS TROTTED HIS LIVELY MORGAN UP THE *Tealwing*'s stage plank, slipping and chicken-footing, in the last moments before it was hauled up. On the main deck forecastle the animal slid to a stop in a seated position on the planking; so Trapper calmly dismounted by no more than standing up, letting on that the maneuver had been on purpose.

Shep's younger brother was eighteen, not as tall as Shep but compact and very supple. His resemblance to Shep was not great. His eyes were a bright, sharp blue and his hair very light in contrast to Shep's haylike thatch. His fair skin tanned evenly, without freckles, to the color of a toasted biscuit, except for his forehead, which was always white where his hatband protected it. As a small boy, which wasn't so long ago, his bright-cheeked rosiness had earned him the nickname of Peaches and made a willing, even joyful fighter out of him for life. He had not, of course, been christened "Trapper." He had a couple of other names, but considered them too fancy for earthly use, so had renamed himself at the age of seven, when he took up muskrat catching, and had never answered to anything else again.

He pushed back his hat now and looked over the people along the rails of the upper decks, his eyes unhurriedly touching each face. Years later he would be able to tell a stranger, "Yes, I seen you aboard the *Tealwing*—upriver run, June of 1860—" that being the kind of memory horse trading develops in anybody who is going to get anywhere with it. As his survey came to Julie, where she stood with Shep, he paused

26

to study her with a country boy's open stare. Shep acknowledged him with a lift of one finger, chagrined that Trapper's
mobility had taken him by surprise.

"Who's that?" Julie demanded.

"Who? You mean that little towhead feller? That's my
brother. I forget his name."

"How come I've never seen him before? I've often enough
seen you."

He didn't like that "enough." "I don't believe Pap's ever
used him on the Missouri. Unless maybe once, about five-six
years ago. Or on the Mississippi either, for that matter. Pap's
been kind of breaking him in to take over the Cumberland
and Tennessee. We never see your boats over there."

"Well, I think he's cunnin'. Go fetch him up."

"Now, Julie, you know you're not interested in all these little shirttail nippers—"

"Little shirt— That boy is eighteen if he's a day! He's as
old as I am, right this minute."

"That's what I say. Likely little feller, isn't he?"

"Hey! Get yourself down here!" Trapper bawled from the
forecastle. And now Shep went down.

Trapper held him at arm's length with a short, hard handshake, and stepped back. The brothers were always glad to
see each other, even when they had been fighting about
something when they last parted—which this time they had
not. But formerly Shep had been accustomed to seizing Trapper under the arms, tossing him overhead, and catching him,
and this had continued into Trapper's teens, to his great mor-
tification. Trapper now weighed some hundred and sixty
pounds, and Shep had only about three inches advantage in
height. No tossing in the air had occurred for some time, but
Trapper was wary of it still.

"I don't know this colt," Shep said, to put off showing any
interest in why Trapper was here. "Not much good, I guess—
I see you're trying to break his leg, so's we can shoot him."

"I never scrappled a leg yet, did I?"

"What about the time—"

"With twelve exceptions," Trapper qualified.

How can you argue with a knothead like that? The criticism was only a matter of habit; neither he nor Pap had been able to cool off Trapper's style of horsemanship yet, nor saw any hope they ever would. It was amazing what chancey riding Trapper lucked his way through.

They put the horse away. "Thought you were supposed to meet Pap, down at Rolla," Shep began.

"That's what I done. And he was in Waynesville before nightfall the next day. About the time you was wheeling slowly into the mouth of the Missouri," he exaggerated. "From Waynesville this is only a piddling eighty-ninety miles. I could have beat you here by a week was there any call to. So Pap and me, we rode out to the Potter farm—"

"I guess I better have dinner and come back in about an hour," Shep said. "Maybe you'll have got to the point by then. What the hell are you doing here? That's what I want to know!"

"I got to fetch a team back to Waynesville. Old Man Potter lost them Norman mares."

"*Lost* them?"

"They was run off on him. Bunch of bushwhackers got 'em. Burnt his barn. Made a try at the house too, but she wouldn't catch. Old Man Potter got his leg bust with a Minnie ball; they saved the leg, but he's bad crippled up. After he was out of it, Saloney stood in for him—she wouldn't tell me if she kilt anybody—but her and the two boys finally fought 'em off. Caylin, the younger girl, she was reloading them old muskets; seems they had a spare. So everybody got in it, except the old woman—she just prayed. Tom Potter lost a finger. I told him not to worry about it, seein's he still had eleven left. But he didn't think it was funny."

Shep couldn't understand it. "The Potters are good, honest Southron people," he marveled. "Loyal to the South every step of the way. How many of 'em was there?"

"About thirty."

"*Thirty?* Seems awful deep in from Kansas for Jayhawkers to be operating. But—hell, it had to be Jayhawkers!"

Trapper said he didn't think so. They didn't seem to need any rightful excuse for robbing and horse stealing down there no more; they'd raid anybody who had anything, on any old lying misclaimer. Burnouts and runoffs in all directions. "You sure Pap's in his right mind? God knows why he's so dead set on keeping them people going at all costs, but he is. I might just as lief take three-four loaner teams down there, while I'm at it. So ... I'll ride with you a piece—maybe overnight; and drop off at Midway, or Boonville—"

"You will not! You stick some cornbread in your pocket, right smart quick, while I holler for the plank! And you get on back the same way you come!"

"Don't want to go back that way."

"Why?"

"Because I kept getting shot at, that's why! Twice. One miss and one graze."

Shep lost his temper. He assumed—wrongly, as it turned out—that this was the big showpiece Trapper had been holding back, while he dragged out everything else he knew first. Probably he had worked on this story, and worked on it, every mile he rode, to make it just as aggravating as he could. "By God, I ought to belt you right in this river! *Where* was you grazed?"

"Coming through them dogwood thickets, along the Osage."

"That's not what I meant, and you know it! By God, I thought you was riding mighty high in your irons! If you haven't got a fresh patch in the seat of your pants, let's see you prove it!"

"It was my other pants." This wasn't true; Trapper had been hide-creased across the back, but he let it go by.

"Now, that better be all you're holding back, or I swear by the Almighty I'll—"

It wasn't all. "Well ... you know ... a minute ago, I asked you if Pap might be sliding into the dodders? All right. Let's hear what you think of this." Trapper picked a long timothy straw out of the fodder bales and chewed on it, speaking carefully, so that what he said next should be right. "Pap sent you a message. He says, 'Tell Shep if he runs across our Norman mares, that Potter had, *he's to let on he doesn't know 'em.*' "

"Wha-at?"

" 'Make sure Shep understands that,' he says, 'because that's an order!' I says, 'Pap, you sound like you know who took them mares.' And he just says, 'No, son, I don't know.' And he wouldn't talk no more.''

Now Shep picked himself a straw and chewed on it, his eyes on the water.

"There's a little more, of a sort," Trapper said. "I cut a circle through the woods, looking for sign. The Potter boys already tried it, when the trail was fresh, but *they* can't track nothing. So I tried it anyway, and sure enough I found where the mares was drove off. And, you know, after all that time— many weeks—I could still have trailed them critters? They're so hootin' big, they sink deep wherever they set foot on damp ground; then it dries, and the track stays forever, almost. Them big dinner-plate hoofs—I swear, a mortified skunk ain't easier to foller. All you do, you keep leapfrogging ten-fifteen miles ahead, and look at all the river crossings. You're bound to turn up sign of 'em."

"And lose 'em at the first steamboat landing."

"Maybe. Point is, Pap forbade I foller 'em. The Potters felt awful. That ain't the first team they lost us, you realize. There was that fly-by-night Yankee banker, taken up that good team of ours for the Potter mortgage. And Pap only said he was glad the mares was there, to be took in place of their farm— and he turned around and loaned old Potter the Normans. You remember?"

"Yup."

"So now, they just begged him to let me track. But Pap said, no, he'd handle it himself; and he promised them these mules I come for. And Old Man Potter, and the old woman, and both girls—they bawled, and hung on him and slobbered over him—it was sickening. And—"

"Who do *they* think done it?"

Trapper said the Potters wouldn't talk much. And neither would other folks, round and about. Either they knew, and it scared them, or they were scared to know. As for Pap, maybe he had some plan he wanted to work out and maybe he didn't, but the way it looked to Trapper, Pap was another scared one.

"Trapper," Shep said, "I've worked with Pap a long time; three years longer than you. If Pap's scared, it's something about losing either livestock or money. Because he don't scare worth a river shrimp off a corpse, for anything other."

"There's something riding his mind," Trapper insisted.

Though they didn't look much alike, there were times when they moved so much the same that it was kind of ridiculous, once you noticed it. So now each took the straw out of his mouth, studied the end of it, and put it back.

"I'll tell you what I think it is," Trapper said, "if you want to know. These aren't just peckerwoods, and swamp-runners, raising all this hell down there. It's holdovers from all those kangaroo societies they whomped up when they was trying to clean out Kansas. Like the Blue Lodge, and the Sons of the South, and the Cavalry Club—you hear those names dropped down around Waynesville, right now. And next, whoever said it, he makes out it was a slip—*he* don't know anything about it—"

"Look, Trapper. Some of the biggest men in Missouri set those societies up. Men like Governor Jackson, and General Stringfellow, and Jo Shelby—"

"Where there's big men there's big thieves."

"I admit that. Some of them would steal a railroad, or a river, or a state. But horse thieves? No!"

"All right. But there was always plenty riffraff swarmed along too, for what there was in it. I figure they're the ones on the road again now. I betcha every time some hellion off a big plantation runs short of cash he reaches for saddle and gun; and you think there ain't plenty rednecks game to throw in with him?"

"And that's the kind of hoot-owlers you think Pap is scared off! I never heard such—"

"I can name one rough-horn old raider Pap don't want to rassle with. Name comes up about every third deal we make in Missouri."

"Who's that?"

"Tyler Ashland."

Oh, Lord. I don't know why I waste words on him. Every time I get the idea he's finally growing up he trips over a fool-hen's nest with a silly's egg in it, and comes up with an outrage fit to stun you. But this whups his record. . . . "No, sonny," Shep said wearily. "Tyler Ashland did not make off with our mares. Nor he didn't steal any pullets off a hen roost, nor any washing off the line, nor anybody's green apples. Just take my word for it."

"He run roughshod over Kansas, didn't he? He helped burn down Lawrence, didn't he? Got his oldest boy killed over there, *I* heard tell."

"Look," Shep said with great patience. "Those people were trying to save Kansas. They might have made the whole Union safe, only the Federal troops come in; and the Missourians wouldn't fire on the flag. Any theory Tyler Ashland's liable to turn around and steal Old Man Potter's team—if you knew him you'd realize how ridiculous that sounds to me!"

But in the same moment that he said it Shep felt a prickle at the back of his neck, and when it was gone it left a chill. What had popped into his mind was Rodger Ashland, Tyler's son, a scapegrace as hotheaded as his father and without his father's brains. . . . He wasn't going to speak of this to Trapper; but now his young brother stumbled onto it for himself."

"Well," Trapper admitted doubtfully, "you know old Ty, and I don't. Never saw him, I don't believe. Saw his son, once, some rods off. Name of Rodger . . . Say—there's the kind of feller I mean it might be!"

"You don't know *him* either."

"No, but I sure heard plenty. Oh, he's made a name! Wilder than his old man ever thought of being. All he does is go helling up and down the Mississippi, pistol dueling, rooster fighting, throwing money around—where does all *that* come from? I heard he's keeping an octoroon woman in Natchez. Now think what that kind of yaller gal must cost to keep up. You think his old man's shelling out for all that?"

Shep thought it over and had to admit it didn't seem likely.

"Some say old Ty's so mad he's cut him off already. But if Rodge is riding nights—in the name of helping the South, of course—that would account for it, wouldn't it?"

There it is. True or not don't hardly make any neverminds, now this sprawl-haid young'un has tied onto it. Just one word

*of it, backtracked to us, and we're through in Missouri. And
every place else, most likely.*

"Now, you look here!" he exploded, in a hopeless effort to
put it out of Trapper's mind. "That's all a lot of blather, without a flyspeck of fact. But it's also gunpowder, and we'll
mighty soon smell the smoke of it if you ever let drop a
word!"

"Well, it sure fits in pretty good with the way Pap—"

"Shut up! Just one hint of such a notion, to anybody, and
we'll leave this country about one jump ahead of the fastest
bloodhounds in Missouri! Forget the whole thing—you hear
me?"

He turned his back on Trapper and went up the after lad-
der. But he knew Trapper would not forget, and neither would
he. Trapper's theory was not a new one in Missouri. Among
a thousand harsh contentions, full of unexpected split-ups,
bitter divisions, feuds, and violences, you could hear every
kind of charge and countercharge you wanted to—including
Trapper's. Useless even to weigh such rumors without you
had certain knowledge of your own, and most likely that was
the last thing you wanted. But . . .

New thing now was Pap's strange caution. All his life the
old man had been game to walk through the middle of a fist
fight between God and the devil without batting an eye. Yet,
plainly, there was something about this thing Pap was afraid
to probe into—if he wasn't pretty sure of the answer already;
Trapper was right, and an involvement of Rodger Ashland
would explain it. Trapper talked a lot of nonsense, but he had
blundered onto a pattern.

Shep didn't suppose that Rodger Ashland himself had
raided the little Potter family. Too much long-shot coincidence in that. But it didn't need to be Rodge, for at least a
dozen families of the planting aristocracy on the Missouri had
wild rattlebrained sons, habitually short of throwaway money
and resentful that they had missed the big raids into Kansas.
Any one of those clans could make Missouri too hot for the
Danielses if they imagined a threat to the family name.
Maybe none of them had had anything to do with the Potter
raid at all, but if Pap believed that some such people were

leading bands of raiders sometimes, that in itself might make him afraid to know.

The hell with it. Pap wants to handle it by himself, so let him. Got nothing to do with me, and most likely never will. Best thing is put it out of my mind.

Then suddenly an unaccustomed pessimism overwhelmed him, and his belief in his own luck left him like the bottom dropping out of a bucket. Whatever was the worst thing that could happen took on the aspect of the only thing likely, or even possible. Of course Rodger Ashland was night riding, if anybody was; he would be the first of his kind to rush into it. Undercover, on pious pretexts, and without the knowledge of his father—but playing reckless hell to his own profit just the same. . . .

From that moment Shep was certain in his heart, as certain as he would ever be, that Rodger Ashland personally, and no other, would someday be their comeuppance in Missouri.

"You didn't bring your brother up," Julie reproached him.

"Couldn't. An accident happened to his other pants."

"Well, I think you're mean to him. Now you get him out of those smelly stockpens, you hear?"

"Yes, mam." Shep went below, picked four mules to go south, and set Trapper ashore.

★ 6 ★

ONCE PAST BOONVILLE, THE *TEALWING* WAS WITHIN A FEW HOURS of Ash Landing, Tyler Ashland's seat of power. People who understood hemp planting assumed that Tyler's prosperity overlaid a considerable foundation of debt, and they were right; but few realized that the plantation as well as the village had actually been built by not one family but two.

Tyler Ashland had married Jim Sam's younger sister, Diligence Delorme, at about the time Jim Sam's rise to fortune was becoming talked about. Ashland made a lot of money, in good years, and put much of it back into property development; but he seemingly spent more than was left over in the lavish hospitality seldom exceeded in Missouri. Jim Sam presently accepted a whole series of opportunities to pour steamboat money into the plantation.

When Jim Sam married, Tyler rose above his debts to build, as a wedding present, the Delorme dwelling now known as the Other Great House, and, as an afterthought, threw in several hundred yards of riverfront; which accounted for the rather peculiar location of what Delorme still called his head offices. Though his main interests had long since shifted to his Mississippi packets, he was by this time more or less tied to Ash Landing by equities, perhaps almost as great as Ashland's own.

It was as Tyler Ashland's business partner that Jim Sam gave the Danielses special rates, and even deadheaded them if he himself happened to be aboard; so that the Danielses stretched their schedules every way they could to ride the Delorme boats.

35

The village of Ash Landing itself was only a one-plantation river stop, somewhat augmented by some installations serving Delorme's Missouri River Line. The little town that had accumulated here was mostly of silver-gray unpainted wood; it looked comfortably settled down and older, more time-mellowed, than it was. Close under the hills that rose swiftly from the Missouri's shore slanted the cobbled levee that Jim Sam had put in, to compensate for the rise and fall of the river. The one-sided bit of road running along the top of the levee was the only business street, stacked high, in season, with mountains of rope and bales of hemp.

The most important building, before which the *Tealwing* made its landing, housed the Delorme offices. It was of two stories, wide and tall, with long galleries across the front, both above and below. From this, a snaggle-toothed row of false fronts and gable ends strung out in both directions along the waterfront, sometimes jogging to go around a big beech or a linden. There was a general store, a chandlery, a harness shop, a livery stable, a fleabag called the Bishop House, three taverns, a block of warehouses, and a church. Upriver, at the end of the street, stood the long, partly open structures of Tyler Ashland's rope walk and at the downriver end lay the pens and sheds serving the plantation livestock, and supplying the village with clouds of flies.

Up the hill behind the waterfront climbed the weathered village, huddling here and straggling there at the whim of the steep land. Distantly, far back on the heights, Tyler Ashland's long rambling dwelling, always called the Great House, could be no more than glimpsed through its maples and black oaks. Nearer the river the Other Great House handsomely crowned its own hill.

That was about all there was to Ash Landing. Whatever might be going on in the great plantation was inland and out of sight; the little town lived by and for the river traffic alone. When a packet tied up, a couple of hundred people might be drawn to the levee and the waterfront awoke to a brief liveliness. Then the boat moved on and the village went back to sleep under the hot Missouri sun.

On this occasion Julie and Jim Sam Delorme were going

ashore for one of their irregular spells of residence at the Other Great House. There would be a series of duty dinners for the elite of the county, to catch up on obligations, while the *Tealwing* went on up the river for her turnaround at St. Joe. A more than common number of villagers turned out to see the great folk land, and Julie stood for a time at the rail of the boiler deck promenade surveying the crowd expectantly.

Hovering near her, available for whatever good-bys Julie might feel suitable, Shep Daniels saw her expectancy turn to disappointment, and the disappointment to exasperation. Calcese hurried below and hurried back again.

"Mr. Rodger is not here," Caleese told Julie.

Rodger. Rodger Ashland. Of course. Naturally. Why shouldn't something be going on, with the two of them virtually raised together? In so far as she's been raised anyplace at all. I never expected nothing no different! Actually, the inevitable association between Julie Delorme and Rodger Ashland had never occurred to him before, and now hit him with a wicked shock. *I forget why I used to think my luck was always so good over here in the Missouri country. I question now if I'm long for this river.*

Julie was riddling Caleese with snappish questions.

"Yes, Miss Julie. No, Miss Julie," Caleese answered with patience. "He hasn't been home in a month. I haven't found out yet when he is expected. Yes, mam, I'm trying to find out—"

"How dare he!" Julie exploded. "He knew I was going to be here!"

"I must ask you to lower your voice," Caleese said with severity. "This is not a seemly exhibition."

" 'Seemly exhibit' be damned!" Julie said loud and clear, startling everybody within earshot. Her landau appeared, and she flounced down the main stair. For the time being, at least, the existence of anybody called Shep Daniels had apparently escaped her.

Even then he could not help thinking he had never seen her more interesting, or more attractive, than when she was mad at everything. She was a little bit like Missouri itself, hell beautiful always, as Shep saw her, but full of deadfalls. He began bracing himself for his first try at substituting for Pap in a deal with Tyler Ashland—the one man in the state his father wanted kept happy at all costs. He approached the encounter with considerable misgivings; his self-confidence hadn't been helped any by Julie's performance.

I sure don't think much of the way things been going. Keep on like this, falling down on the job will be the least worst I can hope for. More likely I get hanged, or something, before I ever get out of Missouri.

★ 7 ★

Tyler Ashland was then working several hundred head of mules and a large variable number of saddle horses, all of which he was continually weeding out, swapping, or adding to. For a long time he had been virtually a captive customer; he trusted no trader but Pap, from whom he would sometimes buy sight unseen. But his value to the Danielses went far beyond the profits they made on him. What was good enough for Ashland was good enough for many others, so that his patronage brought the Danielses many times more business than his own.

Nothing about the look of Ash Landing, whether asleep or bustling, suggested that for four years, ending only two years back, it had been as vehement a source of violence as there was on the Missouri River. Actually, except for a considerable coming and going of riled-up mounted riflemen, it had looked no different then; no fighting ever took place there. But in the years of the Border Wars it had been so active a gathering point for raiding societies that it had virtually amounted to the mouth of a smoking pistol, and might again. Tyler Ashland was the pistol.

The Ashland antecedents traced back to a fire-eating family in the Carolinas, and throughout most of his life Tyler was widely known as a fire-eater himself. He was tall, fierce-whiskered and fierce-eyed; his black hair showed only a token salting of gray. He scared some people, and these claimed it was dangerous to bid him good morning before breakfast lest he call you out on the spot. Certainly he had been of sufficiently violent temperament to lead an unautho-

39

rized company of cavalry in the Border Wars with Kansas and was credited with having cut a broad swath.

What the Ashlands were willing to forget was that for the last few generations their branch of the family had hung on the ragged edge of a poor-relation status. The opening of vast lands in Missouri had given Tyler Ashland's father his chance, and Tyler had built upon his father's beginnings, chiefly, it seemed, by an inexhaustible energy amounting to ferocity; until now he could regard himself as one of the planting aristocracy in his own right. It was a proud ranking, and one of as great security as there was. But having recovered the position that had eluded his people for more than half a century, Ashland almost at once saw his gains threatened by the flood of abolitionist settlers poured into Kansas by the Massachusetts Emigrant Aid Society, with the avowed purpose of hemming him in, pressing him down, and eventually destroying the only way of life he had ever thought worthwhile.

Now, why under heaven did they want to do that? New England's interference was incomprehensible to Ashland. Few among the men who came, or the men who sent them, had ever seen a Negro; almost none had seen a slave. They knew nothing about grand-scale planting or about plantation labor, either its uses or its needs. Loudly they clamored for the turning loose of a million slaves in the Missouri and Mississippi valleys—without any suggestion whatever for their placement, feeding, or control. The plantations would go back to the wilderness, of course; and those hundreds of thousands of chattel field hands would wander homeless, as dangerous as only a helplessly starving horde can be. . . .

The invaders of neighboring Kansas had to be driven out or destroyed; Ashland saw no other choice. In dumbfoundment, but also in high anger, he over and over led his Cavalry Club into Kansas. . . .

This was the man Shep Daniels now had to learn to deal with.

Twenty-three head of subgrade Ashland mules stood around switch-tailing and flap-earing in one side of a divided yard, and Shep's forty head of young stock shuffled themselves in the other. Shep Daniels and Tyler Ashland leaned against the fence, trying to make a deal. If Pap Daniels had been handling the trade, Ashland would probably have said, "Pick me out some good young draft, in place of this chicken-croup museum, and let me know the difference." Trading over. But for Shep it didn't work out like that.

Ashland was in a bad mood, highly incensed that Pap had not appeared in person and resentful of excuses. Pap should know better than to send a boy to do a man's work, by God. He was sick and tired of maunderings about night-rider troubles and didn't mean to stand hitched for one damned word more of it. If he wasn't in bad need of mules he'd tell Shep to take his damned string to hell or Cincinnati, he didn't give a good God-damned which. . . . He finally got around to pointing through the fence at a flea-bit gray, demanding a proposition.

Shep judged that no reasonable offer would do any good. He must either start with a tough offer, and make it hard to whittle, so that he would have room to ease off later, or he could try to disarm Ashland with a giveaway such as would astonish him. He decided on the latter.

"Mules have gone out of sight," Shep began mildly. "Take this big bay here. Last year that would have been about a sixty-dollar mule. Today he'll bring a hundred in the St. Louis yards."

Ashland said that so had his old rack of ruin gone up just as much and he had come on sorry times when he had to stand around being told his business by an apple-cheeked boy. . . . Was this arrogant crank the gracious gentleman famous for his hospitality? Sure he was. Depended on whom he was talking to, was all.

"I'm allowing for your mule going up," Shep said. "I want your mule and twenty dollars for the bay colt."

It didn't work.

"That's preposterous! I say forty!"

Shep was taken off balance. "How's that again, sir?"

Now followed a weirdness in which Ashland insisted on paying double the boot asked of him, and Shep argued against it.

"My price gives me eighty dollars for what I call a sixty-dollar mule," Shep said. "We're not trying to get rich off a market fluke."

"And I don't need any financial favors from you either," Tyler said. "If I catch you lying to me on the going price, I'll know how to make you sorry, quick enough." It was a simple statement, without emphasis, but it carried the conviction of certain fact.

"Pap's going to break my neck for robbery—you know that, don't you?"

Ashland expressed his disinterest in Shep's neck. And that was the way it went, Ashland never softening, never conceding. He insisted on dealing for one mule at a time, never for a span, let alone half a dozen teams together. Shep took to quoting the dead center of the market, while Ashland managed to wrangle by balancing a price too low with another too high—anything for a dispute. It took all day long, and before it was over Shep was certain that something deeper and more abiding was graveling Ashland than his resentment over Pap's absence. Up to now Ashland had never seen him except as a hostler, holding lead ropes in the background, or sometimes demonstrating a critter's gaits. Inasmuch as they had never exchanged two words in their lives before, Shep could not surmise, as yet, what Ashland was holding against him.

"Tell your father it's horses I want," Ashland said, when the bills of sale had been signed. "A lot of horses; fifty or sixty head, to begin. All fast quarter-horse types, standing fifteen or sixteen hands, able to carry well upwards of four hundred pounds; ages four to six; no whites or grays . . ." As he went on with the description, Shep recognized the U.S. Cavalry specifications; stiffened up, perhaps, to an unreasonable degree but plain of purpose just the same. "Do you understand?"

I understand, all right. Never heard such requirements. Adds up to a cross between a beef bull and a kangaroo. We'll play hell filing this bill, ornery as you be. And whistle a long time for our money.

"Tell your father, to hell with city dealers' prices. I want him to search Mississippi and Louisiana . . ."

Plain what he's up to. He's bringing back his old irregular cavalry. Only tougher. Last time they just rode whatever they had. He sees something I don't see. And I'd damn well better figure out what it is before too long.

Aloud he said, "All right, Colonel." It was the first time he had rung in this title, and he saw Ashland notice the recognition of military purpose.

They did not shake hands as they parted; but Tyler did say something that might have passed for an apology if Shep had let it stand. "I realize," he said grudgingly, as if with pain, "I sometimes speak my mind in a manner you're not used to. If we stood on equal footing, and I were not an older man, doubtless you would have been tempted to hit me, a couple of times, today. But . . ." What was he going to say? Probably just that that was the way he was, whether Shep liked it or not. An apology to himself, perhaps, rather than to the other. But as he paused to phrase his thought, Shep flashed a brief ghost of a grin and gave his answer.

"No, Colonel Ashland; I don't think so. I wouldn't dare stand here at all if I thought you could make my temper break. Because if you ever did, I'd hit you, all right. I'd hit you to kill you."

Well, he had got through it, somehow. He had unloaded three horses and twenty-three mules, at prices a little on the high side if anything; but for the life of him he could not have said whether he had done pretty well or very badly. He had a sense of something turning spooky in Missouri, of something hidden going wrong in a lot of ways. A fair number of passengers were going on with the *Tealwing* to St. Joe, but the decks seemed bleak and empty without Julie anywhere. As he went aboard in the warm candlelighted dusk he shivered meaninglessly, in the way some people would have said meant a stranger had stepped over his grave.

★ 8 ★

SHEP DANIELS WENT ON UP THE RIVER, EASILY TAKING HANDSOME profits, not only on the remaining Daniels mules but on the Ashland culls, in the biggest boom market for draft animals he had ever seen. He could have got the job done in a hurry at the normal landings of the *Tealwing* if he had been willing to take first offers. He would have liked to stay with her, on the supposition that Julie and Captain Delorme would board her again upon her return to Ash Landing, but it would have cost him many a hundred if he had done that. He worked as fast as he could, if only to keep his mind occupied, for he was bored and discontented with Julie gone out of his world. Even so, the conscientious milking of each deal took time ashore, and he soon lost his free ride.

All along the river he met the continuing rumors of disorder and chaos in the southern counties of Missouri, but he didn't believe them much. Had they been true, a flood of quick-cash, stolen farm animals should have beaten down the market, which certainly showed no signs of it. A lot of the rumors canceled each other or soon proved exaggerated, if not false altogether. One story had it that a band of a hundred runaway slaves had armed themselves and were terrorizing the Kansas border; this later dwindled to a group of six wretched fugitives who were chased into Kansas and brought back. A tale that the entire town of Lick Skillet, on the Big Niangua River, had been sacked and burned by Jayhawkers came to nothing at all, for Lick Skillet was still there and had never heard of it. Something seemed to be happening down there, in the back country into which Pap and Trapper had gone, but communications were so bad it was impossible to judge just what it was.

Pap had hoped to meet Shep in Kansas City, but he wasn't there, nor any message from him. It was not surprising. They were always being delayed, or making an unforeseen detour, or starting for one place and ending up at another. Livestock was where you found it, and so was the demand for it. Commonly you chased will-o'-the-wisps of misinformation and just stumbled on what you wanted. Shep was already out of stock in trade and, without instructions as to his next consignment, there was nothing he could do about it. He took the fastest packet he could find and went booming down the Missouri to St. Louis, where word should have been waiting if Pap had been able to send any; and was let down to find none there either.

But now something else happened to change Shep's way of life, for the second time that summer. Captain Delorme most abruptly gave up hiding his too-marriageable daughter up the once wild but now steamboat-teeming Missouri. He returned with her to the Mississippi, where he established his headquarters aboard the *Royal Oaks*, newest and biggest of his packets, a great showpiece, automatically flagship of his lines. He had a reason for this decision, which Shep would presently find out. It was in no way pointed at Shep, who probably did not exist at all in Jim Sam's mind when out of view; but it affected Shep anyway, to an unreasonable degree. Except for a short run now and then, Shep never had any call to ride the Mississippi. What he saw at once was that only by an occasional miracle would he ever see Julie again—to talk to, at least—in the course of his natural life.

There was no sensible reason why this should have been important to him. He had no plans connected with her; if a sneaking hope was hiding in the back of his mind that he might somehow come to mean something to her someday he was not even aware of it. *It's better this way,* he tried to tell himself. *She'll get married, in any case, and be gone from the rivers, pretty soon. These things wear off. Someday I won't even remember who it was used to lean on the rail beside me, watching the fireflies in these long twilights.*

He sat in the tilted-back splint chair on the veranda of his hotel, bored and disgusted, listening to the moaning of the steamboats on the Mississippi. After a time the mosquitoes rose in clouds from the shrubbery to sing about his ears:

> Bazoo, bazee,
> Honey, you're for me—
> That's the Mosquito Song.

And presently it occurred to him that maybe he did have an excuse for taking off down the great river. Looking for Pap was out of the question. He had once lost six weeks trying to catch up with Pap in the back country and had caught hell for it. Meantime he had Pap's orders to please Tyler Ashland at all costs, and he had Ashland's request that they search Mississippi and Louisiana for horses. He could get started on that. There were a few holes in this line of reasoning: St. Louis was where Pap expected to reach him, and it was where he would be handiest when needed. But Pap could snatch him back by telegraph fast enough, couldn't he? He sure could. He left his forwarding address as "The *Royal Oaks*, southbound run, en route," and got out of there before he should get some word he didn't want.

★ 9 ★

Julie Delorme had not known Shep was aboard the *Royal Oaks* when she unexpectedly ran into him upon the promenade. She greeted him with astonishment and an open delight that dumfounded him, considering that she had forgotten to so much as wave to him when she went ashore at Ash Landing. She went through a soundless clapping of hands, and even a small, token jumping up and down, as if she were a little girl. For a moment he hopefully thought she was about to throw her arms around his neck, but she wasn't *that* glad to see him.

The hundred or so passengers traveling south from St. Louis included few eligible young men—those would come aboard farther south; and now Shep and Julie picked up where they had left off before Ash Landing. They settled at once into a happy familiarity, in which she hung upon his arm at the least excuse, or with none, much as if they had known each other all their lives instead of during only one slow trip up the Missouri. Oddly, Shep found himself continually humbled, rather than excited, by Julie's treatment of him as her best and oldest friend ... most of the time.

He was daunted, at first, by the *Royal Oaks* itself, for he supposed it to be Julie's natural setting, in contrast to which the *Tealwing* was a scrubby fishbox on a raft. The *Royal Oaks* wasn't the biggest packet on the river; her 328-foot length was thirty-five feet under that of the vast *Eclipse*. But she had three decks, not counting the unroofed hurricane, or the texas, half a deck higher, with the gold-leafed pilothouse towering above that. She had carpets so thick that waves were

47

said to run across them if a breeze got in, and an oil painting of Victoria Falls, or something, on every stateroom door. During dinner an orchestra played, and a brass band serenaded the important landings. Thirty stewards were carried to work the dinner tables alone.

The *Royal Oaks* could probably make her upstream run, from New Orleans to St. Louis, in five days if called on. But Captain Delorme never put speed ahead of business, and took anywhere from three to four weeks for the round trip.

Shep made inquiries for Pap at Cape Girardeau, where they sometimes left messages, and at their bank in Cairo, but the Missouri wilderness had swallowed Pap and Trapper without trace. Shep was relieved, rather than bothered; his feeling about it, this time, was that it could keep them for him a while, and give him a little time to himself right where he was.

Now that he was with Julie again he couldn't remember how he had ever thought he could get her out of his mind. He would have been dumbfounded had he known how many nights she lay awake worrying for fear she wasn't pretty enough. Middle-aged women of the deckchair brigade usually placed her as "a lovely girl," by which they meant she had the lucency of youth in her favor, if not much else. Words like "pretty," "beautiful," "lovely," never came into Shep's mind in relation to Julie. He found it equally difficult to keep his eyes off her whether she was biting a hangnail or romping out a reel; and he was certain no other girl on earth could ever replace her.

He had trouble keeping his eyes from drifting to her when she was nearby, yet politeness prevented his staring at her. It had been different in the days when he was confined to the cargo deck. Sometimes, then, he had studied her from no great distance, making blunt-minded speculations he was ashamed of now, secure in the conviction that a muleboy in butternuts was invisible to the likes of her. But he wasn't invisible any more, so instead developed an acute awareness of where she was whether he could see her or not. He might be in the stockpens on the main deck, drenching an ailing horse, and she might be three and a half decks above, in her cabin in the texas, yet he would be as clearly conscious of her there as if the decks had been glass. If the notion came to him that she was brushing her hair, it carried such conviction that he seemed to *see* her brushing her hair.

South of Cairo an occasional rival began to come aboard, and from Memphis on down they appeared in numbers. Probably there were not more than half a dozen of any significance, but to Shep they seemed to swarm. They were planters' sons, mostly, easygoing young men, who laughed a good deal. Why shouldn't they, without a care in the world? Among them Shep remained a loner, neither snubbed nor cultivated. He had nothing they wanted, nothing they could fear. Main thing they all had in common was their interest in Julie. Still, Shep managed to spend his share of time with her, and considerably more. Plainly, she was helping him to maneuver this. Sometimes she might seem to forget him for half a day; but mostly she kept up his illusion of being her best, her closest friend. As when something struck the two of them as ridiculous, unnoticed by anybody else, their eyes would seek each other's, and hold for a moment, expressionlessly sharing the joke.

And there were times when she had a special magic, not to be expected in any human being. The *Royal Oaks* had dancing every night; but though Julie sometimes dragged him out to dance with her, and coached him when she had a chance, he didn't take much part in it, there were so many to cut in who were better at it. So he often watched from the shadows, seeing nobody but her. Caleese, who made most of Julie's clothes, must have spent the entire winter copying everything in New Orleans. In her off-shoulder ball gowns Julie was two things at once, like a mermaid. Above the so-called neckline, which was below the armpits, her bare shoulders were flesh and blood, but where Julie left off and the dress began she became something else. Caleese had a trick by which the outer layers of the hooped and swirling skirts were made of gauze, so that below the armor-bearing bodice there was no girl at all, but something like a pearly vapor. *Like a butterfly,* he thought. *No, butterflies flap. She kind of sails along, the way a pie tin goes spinning downcurrent. Maybe like a little hunk of river mist, when rays of sunlight strike in, and get lost in it. With about as much rainbow all through as one dewdrop has. Yes, that's more like it. Some living thing, made out of mist. . . .* But whenever he tried to tell her how magical she seemed— "That's a right purty dress" was all he could make out to say.

Long before Natchez all those eligible, well-fixed young men had shown him the immediacy of his danger. At eighteen Julie was already beginning to think of herself as an old maid. *She can marry anybody she wants, by no more than lifting a finger. She'll do it, too, and mighty soon—never mind how her old man hollers. Only hope is to marry her myself. Some way or another.*

He had to admit to himself, though, that it couldn't very well be done at once, or anything like it. Here in Julie's world he was no more in command of his fate than a minnow in a butter churn. Where would he put her?

The Danielses' home base was at Paducah, only thirty some miles up the Ohio on the Kentucky shore. Here, behind the pretty river town, they kept up a small farm, rich-soiled but not big enough to be used for much more than a holding yard. The house was pinched and flimsy; they had never got around to replacing its peeling paint, and probably never would, for it didn't sem to matter any more, now that Ma was dead. But the barns were magnificent, and the land itself was cut up into paddocks by an expensive amount of white-painted fence. To run it they had a distant relative named Henry Hazen, called Cousin Henry by both Pap and the boys, though he wasn't as closely related as that. Cousin Henry was a plump, rosy-cheeked, white-whiskered old fuddy-duddy, full of benevolent intentions, and without an enemy in the world. He thought of himself as a lawyer, or sometimes as a storekeeper, having failed in both professions. Actually he was a back-country farmer, of the type very likely to leave a rake lying around, tines up, and later step on it in the dark. Still, with a couple of aging Negroes to do the actual work, he was capable of taking care of whatever livestock happened to be on hand.

The little old paint-scaled house was dear to Shep, as any

place where you were born and raised is bound to be, but he could not imagine leaving Julie there. He needed time, time to make a deal with Pap, and time to implement it. So he said nothing to Julie yet. He told himself he was holding back lest Jim Sam get wind of his intentions and bulljine the stage plank out from under him before he was set. But in the back of his mind he must have known he was trying to hide a different fear, a fear of putting Julie herself to the test.

From Memphis on down he got to work. What time he was not with Julie he spent talking to every male of consequence on board, endlessly repeating Ashland's description of the horses wanted, though without using the name. The South was not having a good year; every year had been bad in the South for quite some time. Shep got plenty of promises to bring a number of head to one or another of the boat's scheduled landings, on her upstream trip. Most of these prospective suppliers would forget to come, of course, or not get around to it; he could pretty well tell by talking to a man what was to be expected of him. As, when he told a big planter that anything over fifty dollars better come with gold shoes. "Gold *shoes*? Why, suh, my magnificent animals weah the golden wings of Icarus!" *Hopes to saw off a string of crocks,* Shep interpreted this.

This activity, as much as Julie herself, kept Pap and Trapper well toward the back of his mind. A dim spook was haunting him back there, a dark shadow of uncertainty, of anxiety, tinged with some sense of guilt, but he was able to avoid thinking about it much. The *Royal Oaks* ran singing down the greatest of all rivers, loitering at Helena, Rosedale, Arkansas City, Vicksburg, and Port Gibson, besides touching at twenty-five or thirty plantation landings; and tied up at Natchez with her band ablasting.

It was at Natchez that the whole relationship between Shep and Julie changed again; for here Rodger Ashland came aboard.

★ 10 ★

S‍HEP HAD TWENTY HOURS' NOTICE THAT R‍ODGER A‍SHLAND WAS coming aboard, for whatever good that might do him. Seeing he could do nothing to ward Rodger off, the news served to spoil a day for him, and not much else. But it spoiled no day for Julie. She got the word in a letter picked up at Grand Gulf and instantly ran to tell Shep all about it. She was displaying the same kind of little-girl delight with which she had welcomed Shep aboard at St. Louis—shining-eyed, tippy-toed, bubbling—he had never seen anything half so disgusting. His response was a nonplused silence.

"Tomorrow," she harped on it. "He'll come aboard at Natchez, early tomorrow!"

"Why?"

"Because I wanted him to. We agreed on it. We've been writing back and forth all along."

"That's nice."

"You don't like him, do you? I can see you don't. You look as though you're clouding up to rain!"

"Sorry."

"Well, you'll surely like him when you know him better. I'm going to get you two together."

"I see." He could have told her that he and Rodger Ashland had detested each other on sight, long ago; and nothing had ever happened to change that. Instead, he asked her bluntly, "Are you going to marry that rooster, Julie?"

She was taken off-balance, so that she hesitated. "Do you mean, are we engaged? Well . . . no; at least, not now. We had a kind of halfway understanding for a while. But it—it got

52

put off. No. I'm not engaged to him." She went back to her tone of anticipation. "He may ride with us all the rest of the summer. I think you're mean, not to be happy over it. *I'm happy.*"

"I can see you are."

"Oh! You!" She lost patience with him, and went whisking off. *She sure needs taking care of,* he thought, preventing his eyes from following her. *I don't see how I can ever bring myself to trust it to anybody else.* But his own chances of getting it done were on the downturn, worsening badly.

He had noticed the coincidence that Rodger was at Natchez, where he was rumored to be keeping an octoroon mistress. This sort of carrying-on was a commonplace among the gentry who could afford it; the kind of thing you might not talk about openly, or to the wrong people, but accepted as happening, without much feeling about it one way or the other. He set small store by rumors and saw no reason for either believing or disbelieving this one. And yet . . . the thought of Rodge coming to Julie direct from the arms of a high-yaller gal was peculiarly sickening to him.

I may kill him, he thought idly. *No, I won't. I can't do that. I can't ever do that.* He had remembered that Rodger was Julie's cousin. His father was her uncle Ty, and his mother, who had been Diligence Delorme, was Julie's aunt Dil. This consanguinity raised no barriers whatever between Rodge and Julie, in the sentiment of the day—cousins married all the time; yet it permitted a lot of near-liberties, objectionable to Shep in this case. And what was most troublesome of all, it made Rodge inviolate, as Julie's blood kin. He recalled a story about an old woman in eastern Kentucky, whose husband fell to feuding with her family. "Shucks," she remarked as she shot him, "he ain't no kin of mine."

From a distance, as the *Royal Oaks* neared the Natchez landing, Shep got the hiccups watching Julie's increasing eagerness, and guessed his breakfast wasn't setting well. But he stayed to see Rodger Ashland appear, just to make sure the worst had actually happened. Rodge was traveling light, except for guncase, saddle, and bridle, items many gentlemen carried; he looked in good shape, and darkly tanned. As he came up the plank the band, with possibly accidental timing, struck up a popular march called "Hail to Our Fire Chief," and Ashland coolly lifted his hat. Shep had had enough. He got out of there, in no mood for witnessing a nauseating reunion.

Rodger Ashland was almost as tall as Shep, and could turn himself out with unsurpassed elegance when he wanted to. This was not often, for he had the cannon-metal cheek to appear at breakfast barefoot and unshaved if he felt like it. He had his father's black eyes and hair, and the same white forehead Trapper had, from always wearing his hat. Like his father, too, he was lean-cheeked, with the same high and bony nose; except that Rodger's nose had a slight crook in it. Shep had put it there, when he was fourteen and Rodge two years older. Now that young ladies could be found to say that Rodger Ashland was the handsomest man in Missouri, Shep Daniels supposed he could blame himself. He considered that he had improved Rodger's appearance immensely by breaking his nose.

The ambuscade in which this happened had not been about anything. Rodge had been fooling around the forecastle, as the open main deck in the bows was called, asserting his right to get in the way if he felt like it, and Shep, of course, was bringing some mules aboard. One of these tripped himself in a coil of rope, while Rodger Ashland somehow managed to set foot in another loop of the same rope. To the credit of Rodger's agility, he did not actually fall. He was jerked almost into a somersault, but turned in the air, partly caught himself, slipped, caromed off a winch; grabbed a hanging rope that was not fastened at the other end; and finally pulled up, flailing for balance, on the guards. It seemed to go on for a long time, and everybody in sight, which included most of the passenger list, was howling; except the black deckhands, who had no laughing licenses, so turned their heads away.

Shep freed the mule, and still had time to snatch Rodge back before he fell in the river. And next, by pure accident, they put on one of the oldest, most sure-fire clown routines known to man. Rodge took a mighty swing at Shep's head, just as Shep stooped to pick up Rodger's hat, so that the blow whistled over; and as Rodge recovered his balance, Shep was offering him his hat, unaware of the attempt Rodge had made upon him. The crowd roared again, and Rodger charged; it was Shep's left hand, stuck out to fend him off, that broke Rodger's nose. . . . The incident had set the pattern of their relationship. There are people who are strangely unlucky for certain others; and Shep had continued to be poison to Rodge throughout their early years.

For two days, after leaving Natchez, Rodger and Julie Delorme were inseparable, oblivious to the existence of everybody except each other. Their behavior was more nearly that of honeymooners than anything normal. Shep was soon aware that he should have begun making love to Julie long ago. He certainly could not start now, with the two of them so hideously glued together as they were. For those two days it looked as if his chance might never come again.

Abruptly something busted; throughout the third day Julie and Rodger scarcely spoke. Rodge even had his baggage brought on deck at Baton Rouge, but Julie sent it back to his stateroom. After that they were friendly again, not as honeymooners this time but at least as old acquaintances. This lasted a little while, then blew up again during the New Orleans turnaround, when Rodge and Julie shared a late night ashore with Caleese. And that was how it went, on again, off again, for a thousand miles; except that on the upstream run Julie was treating Shep and Rodger Ashland exactly alike, in so far as such a thing was possible.

Shep was trying to make up his mind whether or not there was any likelihood that Rodger Ashland was a night rider, as Trapper imagined. He was getting more opportunity to study Rodge than he considered should be forced on a hog, but he wasn't learning much. He could often recognize a dishonest or dangerous man, but he could never place a stranger as definitely honest. And though he was pretty good at judging what a man was likely to do next in an immediate situation, such as a horse trade, he could not predict what the same man would do in some other situation in which Shep had never seen him.

There was plenty of money behind Rodge, and unless he

got himself disowned, it would all be his someday; though probably he couldn't lay hands on much of it right now. Tyler Ashland was a man who stood no nonsense from anybody, and this included his son. To Rodger Ashland, Tyler had applied, or tried to apply, a harsh righteousness of discipline he had never experienced himself. Shep had never seen Tyler Ashland talk to Rodge for more than two minutes at a time without beginning to chew his mustache and get mad. It was not hard to see how Rodge might find himself hard up for cash or why he might seek adventure as far away from his father as he could get.

On the other hand, Shep could see no sign of his spending much. He didn't need money to ride the Delorme boats, and his gambling losses were trivial. His clothes were good, but he carried only what he needed. Tyler Ashland would allow his son as much money as Rodger was visibly using, for the sake of appearances alone, and no quarrel short of outright disinheritance would be likely to cut off the supply. If Rodge was night riding, Shep could see no evidence of it.

He was fighting off a deadly fear that Julie was going to be lost to him; perhaps was already lost. If Pap had taught him anything, it was that fear was a sickness, not only disagreeable but disabling. It could make a dog bite you, or a mule kick you, or turn people against you, though they never knew why they turned. It could bind your muscles and turn them clumsy, and make your rifle miss. So he rejected his fear and made himself consider coolly just how much time he could figure on before he must make his move. He knew now that he could count on Jim Sam to sit back in the breeching, hostile to all suitors alike, but the uncommonly strong ties between father and daughter were fraying out at one end. Caleese would keep a tight rein while she could, and that would have been decisive once; now, though, Julie was demanding obedience, in room of the discipline Caleese had always exacted. If between them they could get Julie through this one more summer . . . Shep wouldn't bet a nickel on it. Disarmed and empty-handed as he was, he would have to make his move this year, this summer—this very trip.

What steadied him more than anything, and saved the journey from becoming a nightmare, was that on the upstream trip he had plenty of work to do. At Baton Rouge, where the *Royal Oaks* stopped only half an hour, he got the first indication that his buying might go better than expected. A portly and red-faced gentleman was waiting there with ten head, every one of them held on lead by its own Negro hostler. "The cream of the crop, suh," he told Shep Daniels. "The pride of Singin' Tree plantation!"

Shep saw two among the ten he might barely make do in a pinch. But in the background four more horses were being loose-herded apart, as if in an unsuccessful effort to hide them. "What are those back there?"

"You embarrass me, suh. I hadn't meant to bring those; they broke out and followed the others. I fea' they are very expensive hosses. But in wretched condition, not up to themselves at all ..."

Oh, is that so? Fat, though, and groomed to the teeth. Also they were the horses he was obviously expected to buy, discovering them for himself, and paying a premium. Shep was badly cramped for lack of time to haggle, and had to foreshorten or drop out such accepted procedures as pretended loss of interest and trifling offers on animals he didn't want. Jim Sam was shouting at him from the hurricane; bells began to ring. "Throw in these two here, and it's a deal on the four," Shep said, waving the counted-out price to which he had beaten down the owner.

"Split the difference! One hoss—your pick, suh—for lagniappe!" And five head went aboard.

After that there were horses waiting for him all along the river. The word had spread, and the *Royal Oaks* was sometimes flagged down for horse showings he had not arranged, at woodyards and one-plantation landings. Shep could have bought the same horses cheaper if he had had time to work on it, and he assumed he was picking up some snides among them. But he was getting horses, by ones and twos and little bunches, more than he had dared hope. And over all he was buying low, compared to prices on the Missouri and on the Ohio. On the way north to Memphis he accumulated forty-seven head.

And sometimes a rare sunburst lighted up the darkness of his prospects. The brightest of these were unwittingly set up by Captain Delorme. Jim Sam always had a captain's table, preferring to choose his own company. But, though he disliked Rodger Ashland and was annoyed to indigestion by the sight of him beside Julie at every meal, he could not very well bar Rodger from his table. Not his own nephew, his own blood kin. So, to dislodge him, he moved Julie to the seat on his own right, and installed Shep Daniels on the other side of her, as a buffer. What he liked about Shep was that he considered him of no possibility whatever as a son-in-law. Couldn't imagine his aspiring to it. And he had never yet caught him trying to get Julie alone, which had become the chief object in life of all the other whelps in creation.

After the rearrangement, Julie sometimes held Shep's hand under the table. Not always; not consistently, nor predictably, but sometimes. It was another off-again, on-again kind of caprice, without relationship to anything that had been said or had taken place. But when it happened, the steamboat turned to gold, the candle flames became jewels; and Shep believed in himself, and the future, and even in his own luck, for quite a while.

Obviously, Rodger Ashland never thought of Shep as a rival, but as a nuisance, like a buzz-fly that circles and lights on you, circles and lights, too quick to slap, too persistent to be driven off. But one thing Rodge knew to perfection, better than all the other eligible young men put together, was how to get in Shep's way, effortlessly, without seeming to try; he could block Shep out of a conversation or leave him pinned while he walked Julie away. Actually, these methods worked better on all the others than they did on Shep. The clouds of young gentry began to drop away, and above Memphis had disappeared from the *Royal Oaks*. But Shep and Rodger Ashland held on, deadlocked; neither one of them could get Julie alone any more.

A head-on collision was inevitable. Shep knew that, though he was unsure which of them would run out of patience first; and he failed to predict Rodger Ashland's choice of time and place.

⭐ **11** ⭐

SHEP ALWAYS REMEMBERED THE CLEAN EVENING LIGHT, AND THE sense of peace upon the quiet water, as he finally stood alone with Julie for a few brief moments at the forward rail of the promenade. He said, "I'm in love with you, Julie. You know that, of course. Will you marry me?"

She must have seen it coming for a long way and kept an answer ready at all times, though perhaps it was not the same answer from day to day. Without any special hesitation or lifting her eyes from the water, she simply said, "Shep, I don't know." And right after that Rodger Ashland came along the rail.

Rodge ignored Shep, as he very often did, speaking only to Julie. "Are you sure you can bear it here?" he asked. "There's an overpowering smell of mules. . . . Oh, excuse me, Shep—I didn't see you there." It was fairly raw, and a weak link in his gambit; but once past that flaw it ran smoothly for him, and Shep could not have come out undamaged whatever he had done.

"You see me now," Shep said, and flicked the back of his hard fingers across Rodger's cheek. It was the kind of reproof you gave a mule, meant to sting and not to injure, though a sort of whip-snap got into it, so that every finger left its mark. Ashland was expecting it, of course. He did not flinch, or blink, or put his hand to his face. He reddened briefly, in spite of himself, but returned to normal color at once, so that only those four pale stripes remained, conspicuous across his cheek.

60

Julie Delorme turned on Shep in a fury. "You leave that! And quick! You want to be called out?"

"That's up to him," Shep said.

Rodge said, "He knows an Ashland can't call out a mudsill. He never was safer in his life. And he understands that perfectly well."

Shep hit him with closed fist, a blow that should have torn Ashland's head off if he had held as still as before. Rodge partly evaded it this time, so that the blow caught him high on the side of the head, nearly breaking Shep's hand. Even so, Rodge was knocked off his feet. He made a grab at the rail, missed it, and sat down, teetering briefly on his rump before he tipped over, flat on his back, his legs waving absurdly. Then suddenly he was up again, with a spring like a jumping trout.

Instantly Julie had her arms around him, and the panicky tumble of her words swept her into deep-South elisions seldom heard in her speech. "He apologizes—I swea' he does—"

"I do not!" Shep said.

"Now you keep hold you'se'f!" Julie held herself hard against Rodge, her arms wrist-locked around his lower ribs, through a moment of uncertainty. "Just a mudsill—not accountable—you said so yo'se'f—" Rodge began to relax, and Julie got him turned away, her tone slacking off into honey-chile coaxings that bit Shep like a cottonmouth. "You come along, now. That's enough such carryin's-on! We haven't time, you and me, for any such sorry class of people...."

And down come the cobhouse, Shep thought when Julie had got Ashland away from there. *Oh, I done it now!* He supposed they'd have to pistol-fight, of course.

But after that what seemed peculiarly ominous, because mystifying, was that nothing happened next. The incident called for somebody's sudden death, by Rodger's code; but no reprisal came, and none of the three ever acknowledged by any sign that this thing had ever taken place. He remembered his mother's despairing insistence—"You *are* quality—you are, you are!"—and he had never believed her less. *I'll never understand these people, never,* he thought, as if answering her. *Ain't in me to understand 'em, I guess. They live in some different world. . . .*

Before he entirely regained his balance from this bewilderment a new puzzlement hit him from another direction. At Cairo, by the confluence of the Mississippi and the Ohio, a telegram—or part of one—came aboard for him. It was a week old, and its point of origin was Buffington, Missouri. This was end of track for a little sprout of railway that had pushed a few miles into southeastern Missouri, heading hopefully for Texas and California from a point opposite Cairo. The telegraph lines were developing fast, but so far, in the Mississippi Valley, you could count on finding them only where the railroads were. The message said, in handwriting:

> Meet me immediately at—
> Service interrupted. Line believed down again.

It had to be from Pap, of course. Shep judged that the unnamed meeting place was more likely ahead of him than behind. Couldn't very well be Buffington, or Pap would have said, "Come to—" instead of "Meet me." Pap usually sent casual messages, beginning "Mosey down here to—" or like that; so now Shep imagined a tone of emergency, and it fretted him. About the only thing the message told him for sure was that he was about at the end of his string. Time, which he had once thought was in his favor, had all but run out on him.

⋆ 12 ⋆

JULIE DIDN'T KNOW IT WAS SHEP'S LAST DAY ABOARD THE *ROYAL
Oaks*; he didn't know it himself, having decided that Pap had
probably gone to St. Louis. But it was Julie who contrived
that they should have one of their rare quarter hours alone. It
was late in the day, getting on toward dinnertime, so that
Ashland and nearly everybody else was getting dressed for it.
Though the sun was not yet down, Julie had dressed early, so
that her shoulders and the upper half of her breasts were bare,
which was a new thing to him at this time of day. Shep was
used to seeing her so gowned only by candlelight, which
seemed to clothe her of itself as the broad daylight certainly
did not. This, along with the fact that she had sought him out,
distracted him from her improbable look of innocence, which
should have told him she had nothing serious in mind.

He was standing with his back to the rail, and she was gazing with deceptive dreaminess at the shoreline far ahead
when she said, "Shep, you been afoolin' me."

"Who, me?"

"You always told me," she said in stupid-child tones,
"there wasn't any difference."

"What?"

"Between boys and girls."

He started to say he didn't rightly recall coming out with
any such stupefying discovery as that, but she interrupted
him.

"Turn around," she ordered him, and when he hesitated,
took him by the elbows and turned him by hand. "Look yonder, will you? *Now.*"

A bunch of boys were swimming in a still-water cove, half of them perched on a tall snag from which they watched the steamboat, in no hurry to dive in. It was about what Shep had expected, or a little worse; at less than a hundred yards, in that clear light, nothing could be plainer than that bathing suits were unheard of along the Missouri shore.

That sort of foolery had once had a certain warmth of illicit intimacy in it, but he couldn't enjoy it any more. He didn't want anything illicit where Julie was concerned. He supposed Rodger Ashland, in his place, would grab holt and kiss hell out of her. Teach her to fool around. He considered trying it, but shied off. "I can't see a thing from here," Shep lied, starting his change of color.

"Well, I can. Shall I describe for you—"

"God forbid!"

She was beginning to laugh at him again, and this time he suddenly knew he had had enough of it. *Doesn't she know what kind of women speak that way to men?* It seemed to him now that she would never have dared flaunt him with such an invitation to liberties had she not considered him meaningless, as safe under any kind of imposition as only a hopeless dolt could be. There seemed to him a monstrous unfairness in this, for if he had leaned far over backwards throughout their relationship it was because he loved her; better and less selfishly, in his belief, than she was likely to be loved again. *Does she think I'm so harmless that how she acts around me don't signify? No more than talking like that in front of a horse?* Old Jim Sam very plainly thought so; and so, probably, did Caleese.

He said sharply, "Do you talk to everybody the way you talk to me?"

She was still for a moment, then turned to stare at him blankly. "Let me hear that again."

"If you talk to every man you run into the way you talk to me, you're going to get yourself misunderstood."

"If I talk to every— Who, for instance?"

"Rodger Ashland, for instance. There's always plenty of his kind around."

He had not known he was going to say that. But he had

carried too much on his mind for too long, until now he felt beleaguered, beset on all sides.

She stood looking at him, and her eyes had turned an empty black, reflecting surface lights from the water but without any light coming from within. Her face was dead-white, as white as Rodger Ashland's face had been the time Shep had watched him get up from the deck.

She said slowly, "What is it you don't like about the way I talk to you?" She held the words expressionless, but she could not prevent a tremor in them that he heard, so that suddenly he was unable to remember what he had been angry about.

"Nothing," he said, as gently as he knew how. "I didn't mean it like it sounded. It was kind of as if ... I guess it seemed to me like as if we were married already. I wouldn't like to think of you talking to other men like that."

Her tone turned harder, and there was no tremor in it now. "Married? Just how did that get into it?"

"Haven't you ever thought— Don't you *believe* someday we'll be married?" He was surprised again, to hear himself say that. It was an overreach, in the circumstances, and he knew it. But once he had said it he saw no way to call it back. He could only watch her profile, and wait for her answer. He saw now a faint resemblance to her father that he had never sen in her before; less a matter of looks or expression than a projection of spirit. She could never have been her father's daughter without the Delorme streak of explosive pride.

And as he waited he became aware again of the great gulf between them, a gulf no muleboy in his right mind should ever try to span. It was a barrier not exactly of wealth, not even of power; for, though these things had a part in it, they could be attained. Such aristocracy as the planters and packetman of the Missouri had achieved was a hundred years newer than that of the Lower Mississippi, and two hundred years away from the serene unattainability of the Savannah, the Roanoke, and the James; and they guarded their own exclusiveness with a more bitter jealousy, for that. Shep could pull Julie down to his own level of acceptance. She could not raise him to her own.

I can't whip it, he thought. *How can a man go upstream against half a century of time and change what his grandfather was?* The possibility remained that all this might be furthest from her mind; but he could not know that then or imagine what she might be thinking instead. He said aloud, "Maybe I've taken too much for granted, all along." And he waited again.

"Yes," she said at last. "I think you've taken a great deal for granted." She stood silent, looking at the river for a space of ten seconds more, then turned and went toward the stairs of the texas. He wanted to cry out to her, to call her back, but no words would come out of him; and she did not look around.

It will blow over, he told himself. He knew he had done himself no good, though at that time he had no correct understanding of how or why. But he was remembering that he had knocked Rodger Ashland flat, and yet, incredibly, nothing had come of it. He roused himself from his despondency with something like the crack of a mental blacksnake. *I'm not giving up. Not by a long shot with a duck gun. She'll forget it. Maybe she'll even forget it by the time we go to dinner.*

But Julie did not come to dinner that night.

Shortly after full dark the *Royal Oaks* tied up by torchlight at Cape Girardeau, a couple of days below St. Louis. Both Pap and Trapper were waiting at the landing. Shep went down to them at once, for they obviously did not intend taking the boat.

"Where the hell have you been?" Pap demanded, by reflex of habit; but— "Let that go," he canceled the question unanswered. "It don't signify now, I guess. Get your stuff ashore, and don't be delaying the man's boat!"

"I've got forty-seven head of saddle stock aboard, consigned to Tyler Ashland. But they're routed on through to Ash Landing, so all I have to do is tell the purser—"

"Consigned to *who*? Never mind—I heard you! Jim Sam!" he yelled at the pilothouse. "Hold up for me—I got to change a consignment!" He went tearing aboard, Shep and Trapper at his heels.

"Pick out five head of the best and toughest you got," he ordered Shep over his shoulder. "Then come to the purser's office and pull their bills of sale. You go with him, Trapper, and take them he gives you ashore. On the jump, now!"

"What happening here?" Shep asked him.

"Missouri's blowed up in our face!"

Shep gave a steward an uncounted handful of silver to go and ask Caleese if he might see Julie at once; and he went about the work Pap had given him. His livestock and gear went ashore with the fussless celerity that practice teaches. A couple of stewards, who for unknown reasons of their own happened to like him, packed his cabin things with an unprecedented burst of efficiency; everything he had was on the levee by the time his scant paperwork was done. Captain Jim Sam had rung his warning signals to his engineers; the mate, at the hurricane rail, was brawling at his deck crew to stand by fore and aft to cast off.

And still Julie did not appear. Neither Caleese nor the steward who had carried his message brought him any word from her. He was not much surprised. He had watched for her with an irrepressible hope. But since the first moment he had set eyes on Pap he had known he was not going to see Julie again, perhaps not for a long, long time.

The *Royal Oaks* upped her plank as he stepped ashore. The great softly lighted packet still held his eyes as she wheeled, massively, yet somehow daintily, into open water, then breasted the current with a mighty surge of power. He was hoping for a last glimpse of Julie, somewhere along the decks, but she was not in sight.

★ 13 ★

WHAT STRUCK SHEP WAS THAT HE HAD NEVER SEEN HIS FATHER looking so played out; not slowed up, nor willing to let himself sag, but haggard, and hollow-eyed with exhaustion. Yet Pap Daniels took the halter shank of the nearest animal and vaulted to the withers; he had never yet become so tired or so old but what he could do that. Trapper, though carved very lean, and tanned so dark his eyebrows looked white, seemed hard-conditioned and ready. "Let's go where we can talk," Pap said, and led off down the levee at a walk. They sat on a pile of lumber, under the hot, star-peppered night, while the held horses switched and stamped and flung their heads at their flanks.

"I was right all along," Trapper said at once. "Rodger Ashland is night riding, just like I guessed. We tangled with him ourselves."

"Now, how can that be?" Shep objected. "He's been aboard the *Royal Oaks* for the past three weeks, and he's aboard her now."

"Why didn't you tell me?" Trapper exploded. "I could have gone aboard—had him under a paddle wheel by this time! By God, I'll gallop upstream—"

"Oh, no, you won't," Pap said wearily. "Now simmer down, damn it! Trapper's right, Shep. This was a month ago. He could have caught the boat afterwards."

"You want me to think it was Rodge jumped the Potters? His old man would break his damned—"

"Hell, no! He had nothing to do with them mares. As for his old man, *he* knows nothing about it."

68

After Trapper rejoined Pap at Waynesville, they had worked on south for two-three weeks, finding worse news every day they rode. The Danielses' losses in farmed-out brood stocks, colts, and yearlings had been very heavy, perhaps ruinous, throughout all southern Missouri. What you had to remember was that this was the part of the world from which Missourians had ridden into Kansas to kill abolitionists, and did kill them—unchallenged by any effective agency of the law.

Many of the farms that the Danielses had laboriously aligned into a major source of draft stock had been chosen for the very reason that they were small and remote; the best deals, as well as a high average of honesty and loyalty, were often to be found among their like. Since these isolated farmsteads were the most easily picked off by marauders, it was no accident that the Daniels livestock had been spread all through those sections already so hard hurt that they were being called "the burnt counties." A lot of the people the Danielses had known and worked with had disappeared, leaving behind a clutter of worn farm tools and the ashes of their homes. Those who still stood their ground never went unarmed; all of them seemed to be tied up with one armed band or another, for mutual defense, or reprisal, or the recovery of property—always, of course, in the name of the vanished law. And the less you let on to know what they were up to the better you were off.

Both Pap and Trapper rode that country of hills and forests wearing moccasins, instead of boots, for they had taken to deerstalking ahead on foot whenever they came on any considerable passel of riders in the road. Rather than mess with strangers, they went some other way round or else bushed up until the road was clear. In spite of Trapper, who naturally wanted to do all the scouting himself, it was always Pap who went ahead. Being strange to the country, Trapper couldn't tell what he was looking at anyway—only thought he could; whereas Pap was liable to recognize some of the people, so could tell when it was fairly safe to ride on through. Pap made mention of the great wearisome effort by which he had broken Trapper of arguing about that. Fortunately, they didn't have to go all through this every day; scarcely oftener than once a week, when you came to reckon it up. But it was such a nuisance when it did happen, and there was such a jumpiness to the feel of the whole country, what with false alarms and all, it seemed like it happened all the time.

Pap and Trapper had run into Rodger Ashland near the end of July. Shep must have been in Kansas City at about that time. They weren't looking for Rodge, or expecting him; nobody had told them anything about him. The lonely farm where they encountered him was the one that used to be worked by some people named Benjamin, who had pulled out. It was long after dark, and they had some notion of laying over if the place still stood empty. It did not. A considerable milling of ridden horses, and a power of gabble, such as you always get from peckerwoods when the jugs have been going around, warned them from far off that a right smart chance of people were ahead of them. And pretty soon, when torchlight showed through the trees, they pulled off the road. Pap walked ahead, leaving Trapper holding the horses out of sight in the woods and hating every minute of it.

"I'm used to him taking forever," Trapper told Shep. "But what he does, he always come sneaking back on you some new way, so's you never know where he's at until there he stands, about two feet from you. Makes you feel like a fool."

"That's to learn him he ain't the only one can move quiet," Pap explained. "It's needful, to keep him in hand."

"Well, it scares the horses," Trapper got in the last word.

This time, though, Pap came back to Trapper by the shortest way. He had found about two dozen fellers up there, mostly mounted. Those afoot were bee-swarmed around some one point of contention that Pap couldn't make out and about five separate arguments were aboiling like corn juice in a still. But with all talking at once, the general embranglement could have been about anything, from the broaching of a whisky barrel to the burning of a nigger—Pap couldn't say.

One thing he knew. He knew who was in charge. That silent man who sat his horse to one side, backed up by three–four others just as silent, yet attentive to him—that was the man in charge. And he was Rodger Ashland.

Trapper had said immediately that he wasn't a damned bit surprised. He always had thought Rodger was a night rider, and he'd said so before. He didn't know Rodge himself and hadn't actually heard anything to back up this opinion, but except for them little details, he'd virtually known it all the time. He naturally assumed they'd get themselves out of there like a couple of turpentined cats. With their tails on fire.

Pap answered quietly that this was very smart of Trapper. He wished everybody could be that smart. Unfortunately, he was a little slower in the head himself and hadn't known anything of the kind. Not only that, but he didn't know it yet, and he had no intention of swallering any such farfetched surmise without he took steps to find out.

"What are you going to do?"

"I'm going in there."

To Trapper's credit, Pap allowed, the boy never turned a hair. He was inclined to balk a little when he found out they weren't going to ride in there side by side, making it two against two dozen, instead of one, in case anything went wrong. But Pap snaffled him out of it by putting it that he needed Trapper to handle the fighting end if it come to that. He himself was going to ride in unarmed. They took Trapper's horse deeper into the woods, and tied him, snubbing his head down pretty short with a pinch-nose hackamore. In this kind of country, if you saw any chance you'd have to swap shots, you'd best leave your horse out of it. No horse alive understood about getting behind a tree. Pap hung his own saddle blanket under the animal's nose so he wouldn't feel so much alone.

"He just might snooze off," Pap said, throwing Trapper's saddle into a pawpaw bush. "He's pretty well frazzle-assed tonight."

"He'll whicker anyway."

"Let him, then. I don't look for any trouble. But if anything does bust, stay as far away from him as you can get. Might be he'll toll them off you. There's other horses in the world."

They left Trapper's horse pawing unhappily and thrumming through his nose pretty loud, but he didn't whinny. And

Pap showed Trapper where he wanted to be covered from, on top of a point of rocks, overlooking the Benjamin place. It wasn't very high, but it was enough of a barrier to turn the horses aside, and give Trapper a chance to lose himself in the woods. The near-riot in the Benjamin dooryard had quieted some, but it was still noisy enough down there so that Pap and Trapper could talk without lowering their voices, a couple hundred feet away. Trapper complained he couldn't hit anybody from where Pap wanted him to be, but Pap didn't care about that.

"All I want from you is one loud shot—point it down enough to show some flame and smoke—to kind of draw attention. Then pitch yourself backwards down the slope behind you, and get the hell out of there—just as fast and quiet as the shadder of a bat." He gave Trapper his .44 revolver, for safekeeping mainly. It had a tied-back trigger and the hammer polished slippery, which made it fast to fire. "Don't try to shoot it unless somebody steps on you," Pap told him. "You won't hit nothing with it, beyond four-five feet. And don't try to go far. Clamp fast to the ground, in the first brush thick enough to turn torchlight, and don't move again until the last man is long gone. Then foller down the road to the turnoff, and I'll meet you at the Hog-Scald Springs. We hope."

Only thing, Trapper interrupted Pap's story, it mostly didn't work out like that. Ambuscades never did seem to go the way you planned. They were like accidents, forking off into all kinds of freaks and flukes, never satisfied just to happen in some common-sense way.

"All right. Go on and tell him how you seen it, then." Pap was feeling his age. He had seen too many things too often, and he was tired. So now Shep got the rest of the story mostly from his younger brother, with only occasional put-ins from Pap.

Pap went back to get his horse, while Trapper went up onto the point of rocks and settled himself there. He picked out Rodger Ashland at once, without any doubt or trouble. He couldn't see Ashland's face very well, but he knew him by the way he sat his fine horse, straight-backed but easy; by the gloves which nobody else wore; and especially by the four-reined bridle. No movement could be seen in the hands or bit, but the horse stood as if carved of wood, so Trapper knew the gloved fingers kept whispering faintly down the reins.

Over in the corner of the barren yard, in front of the empty barn, was where the fellers on foot were clustered, and it was amongst these that the most of the hollering and disputation was still going on. They had built a smallish sort of fire over there, that some of them were fussing around, so maybe they were fighting over the cooking, for all Trapper could see.

And now the usual long-seeming time passed that Pap always took to get himself from one place to another, whenever Trapper happened to be waiting on him; and with the uncertainties that lay ahead, he knew this was going to be the worst wait of all. *Of course,* Trapper told himself, *he's got a far piece to go. Many inches. Might take me as much as a quarter of a minute. So for him, I better allow about an hour. I pro'bly got time to take me a good sleep. If'n I was sure I wouldn't snore. . . .*

To pass the time he tried sighting in his Sharps carbine on Rodger Ashland's face, and immediately discovered his hands were shaking; which made him so furious that he all but went rigid. He finally got himself unwound by shaking loose the first finger of each hand, as Pap had taught him, and relaxed to a point where he could at least aim the carbine. But his sights were so nearly invisible, out there in the dark, he was glad he wouldn't be called on to make the actual shot. *Better keep well down below his hat brim. What is there about a hat, makes a gun shoot high? Never saw a feller yet, claimed he'd been in a smoke-up, without he showed me a bullet hole through his hat. . . .*

He had to keep talking to himself that way to keep from watching the mouth of the weed-grown wagon track from which Pap would appear. Or else get to straining his ears for Pap's horse, which would be unhearable on the grassy footing, under all the other noises. His nerves would tighten into banjo strings if he let himself do that. *There now,* he thought, looking down his carbine. *That ought to do it. Right through the back teeth, by God. Providing he don't turn his head. . . .*

He turned it. Have to fall back on a gut-shot, I reckon. Fine, high-class piece of shooting. Going to ruin his dang jacket.

Pap still hadn't got there when Trapper saw somebody bring something away from the fire, and it was no spider nor any form of cooking iron but a great hog-leg of a pistol; and even at the distance he could see that the muzzle was white hot. The crowd made way for the man with that thing in his hand, then closed behind him when they had let him through.

"And you know what fool thing I first thought, right then?" Trapper remembered. "I thought, 'They sure treat that like a borried gun. If it wasn't busted before, it's ruint now.' "

All of a sudden all the yammering down there died down and stopped, giving room to a new sound, a dreadful sound, the awfullest Trapper had ever heard in his life. It began as a great almighty screaming, holding on and on before it died down, then rising up again, over and over. Finally it kind of sagged into an endless babbling and blubbering that was the worst of all, with no word to be made out of it; but the voice was that of an old man.

A lot of the horsemen had crowded in, stretching their necks for a look, so nothing was to be seen from where Trapper was, and it was just as well, for he could imagine what was happening much plainer than he was of a mind to. And he didn't know whether he smelled burning flesh or only imagined that part, too. But he was turned sick, and maybe so was Rodger Ashland, for he stopped it finally. He crackled out an order, pretty loud and sharp, and though Trapper didn't get the words, those down below understood it.

Five or six shots sounded, and everybody kind of hauled back, and in the open space they left, three dead men lay.

Trapper never did see Pap come there. In the silence his eyes went to Rodger Ashland, and Rodge was not looking at the dead men but toward the wagon track. So Trapper looked there, and there was Pap, setting his horse in the mouth of the track, just as cool as a hog on ice.

"Can I help you, Rodge?" Pap sung out.

All over the place you could hear the little clash and click of every kind of weapon being brought on cock.

Rodge called back, "Who-all you got with you there?"

"Look for yourself," Pap answered. "You see anybody with me?"

Rodger Ashland said just two words, not loud, but plenty clear. "Kill him," he said.

A gunshot sounded at once, and then a general scattering more. But even before the first shot sounded, Pap made his horse do something no horse could do. He jumped straight sideways, more like a fifteen-hand cat than any horse critter ever done, and he jumped at least twenty feet. ("I doubt it was more'n eighteen feet," Pap qualified later.) And in that same jump he swapped ends in the air, so he was headed back down the trail, and he lit running flat out. All so fast that a wring of the tail was about all you could see, as he whipped around the curve of the wagon track.

Now, how did Pap do that? No whip, no spurs—just his moccasins. Not even a severe bit, just a short-shanked single-rein curb, with a leather chin strap, at that. Either Shep or Trapper would have given any amount to know how such a thing was done, but they would never find out from Pap, who no more knew how he rode a horse than he knew what muscles he triggered when he walked. "Always sit facin' forward," he had told them as little boys. "Never sit facing the tail. Unless you got some reason for it," he qualified even that. From there on he could always make a few thousand scalding remarks about what they were doing wrong, but nothing more about what was right. "A man can ride a horse or he can't," was all he could say.

The ragged volley fired after him must have filled the mouth of the wagon track with buzz-bees, but Pap was gone from there. As he vanished, Trapper swung his carbine to cover Rodger Ashland's belly, and pulled, but nothing happened. To his everlasting shame, after all the hunting he had done, and all the good shots he had made, he had this time forgot to cock the hammer!

Now Rodger Ashland jumped his horse forward, cussing unheard as he whipped his pistol out; and he streaked for the mouth of the wagon track, his hotblood plainly able to gain three yards on Pap at every jump. He almost made it into the woods, but Trapper was stunned now, his brains knocked out by his own mistake, so that his hands took over, and did properly what he had failed to do when he had had time to think. He was looking down the barrel, but without benefit of the sights he could not see, and nothing to sight on anyway, the speed of Rodger's horse requiring such a long lead; and he got off his single shot.

Rodger Ashland's horse was taken in mid-stride. It collapsed in the forehand as the forehoofs struck, and went end over. Trapper had a flash glimpse of the hindquarters sticking straight up, high in the air, before the black powder diffused in a billow that blotted the whole thing out. But when next his view cleared, the horse lay wrong end to, with head twisted under, and the rider lay quiet a few yards beyond—knocked senseless, as it turned out.

Later, in afterthought, Trapper was able to figure out that he had fired at Ashland's knee, allowing that if he missed the knee his shot should get the horse, either through the shoulder or the heart; he never did know which it had been. But actually he hadn't had time to think it out that way. He hadn't even known, consciously, what his hands were doing, until the carbine kicked and the horse somersaulted. And now Trapper's brain got to work again, and he went back to doing nothing right.

He forgot to pull back from his firing position, first; didn't even reload, but just lay there trying to stare through the smoke and see what was happening. That was how he knew that the first riders starting to follow Rodge jumped down to have a look at him, blocking the wagon track. Others came cannoning into these, and in a few seconds the whole thing was corked up, securing Pap from any effective pursuit. It took a Minnié ball, saying "Cousin!" in his ear, to remind him he was supposed to get out of there.

He slung himself down the back slope a few yards, then scrambled up off-balance and plunged down the hill in great uncontrolled leaps, crashing, thrashing, bouncing off tree trunks—protecting his carbine pretty well, but making enough noise to bring rain. At the bottom he tripped in a brier tangle, and fetched up flat on his face at the edge of a cutbank, with most of his wind knocked out. Another ball whistled over from someplace, clipping twigs that dropped down the back of his neck—or at least, he thought that happened; and suddenly he was seized by an unaccountable conviction that the woods were full of people.

To get into bullet cover, he rolled over the bank, producing a great instantaneous splash as three feet of ice water closed over him. He held the carbine up in time to keep water out of the barrel, but its Maynard priming tape got soaked and so did the cartridge box at his belt, which carried the linen cartridges the Sharps was using. He made a grab at his father's revolver, and caught it just as it slipped from his belt, headed for the muck of the bottom; but of course it wasn't going to fire again either until it had been dried out and reloaded. He was clean out of firepower until he should have a chance to dry his powder.

He struggled up, spluttering, and went splashing and floundering into deeper water, where he had himself another total immersion. He had about given himself up as a goner by the time he climbed out of there, fully expecting Ashland's bushwhackers to be waiting on both banks.

Pap and Shep looked at each other. "Makes you wonder, don't it?" Pap said sadly. "I don't know how we ever get 'em raised."

Trapper finally holed up, gasping for breath, behind a log in a wild blackberry patch. It took him a long time to get his wind back enough so that he could listen to the woods. By that time the sky was brightly firelighted in the direction of the old Benjamin place, where the tumble-down old buildings were evidently burning. Except for that—nothing. Stillness in the wagon track by which they had come here, stillness in the woods, not a whisper of any kind in the windless night, other than the barely heard crackle of the flames. Even the small wildlife, that he could usually hear all through the dark hours, had been scared into total quiet.

After a good while he went and got his horse, and rode away.

✯ 14 ✯

PAP AND TRAPPER STAYED IN SOUTHERN MISSOURI FOR NEARLY four weeks more. Pap got stubborn about it, and wasn't going to be run out of there until he had got the job done that he came to do. They didn't run up against Rodger Ashland again, but they heard about him sometimes. Nobody actually spoke his name, but for a while far-traveling rumors ran wild about what had happened at the old Benjamin place, and the killings there were being laid to the followers of a Captain Handy. So, unless the rumors had got cockle-burred onto the wrong man, that must be the name Rodge was riding under—or so they supposed at that time.

Three corpses had been found in the ashes of the Benjamin barn, charred past recognition, but generally said to be those of an old man and his two grown sons. Right there the story split off more than one way, for what was plain at once was that there was more than one attitude toward Captain Handy. A few, mainly those whose blood kin had been hurt by night riders, said privately that he was nothing but a common outlaw; some even charged that he was actually a Kansas Jayhawker, armed and backed up by Damnyankee abolitionists, who had sent him to spread ruin through Missouri. These believed that the Yankees had a vast, invisible network all over the state, and every antisecessionist—pro-slavery or not—must be suspected as part of it. This faction, not very often encountered, claimed the murdered men had been honest Arkansas people, on their way home after chasing a band of slave-stealing Kansans.

But most who had anything to say about Captain Handy,

one way or the other, actually spoke highly of him, referring to his band as Handy's Volunteer Posse, or sometimes as "a citizens' committee." These claimed the victims at the old Benjamin place had been professional slave stealers, looking for a place to stash away the huge fortune they had amassed. And not only that, but they had lately incited four slaves to murder their master, someplace. You could even hear the three dead men were John Brown of Pottawatomie himself, and two of his sons. Since nobody seemed to know just where John Brown was, it was hard to say for sure that this decorative notion was a lie.

One weird detail that kept cropping up in all the stories was to the effect that the old man's eyes had been burned out with a red-hot gun barrel before the three were shot down. You could make discoveries about people you had known for a long time by the way they told this part. A few spoke of it with revulsion, or at least with condemnation; but it was kind of awful how most people just told it in a matter-of-fact way, as a kind of interesting curiosity more than anything else. And some even showed a ghastly sort of relish.

"Now, damn it!" Shep objected. "God knows, Pap, I hold no brief for a man who tried to murder you off. And I've hated Rodger Ashland's guts in his own right for a long time. But what in Christ's name would anybody on earth do a thing like that for?"

"I take it they was questioning him," Pap said dryly.

"*Questioning?*"

"Like, where was their money."

Trapper said he believed every word of it. "I heard the old man screaming, didn't I? I seen the het-up gun barrel, didn't I? And I seen 'em shot down—or virtually seen it—"

"But you didn't see no eyes burned out," Pap said harshly, "and neither did I! It's a damned funny thing we never found anybody who ever set eyes on Captain Handy—or ever knowed of anybody who did! Yet everywhere we went, there was people knew more about what happened at Benjamins' than we did!"

They had gone on with their survey, taking the same precautions as before, but no new ones; and they had no special trouble. Once, traveling at night, they were fired on in the dark, but they just flogged on out of there, and nobody followed. Soon they began to hear of new raids by Captain Handy, at the rate of about one a week—

"Wait a minute," Shep said. "Rodger Ashland boarded the *Royal Oaks* at Nanchez on August fourteenth. And Julie had a letter from him that was mailed from Natchez at least a week before that. He must have left Missouri right after you saw him at the Benjamin place."

"That's right," Pap agreed. "Of course, we didn't know that. But toward the last Captain Handy was reported making two raids far apart on the same night. We knew then that nobody was named Captain Handy; not any one man, anyway. It's just a name they use when they don't want to speak any name. All we ever come to know about Rodger Ashland was just what we seen with our own eyes. Nothing more."

"I don't understand this at all," Shep said. "What did he want to kill you for? Sounds to me like he's been making himself popular in Missouri, more than anything. What's he got to be afraid of?"

"He's got Tyler Ashland to be afraid of."

"I don't see that either. He can claim he was spreading peace and light—same as Tyler himself was doing at the sack of Lawrence."

"That part might go all right. Or it might not. But Rodge made a mistake. Two mistakes, really. The first was when he let his bushwhackers get out of hand. There isn't really very much to be made, jumping on these little farmers. Nothing like they probably hoped. They pick up a few horses they can trade off down in Arkansas, or someplace. Maybe a few firearms, but seldom any that are new or much good. Scarcely any money at all. . . . These old misers you hear about, hoarding their every cent—they generally turn out to be nothing but old scratch-pennies that never made any money to hoard. . . ."

Woolhats liked to follow a man like Rodge, because it gave them the only association with quality they were ever likely to know, but they never did take to discipline easily. Probably Rodge thought he'd better go easy on them at first, and

tighten down on them later. Any army sergeant could have
told him it had to be done the other way round—bear down
hard at the first and slack off later. But Rodger Ashland
hadn't the experience to know that. So, Pap figured, if the
night riders convinced themselves they had hold of some rich
slave stealers, with a big fortune hid out, Rodge may have
thought he had to let them make a try for it their own way
or have a revolt on his hands. Except for that, the whole affair at the Benjamin place could have passed off as a local
lynch-riot—a rising up of outraged citizens, to deal with
known criminals—Rodge standing by to preserve decent order. Or, it could have been handled as the Kansas abolitionists
handled the murders by John Brown on Pottawatomie
Creek—the whole thing classed as a political embranglement,
with so many sympathizers involved that no question of crim-
inal law applied.

But when it came to torturing an old man for his
money—or even sitting by and letting it be done, in room of
taking charge—that was something for which no gentleman
could ever be forgiven.

"The story was bound to get back to Ash Landing, someday. Too many people know that Rodge was there—and so
was I."

"Nobody Tyler Ashland would believe!"

"Except me. Ty knows I don't lie, and his boy knows he
knows it," Pap said. "You don't buy a horse from a man sight
unseen without knowing that much about him. So suppose
Tyler Ashland asked me what happened—and I so much as
refused to answer. He might never give sign that he knew the
truth—but he'd know it, all right. That was what Rodge was
afraid of."

There never would be any legal comeuppance for Rodger, no
matter what; no penalty of the law, or court-tested proof, or sen-
sational trial. Ashland would stand solid behind Rodge, never
admitting to a smear upon the Ashland name. It would be his
own people Tyler Ashland would have to face down. What
would come from them would be a silence, unanswerable because nothing would be said. But inside him he would know;
and Old Ty would never forget or forgive the humiliation of

that. Someday, maybe when Tyler Ashland died and his will was read, Rodge might find out he'd lost himself a kingdom the night he rode to the old Benjamin place.

"I could have saved his bacon for him," Pap said somberly. "I could have told old Ty, no, I didn't see nobody tortured. Heard some hollering. Might have been somebody threatening somebody, for all I saw. I could have throwed it up to Tyler—hadn't he ever heard an abolitionist holler? And anyway—Rodge stopped it, whatever it was, and made them execute the criminals clean, by firing squad. All that is to the letter of the fact. If I had to bend the spirit of the truth a leetle mite I'd have bent it quick enough, in self-defense. I could have made his father proud of him if only he had kept his head."

"Damn it, Pap, Rodge must have known you couldn't afford to carry tales to his old man!"

"Sure, he knew it. If he'd had time to think. But I'd taken him by surprise, and he panicked. All of a sudden he sees me sitting there, and what he sees is the one mudsill in creation Tyler Ashland will believe. 'Kill him,' he says—and down come the cobhouse. Right there he committed himself to murdering us all out of Missouri, without no way to turn back; and we got ourselves a blood feud with the Ashlands—the very last feud I wanted on this earth."

"We'll fight 'em," Trapper said, almost stolidly. "We'll fight 'em into the ground."

Neither Shep nor Pap bothered to answer him, it was so plain on the face of it that this feud was one they couldn't win. "What are we going to do?" Shep asked Pap.

"We're going fishing, I guess."

"We're what?"

"I've got to pick up some rest."

"And after that?"

"I don't know."

★ 15 ★

THEY PUT THEIR HORSES IN A BOARDING STABLE AND CROSSED TO a towhead, where they camped in the willows for several days, fishing a little to pass the time, but hoping they wouldn't catch much; while Pap mostly slept. What time Pap was awake he asked Shep occasional questions, sometimes about his trading, but mainly about pointless things, without any bearing on their troubles so far as Shep could see. It was the third day before Pap began to rouse up, and Shep suddenly saw what his father had been driving at all along. Without Shep's realizing it, Pap had worked out of him all about how things had gone on the *Royal Oaks*; and knew that Shep was in love with Julie Delorme, past all reasonable present hope.

"I blame myself," Pap said. "I should have pulled you off the *Tealwing* the minute I saw she was on it."

"Why? I never got knocked in the head like this before."

That was true, Pap admitted. Most youngsters had an early siege of affliction, when they could no more be held responsible than partridges in crazy season, when they fly blind all night, bashing into anything in their way. If it came on early enough, you could call it puppy love, and let it run its course. But, maybe because Pap had always let Shep run the levees, Shep had never frozen onto any one girl for very long. And that was the worst thing about it, for now it hit all the harder, like mumps in a grownup. Never was any remedy for it, at any age. "You had no chance," Pap grieved over it. "That girl cottoned onto you when she was twelve years old. Even as a little pigtailer she used to foller you around, trying to get your attention. But you never paid her no mind. If it wasn't for you, she'd most likely be married to her damned cousin today."

"What's so all-fired overpowering about me?" Shep asked, hoping to hear more.

"Nothing that I can see. But Tyler Ashland noticed it, a good while back. It's a great tribute to you as a mule drover that he didn't nail your hide to the barn while he had you in a trading position. Thing is, he's so deep in debt to Delorme, about the only way to keep Ash Landing in one piece is to marry Rodge to Julie. Naturally he hates your guts."

"This here is past all swallering," Shep rejected it. "Up to this year I scarcely spoke to her in my life!"

Pap judged *that* had worked in Shep's favor. "Lots of fellers look better with their mouth shut."

Shep said he didn't believe a word of it, and it was a good thing, because if he did he'd shoot himself. "You and Trapper sure played hell when you rode into that murder party. For once in your life, couldn't you have turned tail and rode *away* from the worst contention you could find, instead of right square into the middle of it? No—I supposed not. Too much to ask!"

Pap didn't argue it. "What do you figure to do about this Delorme girl?"

"What can I do? All of a sudden, we're in a feud with her blood kin. By God, if I'd seen it coming I swear I'd have run off with her before we ever saw Natchez! Or tried to, anyway."

"Well," Pap said glumly, "I suppose that's about all that's left open to you now."

"What's left open?"

"Run off with her and marry her. That's what I always done. The one time it ever come up, I mean."

"Marry her on what? I haven't got so much as a chamberpot, or a window to throw it out of!"

Pap said that if he had stopped to skin fleas any such niggling way, Sheep wouldn't be here now. "I was married on a dollar and thirty-two cents. If I've raised a boy can be held back for lack of a sum like that, by God, I'll pay it out of my own pocket!"

The whole discussion had become unbearable to Shep. "What you better start worrying about is what we're going to do about your mule business," he said, letting a faint emphasis fall on the "your." It was an unfair thing to say, but he had been sealing off more bitterness than he realized. "Way we been going, you soon won't have any thirty-two cents! You know that, don't you?"

Pap thought about that for quite a while. "I'll let you know in the morning," he said at last; and he went back to sleep.

Shep and Trapper returned to their fishing. Trapper tied a small stone onto his hand line, and slung it far out.

"What kind of bait you call that?"

"If I put on bait, I'll catch something. I've et all the fried cat I can keep down." As it turned out, Trapper landed a sixteen-pounder on his empty hook; but that was later. "What are we waiting on? Sure—I know—Pap has to make up his mind. To what? We got to get our critters out of Missouri, what's left of 'em, and such as we can. Until that's done, there's nothing to decide."

He was wrong. Next morning Pap was up before the first light, cooked a big breakfast, and woke up his sons in a mild pink and green dawn. "Shep! Trapper! It's quarter of four! You going to sleep all day?"

"Well, did you cipher out anything?" Shep asked with pessimism.

"Yup."

"What, then?"

"Eat your breakfast."

That is a mighty handsome decision. Well, it beats what I expected What's happened, Pup's gone to work and aged out on us, that's all.

Just then Pap startled him by speaking out almost the exact words that had run through Shep's mind. "Tell you what I think has happened," Pap said. "I've gone to seed on you."

Shep and Trapper went through identical motions, in that curious way in which they sometimes both responded at once to the same situation, while not otherwise looking alike at all.

Each was stuck motionless for a period of some three seconds; then, at the same instant, their eyes slanted to Pap's face, and held there, woodenly expressionless.

"Somehow I can't seem to remember, no more, what was my theory, riding myself to death for the sake of the mules. Used to know. But since Ma passed away, I believe I've just kept on so's you boys would have some kind of a start. Well, that horse won't pull no more. We been losing ground, in room of getting on with it."

"That's no fault of yourn," Trapper said.

"Whatever there is we can save out, it all goes to you boys when I die off. How long is that going to be? Ten years, twenty-five? Could be forty. The less you give a damn, the longer you last, seems like. Any start you get from me is liable to be of no boon to you until you're about sixty years old. . . . No. When you need your start is now. So . . . I'm going to divide the whole thing between you, as soon as we've pulled what we can out of Missouri. That's a right ticklish job; I don't know if you realize how ticklish it'll be. So I'm in charge until that's done. But after that—no more."

Trapper reacted first. He said, with reluctance, with hesitance, "I'd always kind of figured . . ."

He let it die out, but both Pap and Shep knew what was in his mind. Pap assumed, without any questions, that Shep would want to stay in the land where he had been raised, working with the tools he understood, and Pap was right. The country Shep felt was home stretched over a couple of thousand square miles, from middle Indiana to southern Mississippi. It had Illinois prairie and Kentucky bluegrass, flood-silt bottoms, timbered hills, country a red hog couldn't hardly stand up on, and seven kinds of farms. It was a broad reach for a man to sprangle out over, but Shep had sunk his roots deep into it, nevertheless. To him, the Mississippi basin was America, all of it he knew or cared about. But Trapper had inherited the same push-on instinct that had brought their family into the mid-continental wilderness to begin with; every spring and every fall, when the wild geese went over, Trapper felt the same irresistible call the geese answered. He wanted to try the California trade, as a common bullwhacker first, to learn the way; then meat hunter, guide, scout; then a few wagons of his own, and finally his own train. The gift of an established business or half of one, however profitable, appalled him as a hopeless millstone around his ankles.

"I know what's in your mind," Pap said to Trapper. "But I want you to stay with Shep until you're twenty-one. Why? Because he'll need you, that's why. Hell, boy, you can't even sign papers for yourself before then, if'n anybody wants to make an issue of it. After that you can sell out to Shep, or make any deal you want to work out between you. I'll have nothing to say."

Trapper nodded, slowly, in acceptance; and for a while they were silent, embarrassed for want of words. What they were looking at was the last of many things. They were a small family, but they had worked together as a single organism, however much they might have disagreed among themselves. Now it was going out of the world, and they were sobered by the finality of that; but they did not actually feel it yet. Each of the boys wanted to say some adequate thing to Pap, in gratitude and a decent simulation of regret. But nothing came to them to say.

Shep finally said, "What are *you* going to do, Pap?"

"I figure there'll be enough money for you to build a fine house, down in the stylish part of Paducah. I want you to do that right away. Not keep putting it off, and putting it off, making do with the old, like I always done, until it was too late. And that's part of the deal, while I'm still in the saddle."

"But what about you?"

"That's a horse I'll handle when I get him roped." He wouldn't say any more than that, for now.

Trapper started to ask how soon Pap thought they'd be out of Missouri, but it was a fool question, and he snatched it back half said. They all knew they'd be lucky if none of them stayed there. Pap drew a deep breath, and held it, then let it out slowly, his eyes lost in the mists beyond the river; and Shep knew he was thinking of Ma. She would have wanted him to forget the livestock and turn his back on Missouri at all costs, if only for the sake of the boys. But what right has a man to force cowardice upon his sons? Pap taught his boys prudence, or thought he did, in so far as he knew what it was. But he always had balked at making them shy off from risks he would have accepted himself, and he could not change that now.

So they bailed out the johnboat, and plunged into the Missouri wilderness; and for five long months, Pap set them a pace there.

✷ 16 ✷

ON NIGHTS WHEN THEY DARED HAVE A FIRE, PAP DANIELS SAT cross-legged beside it, writing up the ledgers he had heretofore carried only in his head. He had one for each state in which they had interests, but Shep knew Missouri, which had produced the bulk of their mules, and Trapper knew Tennessee, where most of their giant jacks were raised. Pap was chiefly recording accounts the boys didn't know about, in eastern Kentucky, Arkansas, and Mississippi. Here and there he wrote in little notations, such as might help deal with individuals he had found difficult in some way:

> We got lots of friends up the Staggerbuck Valley, owing to I always took them candy when they was little. There is plenty middle age people look for me to bring them candy yet. But don't never take any sticky candy, their teeth get loose in winter up there, it won't help us none if we pull all their teeth out.

They rode armed now, all the time. Trapper always had, but Pap had carried a hidden pistol only a part of the time and Shep had generally kept his heavy cap-and-ball revolver in his bedroll. Now Pap and Trapper had Spencer carbines in their saddleboots and Shep had the breech-loading Sharps single-shot that had belonged to Trapper. There weren't many Spencers around; to buy one you had to find one. Shep had located two, for himself and Pap, but Trapper had been so disappointed that Shep had traded with him.

They took their longest swing to westward first, covering

89

the neighborhoods of Lebanon, Woodbury, Hartford, and Wolf Creek. September was very hot, very dry, with the locusts sawmilling around the clock and the fireflies stirrup-deep all night. The roads were powdery, and thick to breathe, but fast and easy on the critters' feet, so that they made long distances every day. In that first month they serpentined for hundreds of miles across lower Missouri, always on guard, always wakeful—while nobody interfered with them in the least. They heard no more of Captain Handy, and the few rumors of other raiders came from far away. They were in a lull most ominously like that before a far greater storm. Where were the night riders? Maybe it was a time of regrouping and the licking of wounds, following devastations of such unforeseen extent as should have brought grave forebodings to all connected with them.

Or maybe they owed the truce to nothing more profound than the harvest season, which at the same time was proving to be the Dainelses' greatest impediment. Pap would never pull work teams out from under the laggards whose crops were still standing. Again and again the drovers tied in to pitch hay or pick corn, to get the work over with; or else doubled back to cover the same ground once more.

Some of their breeders gave trouble over yielding up loaned brood mares, or young mules brought to the collar, but these were fewer than they had feared. Many small farmers were giving up, to move to less disturbed areas; others were already gone, and the Daniels livestock with them, unlikely to be seen again. But all losses together were running lighter than they had been led to expect in the west, under the very guns of the Kansas Jayhawkers. They might yet be able to settle for an over-all loss of only twenty-five or thirty per cent.

And they found they had more friends left than they had supposed, with whom gathered livestock could be safely left in small bunches, to be picked up on their way back. After they turned eastward, a dozen or so often rode with them for a long way, an unpaid armed guard who made a picnic out of every mile. And thus they reached the Rolla railhead by mid-October, unscathed.

Pap used the fretful period of delay at Rolla to write inter-
minably in his ledgers:

Up Whippy Creek is the only place I ever knowed a 8
year old child to have a baby. Some up there say, Well
wy not, she was married when she was 7. But others say
no, it was only a catch colt, the marryin story was just
made up by dam yankees to make them look bad. The
rest of the district is republican.

While Pap worked on his ledgers, Shep sweated and suf-
fered over a letter to Julie. He hadn't had time to write to her
when they saw their last of the Mississippi at Cape
Girardeau, and there was no reliable way to send mail out of
the back country any more. So now he was trying to tell her
about his plans and dreams, in a way that would hold her, he
hoped, and forestall a misstep that would spoil both their
lives forever. It was the most important letter he had ever
written in his life and he couldn't get it right, or even any
good at all; he kept burning what there was of it, to start
again. But finally their stock was loaded, and he sealed it up,
less in hope than desperation, and got it into the mail in the
last minutes before it left the end of track. They were past the
middle of October, and Julie must be in New Orleans by this
time, two thousand miles away, as rails and river wandered.
But he judged his letter ought to reach her before the last of
November.

From Rolla, after another week and a half of writing, they
shipped a hundred and four head of mixed stock—heavy
brood mares, mule foals, yearlings and twos, young work
stock, and a handful of jacks. Less than they had hoped, but
worth six or seven thousand dollars on any market—a pretty
rich haul in its own right, if you forgot the losses. On the
whole, it had been a good month, an encouraging and hopeful
month, though a slow one, stretching out to seven weeks before they were done with it.

With the cooling weather, the night-riding bands that had
lain idle through the dry heat of Indian summer now stirred
to life, as unpredictably as they had eased off. Jayhawkers

made a deep foray across the Kansas border, first, into the rich lands near the Missouri. Other disconnected outbreaks followed, spreading slowly southward and eastward, as before. Pap judged that the imminent presidential elections might explain it. Deadly tensions, first induced when the Border Wars turned inward upon Missouri, were becoming unbearable, in the shadows of vast uncertainties soon to be resolved. But the Danielses were riding southward, threading the heart of the Ozarks toward the Arkansas border, and the fresh outbreaks were behind them. Nobody troubled them yet.

The news of Lincoln's election was ahead of them at West Plains, and nobody was more dumbfounded than Pap Daniels. In the stormy political climate through which they had traveled, no possibility of a minority abolitionist President had ever occurred to anybody. Die-hards refused to believe it; the early return had indicated a Douglas landslide, and they could not get it out of their heads. Most, though, understood what had happened. The party-bolting candidacies of the secessionists Breckinridge and Bell—themselves in disagreement—had split the Democrat vote three ways; each had tolled off enough votes to have elected Douglas, a Unionist, to be sure, but a stout proslavery man. Thus the power of the Presidency had been lost to the South at last. Regionally there were periods of strange stillness, as if Missouri lay stunned.

What Pap saw was that new uncertainties had now riddled a situation already about as shaky as it could get. Without a guess as to what would happen, he judged that whatever it was would move faster now, and he reacted sharply, trying to speed up their retrenchment.

And next the rains came, opening up with monstrous thunderstorms that sent lightning dancing in hundred-mile jumps all over the Ozark peaks and deluged the state. Once begun, the rains held on in a steady drizzle-drazzle, broken by downpours; every day their livestock moved more slowly on the worsening roads. The pace at which they moved was limited by the weaker stock, so Pap now got rid of a good many of the slower, any way he could, and redoubled his own efforts to keep them safe and moving.

From West Plains they looped eastward, still picking up

livestock, plodding back toward Rolla by way of Eminence and the headwaters of the Current River, a far longer way than that by which they had come. November was old when they drove seventy-odd head through the little timbering village of Salem, and camped beyond it, no more than three days from Rolla. Pap dropped back, in the early winter dusk, and loitered for a while in Salem to see what he could learn. It was after dark when he rejoined his sons, where they had camped in the dripping timber, and immediately changed his saddle to a fresh horse.

"Heard something," was all he told Shep and Trapper. Then he packed a wad of raw cornmeal in his cheek and trotted northward on the Rolla road, pressing briskly.

Two hours after midnight he was back, his horse played out and lathering, and shook his sons out of their blankets. "We got to turn around. Right now. We're blocked off from Rolla."

"How many men?" Shep asked.

"Fifty to sixty near as I can judge. Camped about sixteen miles ahead. Been working southward, toward us, by all signs."

"You think they know anything about us?"

"They know. Never mind why I think so. I'll explain you that later. Someday, when we got time for it."

Shep was studying on the sixteen-mile start they had, thinking how easily they could be found and overtaken wherever they might go. But it was so obvious a likelihood that he didn't remark on it, and neither did the others.

Trapper wanted to keep on toward Rolla, and fight on through, if they had to. "Might even be friends . . ."

"Well, they ain't." Pap didn't bother to mention the odds against three men whipping sixty. "There's a reason we can't fight these people, and I got no time to go into that neither!"

Trapper wanted to argue it; he was itching to try out his repeating Spencer in a real fight. But Pap turned on him in a brief blast of such fury that Trapper was silenced for hours. They took the road again, in the bitter cold of the night rain, heading back the weary way they had come.

⋆ 17 ⋆

BEFORE DAYLIGHT THEY TOOK A DISUSED LUMBERING ROAD
through the woods to avoid Salem, and gained the main road
eastward, such as it was. They were trying for Ironton, a min-
ing town a long, long way farther to the east than the
seventy-five miles they called it, on evil roads that never did
seem to go the way they wanted to. The rains kept on, and
though the nights were bitter cold, it was a wet cold that did
not firm the footing; often the small hoofs of the mules sank
belly-deep in gumbo. But Ironton was the terminus of a railway spur from St. Louis, and if they could ship their animals
on the steam cars from there they would save almost a like
distance farther to Ste. Genevieve on the Mississippi. Pap
Daniels traded for a calf wagon, in which to haul the weaker
of the foals, and a second wagon for corn and forage, which
they paid cash for every day, somewhere along the way. This
made travel barely possible; nothing could improve their
speed. Sometimes they bushed up, deep in the timber, to let
small parties of riders go by who looked like bushwhacker
scouts, and then they were briefly grateful for the swimming
roads that erased their trail. Other times they took circuitous
evasive actions over cutoffs much slower than the long way
around.

Shep tried to find out from Pap what night riders, other
than Rodger Ashland, he had recognized at the Benjamin
place, and whom he had seen camped on the road before
Rolla, but he couldn't learn anything. "Won't do you any
good to know names. Not now." Pap's reputation for telling
the truth was deserved, but he also knew how to keep his

94

mouth shut. "I'll tell you what you need to know when you need to know it. Not before!"

It took them three dreadful weeks to reach Ironton, with a herd reduced to sixty-three head.

At Ironton they again waited for cars, in the shakiest kind of security, standing guard in rotation upon the stockpens, while the anxious days dragged by. They were still there when they learned that South Carolina had seceded, and they spent much thought on what this might mean to mules, but without coming to any useful conclusions. And thus their Christmas was spent.

While they waited they argued over what they would do next. It was Trapper who was possessed by the stubbornest notion. He wanted to go back to Waynesville, and he thought up forty exasperating reasons for claiming this was logical. He even tried to toll Shep onto his side with a special holt. "That younger Potter girl, the one they call Caylin—she's mighty sweet on you, Shep. You know that, don't you? I could see it plain while I was there. Couldn't talk about nothing else but you and asked all kinds of questions—"

It was the last bait likely to get Shep to Waynesville. What Trapper said was true, all right, and Shep had known it for a long time, to his great embarrassment. Caylin was younger than Julie, and always undersized for her age, but very early in maturing. She was sweet-eyed, winning as a kitten, and somehow kind of pitiful in her unconcealed adoration. But Caylin simply didn't attract Shep, and Pap's rule against meddling with the womenfolk of business connections had never been needed in her case.

"You been fooling with the Potter girls?" Shep demanded.

And now the truth came out. Trapper had left his Morgan saddler at Waynesville to rest up, and he wanted to go get it.

"Oh, hell," Shep said, disgusted. "Is that all! One more word about that dang plug and I'll belt you!"

Shep himself would have been willing to write off the rest of the Missouri livestock and get out of there while they could. He wanted to get down to New Orleans and have a try at sweeping Julie Delorme off her feet. Marry her on the spot, if he could; or else run off with her, if she would go with him. He was haunted by the conviction that every day that passed was working against him. But Pap had set his teeth in this job and would not let go.

"One more swing," Pap insisted. "The last, the shortest, and the surest. I've planned it from the first. It shouldn't take long. And after that, I promise you, we'll call it a year."

They finally got cars and finished their loading after dark. Shep had accumulated a whole stack of little short letters to Julie this time, and hoped they would help his case, though he wished he could get one to her every few days, instead of dumping them all on her in a heap. But now he only had to write a brief note more, telling her he hoped to see her soon. He was asleep before Pap finished his nightly stint with his ledgers, now nearly done:

Clapperjaw Holler is one of these here places, they got a wild man running loose. Or so they claim, and I think they believe it, so maybe you better let on to.

This one they say is 8 foot tall, and shaggy like a bear, and leaves tracks 2 foot long with toes like a man, no claws.

Very often this thing drags some woman in the bushes, and gets her in trouble, and they give her an abortion, and all the neighbors gather round. In sympathy. Or maybe in thirst, them people never can clot up without they fetch out the jugs and fiddles, it turns into a regular abortion bee. But they dont call it that, I dont know what they call it.

Personally I dont believe in no such critter. Though I seen some of the tracks. I have about give up on accounting for everything.

As 1861 began they saddled in the bitter blackness before daylight and headed south toward the last adventure into which the three would ever ride together.

✶ 18 ✶

Their last swing, this one through southeastern Missouri, went quickly, at first, as Pap had promised. The wilderness they rode was less muleful than they had hoped, for they were combing the southeastern borders of the burnt countries. But some light, hard-packing snows rebuilt the roads for them, and they made good time for a while.

During January, five more states joined South Carolina in secession. Florida, Alabama, and Georgia had been expected to go out, and the enormous state of Texas, which followed on February 1, seemed far away. But the defection of Mississippi and Louisiana cut in two the great river itself, the all-important highway of Middle America, and the West's outlet to the world. An overwhelming cataclysm had abruptly become real and close to home. The departure of the seven was no extension of the windy declarations that had gone on for years, but this time a rebellion in armed force. In the first month of 1861 the seceding states seized thirteen forts, four arsenals, and a navy yard; a supply ship, carrying relief stores to Fort Sumter, was fired upon, and turned back from Charleston Harbor. The breakup of the Union was an accomplished fact.

But now the rains came back, with brutal thaws, and animals began dying in the mired roads again. Somehow, in spite of all their efforts, January got away from them, and the Danielses' final all-out effort to get out of Missouri left them no time to think about what meanings the incredible dissolution of the nation might have for them.

Pap was changing horses twice and three times a day,

scouting great distances both ahead and behind. His eyes appeared to sink deeper into dark pits, but behind them red fires often glowed. Except that he admitted now that he planned to spend the rest of his life in sleep, his furious energies showed no signs of slacking off. Moving with great difficulty, but encountering no interference, they neared Greenville, where Pap had prearranged to buy thirty or forty head of low-priced saddle horses. Beyond Greenville they would strike directly for the Cape Girardeau plank road; they would be as good as on the river once they set hoofs on that. Then suddenly they hit the end of their rope. Blocking their way into Greenville were camped perhaps a dozen armed men, whom they dared not try to pass.

They turned back undetected, and drove southward, across country, down the Big Black, to the road through Poplar Bluff; then eastward again, trying now for the little railway spur at Buffington, which would take them to the Mississippi opposite Cairo. A hard, slow week—and they were cut off again, this time by a small, unknown number of bushwhackers, very obviously watching the road, almost within sight of Buffington.

Pap called a family council. He believed it hopeless to try for Cape Girardeau again, by whatever way. He was willing now, if his sons were, to abandon the livestock to whoever it was wanted it so badly, and get out of this wet nightmare of a wilderness forever. But they still had more than fifty head of mixed stock able to keep on, and neither Shep nor Trapper wanted to let go. Pap said he guessed he would have to blame himself; he never had brought them up to know when they were licked. And he admitted there was one more way by which they might possibly win through to the river.

Once more they cut across country, then westward toward Greenville by the St. Francisville road. Toward the end of the third day Pap led them into trackless country again and stopped upon a ridge from which they could see the lay of the land.

"Yonder lies the Black Mingo. It isn't the meanest swamp in the world, or even in Missouri. But I guess it's bad enough to serve the purpose, the way the weather's been. I want you to skirt the west edge of it to the old trace. If you can claw through, it'll bring you to Fiddler's Bend. Whatever used to be there got washed away long ago, but there's a big towhead forces the steamboats close to shore. Shep, you remember how to get on the Black Mingo Trace?"

Shep believed so, but—"Where are you going to be?"

Pap said he was going to make a quick ride to the west, for one more try at the horse herd supposed to be waiting for him at Greenville. If the night riders who had kept them out of there before were still around, he would come away; even if they were long gone, they might have taken the Greenville horses with them. But if he could get the horses out, and hire himself a little help, he could catch up to his sons in the Black Mingo Trace, in maybe three-four days.

Shep and Trapper looked at each other. The horses might show a worthy profit, but the risk was very great. They would have stopped Pap had they known any way to do it. But here was his one last, bold, unnecessary feat of audacity and endurance, the one thing more, over and above what any other man of any age would try to do; and they knew they could take it away from him.

"I ask of you just one thing," he told them. "If you're cut off again, or overtook, leave the stock in the road, and take to the swamp—on foot, if you have to. But above all, you must make no fight of it. You'll only be whelmed under if you try that." When Trapper wanted to argue, Pap knew how to put a cork in it. "You don't want to get your old man killed, do you?" he demanded fiercely. "Ask yourself, with you ahead of me in the trace, what choice would I have but to ride straight into the sound of gunfire? You know there couldn't be but one end!"

That night Pap had one thing more to say to Shep alone. "You, most especial, have all the reason in the world to get out of Missouri without a fight. Suppose it turns out to be Rodger Ashland you run into—"

Shep didn't want to believe that was likely. "What makes you think Rodge is man enough to ride all winter, just to—"

"Because I've seen him. Twice. Once when we was shut off from reaching the steam cars at Rolla; and again when we couldn't get into Greenville. And that's but one of many things I didn't want to tell you till I had to. He's here, somewhere, all right; and in a way it's good news for you, son."

Shep wanted to know why.

"Because it means she's give him the mitten again. Wouldn't he have spent Christmas, at least, with Julie, if she'd married him already? Or even was about to?"

Pap even thought there was a chance of peace, of sorts, with the Ashlands if they kept their heads. "We've spread no tales. He's bound to see, someday, we're willing to back off from it if he is. If ever I run into him face to face, where he can't shoot, like on a steamboat, you know what I'll do? I'll make a joke of it. Claim I realized he didn't recognize me, at the time he fired on me. As for you—give him a wide berth if you can. But if ever he corners you, you might try the same thing. I don't believe he's game to shoot you down if you're unarmed, and with your hands up. Not with witnesses, anyway. Might be we'll yet come out of this without a killing on either side."

Shep wasn't ready to think so, but he promised to avoid a fight if he could. Anybody but Trapper should be able to see they had nothing to gain by it.

"Never forget," Pap tacked on as a clincher, "once you corpse Julie Delorme's blood kin, no excuse of self-defense can get you forgiveness so long as you live. If by any chance you do live, I mean," Pap finished.

That night Pap wrote his last ledger entry, and it was strangely unlike him. When the boys were little, Ma had sometimes recited the Twenty-third Psalm for them at bedtime, to settle them peacefully for the night, and Pap had sometimes filled in for her. Now, as if reaching for happy days long gone, he tried to write it down; but over the years a lot of it had escaped him, so that he got lost in it, and trailed off.

> The Lord is my Shepherd,
> I shall not want.
> He leadeth me into green pastures,
> My cup runneth over.

In the Valley of the Shadow of Death
Beside the still waters,
He anointeth my soil.

Here he gave it up:

God bless you both.
I love you very much.

He clapped the last of his ledgers shut and rolled into his blankets. When his sons roused in the first dawn, he had already saddled and gone.

✶ **19** ✶

I T WAS THE MORNING OF THEIR SIXTH DAY IN THE BLACK MINGO
Trace when Shep doubled back for seven miles along the way
they had come, to get a look at their back trail. He had become aware the day before that a considerable number of
horses were somewhere behind them in the trace. Though
they were too far back to be identified with certainty, he had
felt reassured, satisfied that Pap was at last overtaking
them—belated, and gaining only gradually, but coming
along. He thought he was exercising undue caution, actually,
in taking the trouble to make sure who was coming up from
behind.

He was wrong. He wode rearward before dawn, to take advantage of the hour before the night frost melted into mist,
blinding the distance; and at daybreak he began climbing
trees to look for a backsight. He found what he wanted in the
upper branches of a pin oak, on this third try. What he had
there was a narrow hole through the leafless woods, opening
upon a scant thirty yards of the trace behind them, at any eye-
line distance of perhaps a quarter of a mile. It was enough.
An uneven file of badly mounted riders was visible upon the
bit of miry trail he could see; he could make out the long-
barreled rifles that some of them carried cross-saddle in front
of them. The horses moved laboriously, noses swinging low
to the mud, yet were pressed steadily along. He could not tell
how many had passed before he got a look at them, but at
least fourteen crossed the gap while he watched.

Then, at the end of the file appeared one rider more, sitting
straight and lightly upon a tall, well-balanced horse; and Shep

instantly recognized Rodger Ashland. He would have known him by the position of his hands on the reins alone; he would have known him at four times the distance, or at the ends of the earth. . . .

He did not kill the pretty-good saddle mule he rode in catching up with Trapper; no mule of sound mind would let even Shep Daniels do that. But he rode it hard enough to lose it forever, just the same. The mule let itself be forced almost to the hindmost of the failing yearlings before it quit. Here it raised its tail, fixing to bray, but instead sank to its quarters, let its breath go in a hollow whistle, and lay down. Shep pulled saddle and bridle off it, and left it slowly settling, with the unequaled tranquility of mules, into the mud.

"I figure them for seven miles behind," Shep told Trapper, "allowing for that long slough between me and them, when I saw them. They ought to be a few hours looping around that; God knows it gave us trouble enough. Point is, they've got in between us and Pap . . ."

They agreed to press on as long and as far as they could. They had originally expected to make Fiddler's Bend two days back, maybe they could still make it today; all depended upon what they ran into ahead. Meantime, Rodger Ashland was probably trying harder to close on them than Pap was; Pap was unlikely to pile up onto the night riders during this one day more. If they could reach Fiddler's Bend with even one hour to spare, one of them could hold the herd in hiding, deep in the swamp tangles and the dark, while the other circled back around the bushwhackers to warn Pap. They might yet save livestock and all, with luck.

They pressed on for seven hours more, locked in a weird, unnatural horse race. It was a chase, but a chase like a fever dream, in which time hung suspended while they plodded forever in the same place. A mule colt fell, and could not get up; they left it where it was, its beat-out mare standing low-headed over it. An hour later a big mare, heavy with foal, went into premature labor, and they lost her too. Shep could no longer imagine this winter, this road, this day, ever having any end. The barren woods, under dark and ragged winter skies, had never looked bleak or desolate to him before. Their smoky color was linked in his mind with the good smells of frosty fodder, dried leaves, burning slash, and potatoes frying when you're hungriest; all these in days when he hadn't had a care in the world, and trifling matters, such as finding something to eat, and fixing himself a comfortable way to sleep, were the nearest things to problems that he had.

And in other years, if mud and slush finally came to seem unending, he would have begun lying awake nights to listen for the harsh, sweet clamor of wild geese going over, far off in the high sky. Once he had heard them, the bright days of spring would begin pulling him along, as if they were just ahead instead of a long way off. From then on he could look at the sullen grays and purples of the hardwoods, perpetually wet without glistening, and see the first pale mist of opening buds and the increasing leafage, through which flocks of tree birds would soon be chattering their way north; he could almost smell the fresh warmth, and the greenness of new shoots and sprouting seeds, under the clean reborn sun weeks before these things were due.

All those things were gone out of his life now, and they were not coming back. He could expect to hate the winter, and all its sights and smells and flavors, for the rest of his life; even the spring might be spoiled for him by the taste of bitterness this year had brought, when he had prayed for spring too long, and it had not come.

Shep figured that by now the pursuit should have closed half the distance; their enemies must be three, maybe three and a half miles behind. Ahead of them wound the last of the deadly trace; five miles more—perhaps no more than four—should bring them within sight of the river, and their answer. Hard to believe they couldn't make it somehow. But slower than turtles they seemed to move, slower than snails, as slowly as clams upon the bottom of a creek. It was as if an animal with a broken back dragged itself with its forepaws in a hopeless effort to escape. These beasts had almost no chance of staying ahead of the pursuit even this little distance more. Yet darkness could not be more than two hours away; they might still last until nightfall, which was as good a goal.

Shep Daniels turned once more, to read the sky above the

wilderness through which they had come; and this time what he saw broke up his thin, long chain of maybes once and for all. Far back, a speck shot into the sky. It wheeled upwind, climbing above gunshot before it circled and hung; and the drover knew it to be a marsh hawk that had gone through the same evolution earlier, when they had passed its lookout beside the trace. It told him where the armed riders were, behind, and hope went out of him, they were so much nearer than he had believed they would be.

After the first impact of that discovery, what Shep felt was a strange lassitude of acceptance, almost a relief. Perhaps he never had believed that this one more farfetched venture could succeed.

Trapper came slashing back, on the rawboned and hammer-headed claybank he had chosen for the Black Mingo Trace. His pale hair and the bright blue of his eyes seemed to give out a light of their own, in contrast to this drab wilderness world.

"Guess you saw that hawk?" Trapper said. "I figure we got maybe an hour more."

"Maybe less," Shep answered. "We're moving slower by the step."

"I know."

Shep saw how shaken his brother looked, so gray-faced he looked green; and he was puzzled, for Trapper never scared easily. Not like this.

"I was scouting ahead, just now," Trapper told him, and his words came hushed, in a way not made needful by strangers still a mile behind. "I been kind of on the lookout for somewhere we could maybe hole up, until them people go on about their business. There's a track up here, leads off to a little house, and a barn—not burnt out, nor nothing—only—there's a corpse there, in the barnyard. Maybe more'n one—the wild hogs been at it. Got it so tore up and strewed around—some drug-out guts one place, and a chawed hand another, and an awful-looking head without no—"

"How long—" Shep heard himself imitating his brother's lowered tone, and started again, speaking out loudly this time "How long dead?"

"Some days anyway. The stink's awful. It turned my stummick on me."

He was past the worst of that experience, with the telling of what he had seen, and the color began to come back into his face. Shep did not blame Trapper for turning green; such things affected him the same way. A question crossed his mind as to how a man would look in a fight with his stomach kicking up on him. He guessed Trapper, at least, would be all right, for he could see now what his brother was thinking even before he spoke.

"You ought to let me try it, Shep," Trapper said, but mildly, as if without much hope. "I could get it done. I know I could get it done."

He believed in his homely but tough and powerful claybank, probably the best horse in the Black Mingo as of right then; better than Rodger Ashland's even, considering the type of work. And he believed, in his Spencer, which reloaded with tubes of fixed ammunition, seven rounds at a time, almost as fast as the Sharps breechloader could be loaded single-shot. So now what he wanted to do worse than anything in the world was to fight a one-man rear-guard action from the brush, while Shep, of course, was dead set that his brother was going to try nothing of the kind.

"I could very easy pick me a duck stand, like," Trapper said, perhaps for the tenth time but as wistfully as a little child. "I know, I know, I could reason with them fellers, with this here Spencer. One by one, as they come in view . . ."

In short, his half-baked brother thought he could tie into any number of Rodger Ashland's ruffians, in a wilderness they knew and he did not, and whup them to a frazzle. But Trapper couldn't see it like that because he couldn't see himself as Shep saw him. What Shep saw when he looked at Trapper was a kind of composite boy, made up of all the boys, aged from six on up, that Trapper had ever been; along with all his childhood mistakes, and all the funny things he had said, and all the exasperating yet precious quirks of nonsense by which one child can be told from another as he grows up. It didn't add up to a good estimate of Trapper as he was now or ever had been, but Shep was stuck with it.

"Scarcely any risk to it at all," Trapper said.

"Except to Pap," Shep spoiled it.

"He should be so far back he'll never get wind of it until I got 'em licked."

"But he's in the trace, isn't he? So far as we know. What about the ones that get away?"

Trapper looked at his brother sharply to see if he was being sarcastic. Shep didn't look so, but Trapper couldn't tell.

"Some few are bound to escape this awful slaughter," Shep laid it on, letting the ridicule in it show through. "You don't think them in the rear will keep coming right on, do you? About a dozen are liable to go whanging back down the trace—with you hot after 'em, I suppose. If Pap ain't shot up, he'll get trampled, by God!"

It wasn't as ridiculous as all that, the way Trapper saw it, but he had no satisfactory answer. Pap's situation held him balked and helpless. He shut up, and Shep went over the procedure he had worked out and explained to Trapper early on. They would press on as long as they dared, then Trapper was to take to the tangles. He would take with him the Jack of Diamonds, the enormous young jack that was probably worth a small fortune himself—they might as well try to save that much. Shep would push on with the herd for a piece, to pull the bushwhackers past the point where Trapper bushed up. As soon as the trace was clear, Trapper was to double back to find Pap and warn him. And that was as far as they needed to figure, for Pap would take charge then, and he was welcome to it. Shep, naturally, would wait until the last minute, then take to the swamp on foot. Given ten yards start into the tangles, he promised, and nobody was going to find him, or flush him out, or catch him—not with all the mounted men in Missouri.

"My Colt forty-four," Shep said. "It's in my bedroll, under the wagon seat. Better take it with you, I should judge."

"Don't you want it?"

"Hell, no. Never got around to filing the front sight off."

"Well . . . all right."

"Now get up there and move those mules!"

Their strung-out column had closed up some in the time

they talked, for while Trapper was not with them the lead
mules lost what little pace they had. And now they saw the
lead span swerve and stop altogether, heads and long ears
coming up, uncommonly concerned, for such tired animals,
over something beyond.

"They caught wind of the dead man," Trapper said. He
went charging and churning up to the front, for if the mules
set into a balk now they'd take root to stay. Shep weighed
which of the mares he would put into the traces, if the mules
had to be left there; but the mules went on, once the claybank
was at their heads, and the rest of the stock followed. Shep
was glad now he had said nothing when Trapper had fed his
claybank double rations of grain that the other animals
needed worse.

The ancient saddle mule Shep was riding shivered, and
plodded a little faster to get past, as the tail of the straggle
came to the bend where the leaders had faltered. Here the
wagon track Trapper had explored forked off, and a chimney
showed through the trees, well back from the trace. A stir of
air brought a dreadful stench, oily and choking, as if it tangi-
bly wrapped around his mouth and nose. When it was gone,
he rubbed his mouth on his sleeve, before daring to lick his
dry lips.

The brief uncleanness upon the dank air did not turn the sky
darker nor change the tones of the tangled forest; yet the
swamp was changed by it, and the daylight changed. The clutch
of the mire seemed more deadly and the fading day become
more somber, as if the world were sinking under them into the
depths of a sadness beyond hope. This swamp had become the
abode of something unnatural and sinister, evil past human
comprehension.

From that point on, too, a true chill came into the air, a
cold that came on with the approaching dark and was not
imagined. The surface of the mud began to crisp, though it
would be an hour or two before it would bear any weight, and
a thin skin began to form on standing water. A rising wind
was beginning to moan in the forest, bringing a tingly smell
of snow. It would be a bitter night.

For another half hour Trapper led on. Now that he had

given in, nothing was left to be said. Earlier they had argued awhile over whether they should neck-yoke the jack between a couple of big mares, and concluded it wasn't needful; and they had talked about tying his tail down to keep him from singing. Some mulemen believed that jacks and mules had to get their tails up before they could bray, and some didn't; trials never settled it. What generally happened, the animal paid the rig-up no mind, at first—seemingly only discovered the outrage when he next wanted to sing. But when he did, he was right liable to try kicking the world through the walls of hell without opening the gate. So you didn't know whether he was unable to yell with his tail down or was only so upset he forgot to. Either way, the whole idea seemed kind of impractical, and useless to know about, in most circumstances, and they had decided against experimenting with it now. . . .

No more signs appeared in the sky behind to tell them where the enemy was. Presently Trapper stepped from his saddle into the rolling wagon, to get the Colt revolver Shep had offered him. When that was done, Shep signaled him that it was time to leave the trace, and Trapper waved that he understood. For the moment, though, he returned to the lead and just kept on. Shep let him alone for a while, longer than he thought he ought to, imagining Trapper to be looking for a spot to his liking, but had to whistle at him in the end. Trapper didn't hear him the first time; or else, as Shep suspected, he pretended not to. Doubtless the bushwhackers knew where they were, well enough, but Shep didn't want to pull them into a final spurt of effort by telling them they were nearer than they had supposed. It took a real railsplitter of a whistle to make his brother turn, and even then Trapper only pulled aside and stood, so that Shep tried to lift his ancient mule into a trot, and could not.

"What are you waiting for? Grab your Jack of Diamonds and bush up!" He unchained the jack from the tailgate and shoved the lead into Trapper's hands. "Now, for God's sake, get done crashing around in there before the bushwhackers come up. And pick yourself a stand free of cracklebush, you hear?"

"What if you can't find no way through to the river, only this one here?"

"Then I'll grow myself web feet and live here! God damn it, don't you never listen to nothing? I sure thought I jawed you enough!"

"Looks like we ought to settle on someplace where we could come looking for you."

"I'll see you in Paducah—or hell, or the Promised Land, and what's it to you?" Trapper was stalling, and Shep knew it. Might be game to balk even yet, given half a chance. "You get into the swamp, you hear me? Because they're going to be on us quicker'n you can by God pee your pants!"

"Sure, sure. Take care of yourself." Leading the Jack of Diamonds, Trapper turned off into the wilderness.

Shep did not answer in kind or watch him go; and the reason for this was one he would not have believed could be. He had not cried, or shown a tear, since he was five years old—he knew this with exactness, because he had kept a watchful score on himself those early years. But now tears jumped into his eyes without warning, and an ache like a thumb gouge caught him by the throat, so that he didn't dare to speak or let Trapper see his face. He did not belive Trapper was in any danger—this boy certainly should not be, if he did as he was told. Only—what Shep had been thinking, as Trapper splashed into the bog, was that his brother looked like a man, and he worked and rode and handled a long team like a man, until after a while he had you pretty near fooled by all that. Then all of a sudden he'd turn around and flabbergast you with some boy-sized plan, for whupping half of Missouri, or something, such as would do sorry credit to a little shirttail feller, like needed watching over, and caring for, all the whole time. . . .

He had himself in hand, after a moment or two; but the jungle had already closed behind the claybank and the jack. His blacksnake licked out, stinging and welting now, but pistol-cracking no more. For a while he could hear his brother crashing rearward through the thicket, too close, and moving too nearly parallel to the road. He began hollering a song, in hopes of warning Trapper to go deeper before it was too late.

> Oh, Jack of Diamonds,
> You Jack of Diamonds,
> I knowed you of old, honey child,
> I knowed you of old . . .

What came handiest to the top of his mind, without any thinking about it, happened to be this old, old river song, that had now turned itself into a song about the great golden stud, and nothing else.

> You rob my pockets,
> You rob my pore pockets,
> Of silver and gold, honey child,
> My silver and gold . . .

When he listened again all the brush-beating in the swamp had ended, and about time. In another hundred yards the trace doubled back on itself, and the woods thinned; and soon after he rounded the turn Shep could briefly glimpse Ashland's straggling riders, coming on without haste but very steadily. The muck squelching of his own animals covered all sound from back there, so that the pursuers seemed to move as silently as ghosts, between the trees; but it was time for him to go. Shep pulled his carbine from the saddle scabbard under his knee, and stepped to the ground. His boots crackled through the muddy scum that was beginning to stiffen with the cold, and he stood for some moments in four inches of water, feeling himself settle very slowly deeper into the muck. Then, unhurriedly, he replaced the carbine, and returned to the saddle. The old mule staggered under his weight; it could not carry him much farther.

Shep did not share Pap's hope that Rodge would not shoot him down—or have it done—if he faced him without defense. If Pap was right, he might have the whole contention over within the next half hour, but to Shep it seemed a long, bad gamble. The suck of the mud combined with the chill that came into his leaking boots in a deadly forewarning of the night ahead. Probably not many men would have known how to survive, wet to the neck and floundering, as the tem-

perature dropped in that trackless morass, but Shep thought
he could. He had intended to put his cartridge box and his
carbine in his bedroll with his dry clothes, and carry it high;
so equipped, he was not afraid he would die there. No proc-
ess of logic or reason accounted for his remounting his animal. Only—

It had suddenly come to him that he would not and could
not, now or ever, crawl the night swamp for the likes of
Rodger Ashland. He sat quiet now, facing the back trail, waiting for the first of the night riders to appear.

★ 20 ★

SHEP DANIELS STILL HELD HIS COILED MULE WHIP, BUT OTHER wise his hands were folded before him upon the reins, as the first of Ashland's night riders appeared. They came around a clump of baldy cyress into full view, five of them in a loose bunch, no more than sixty yards behind. Shep half raised one arm, in the grudging gesture commonly used by riders who met on the lonely back roads of Missouri, but this was not answered. The front-riders hesitated, weapons ready, as they saw Shep, sitting quiet on his droop-lipped mule, then came on more slowly, looking to the rear for orders.

More appeared; the long straggle came on and on, twice as many of them as the fourteen he had known about. He knew none of them but they were about what he had expected. Mostly they were swamp-runners, and deep-hills woolhats, of the narrow-shouldered, buck-toothed breed left behind in these backwashes when the frontier passed on. Their type was common in the great areas of wilderness remaining upon the undrained or inaccessible lands, yet he would remember for a long time every face he saw here. To Shep's horse-trading eye they looked inbred and underfed. But a bad thing about them was that not one good bush of whiskers was to be seen in the whole shaveless troop, which said these were youngsters, boys who had but barely got their full growth. Malaria, corn squeezings, and a diet of grease could be counted on to pull their corks in the early years of their maturity. Only in this reckless interlude, before creaky joints and hookworm overtook them, were they given to the convulsive spasms of violence in which they were truly dangerous.

113

And of course they rode well; they would have to ride well to come this far on the played-out racks of bones they rode. Blood showed on many a spur, but they were here, sitting their sorry mounts with the unconcern of riders who always traveled so; and this in itself had to be reckoned a feat of horsemanship.

The rider in front said, "Hobe. You and Elmer go on a piece. Ne' mind the stock. Just fetch that other hoss thief back." Two of the gaunt horses wrung their tails and lurched into a gallop, trailing red froth from their bit chains, as their riders spurred forward.

Shep said, "There goes two dead men, son. There'll be more, you keep on with this."

The front-rider looked directly at Daniels for the first time, his eyes hard in a long-jawed face, but he did not answer. He swiveled in his saddle again to look back.

Up from the rear on his good horse, lacing around the bend in a high splatter of mud, came Rodger Ashland. Shep found it strange to encounter him in this muck sump, having last seen him at the opposite end of creation, aboard the *Royal Oaks*. Rodge stood out conspicuously from the others, though apparently without intending it. He wore a buckskin coat-shirt, without fringe, and cavalry boots made less evident by butternut jeans worn outside, instead of stuffed in the boots. But his slouch hat was of high quality, and so was he. His lean-cut face and high-boned nose, with the faint ripple in it that Shep had put there, contrasted with the slack features of the rabble around him.

Shep said, "Hi, Rodge." And Ashland said, "Captain Handy to you." Shep had meant to say he was glad to see him, in place of somebody who might have turned out unfriendly; but he couldn't seem to get it out. "So these are Handy's Raiders," Shep said. "I expected something better, Rodge, after all I heard."

Ashland spoke to the front-rider by name. "You, Yancey. Where's the other one?" Yancey explained about having sent Hobe and Elmer forward.

"You planning to go on through here?" Shep asked. "Because if you are, might be I could help you make it."

Ashland made no answer, but spoke again to Yancey. "Why haven't you disarmed this Damnyankee? Well, do it now. Help him, Henry."

Yancey and another, a lank beanpole, put their horses forward, hard against Shep's mule on either side. He was coiling his blacksnake as they reached him, slipping the braided rawhide through his fingers to dislodge a poundage of wet clay. He had judged with care the distance to Rodger Ashland's throat, and was satisfied that the sixteen-foot whip would reach. Once coiled, the lash could lick out with a snap that would slice halfway through to the backbone in the next tenth of a second—might near take off a man's head if it stuck right. His hands moved unhurriedly, avoiding any quick movement that might be a warning; and his timing came out a shade too cool, too careful, in the end. At the last instant a pistol barrel cracked across the back of his hand, and it was the blacksnake that went into the mud. It was his own split-second mistake, and he could not forgive it, for he could not expect the chance at Rodger Ashland to come again. That the same mistake had saved his own life he could not appreciate, he set so little store by it, just then.

They took the carbine first, of course, then poked around him in a gingerly way, covering him with enough gun muzzles to be dangerous to each other. One of them found his seven-inch folding hoof knife and held it up. "This here's all he's got on him, cap'n." These willing murderers, as unregarding of law or humanity as wild hogs, showed a notable deference toward Rodger Ashland. Their respect for the twin pistols he carried in his saddle holsters was understandable, but there was something more. Part of it was that these men who had been raised barefoot on dirt floors looked up to the quality Rodger Ashland represented; yet whatever real authority he had came from the man himself. His total assurance, his certainty that he would be obeyed, had to come from the great plantations, and from no place else. Yet his hold upon them was unlikely to reach very far out of his sight. They could be expected to run wild on their own the first moment that he turned his back.

They got rougher as they went along. Shep's coat split

down the back as they ripped it off him, and there was some cussing from those who had had their eyes on it. If he had had a horse like the claybank under him, he would have known some things he could try; and he should have kept his revolver with him. He could not remember in these moments why he had chanced this kind of an end-up, sitting helpless with no way to fight back. One of the horses crowding Shep's mule had a hoof on his whip, sinking it in the mud. Shep made a try at diving for it anyway, but Yancey jammed him in the ribs with the same pistol that had struck the whip from Shep's hand. Shep twisted, trying to get hold of it.

He did not get it. But now at last he saw what pistol this was; and he knew in a flash of instant recognition that Pap was dead.

This was the pistol with the shortened hammer and the tied-back trigger, for slip-firing without fumbling to get a work-stiffened finger within the guard. Neither he nor Trapper would ever forget that weapon, they had watched Pap practice it so many times, fascinated by the probability that he would sooner or later let slip at half cock and blow off a handful of toes. They had dreaded to see this happen—yet, at the same time, were left kind of disappointed that it never did.

Shep lashed out at Yancey, who saved himself a fall by snatching at the saddle, and the pistol fired wide. Hands grabbed Shep from the other side. He seized a wrist, unhorsing its owner, and heard the crack of breaking arm bones, the man's yell ended abruptly in a bubbling sound as he was slung face down in the mud. Then a gun butt took Shep under the ear, draping him upon the neck of his mule.

Rodger Ashland had been looking entertained, but now he interfered. "Don't you kill that man!" he shouted, and let off one of his own pistols to get attention. "Get away from him! I'll know when it's time to hang him!"

Shep Daniels sat up slowly, numbed less by the blow than by his certainty that Pap was dead. Maybe Pap's theory that the feud could still be called off, that Rodge could not kill him if he held back from a hopeless fight, might have held true before Pap was killed. When had they done it? Three days ago? Two? Maybe he had spent twenty-two years getting ready to build himself a life, and had lost his last gamble by only two days. . . .

"Where's your brother?" Ashland demanded of him.

"What brother?"

Somebody said, "Hobe's likely got him by now. Should I ride up and—"

Ashland put two fingers in his mouth and sounded a far-carrying two-note whistle; it was the kind of signal the swamp-runners used across the impassable bogs. From far up ahead a three-note whistle answered.

"Well, Hobe hasn't got him. And won't get him, either. Might get himself shot from the brush—that's the nearest he'll come." He whistled one more signal, evidently a recall, for Hobe and Elmer presently came back. "But there's a better way. Call your brother in, Daniels."

Shep worked his jaws to see if his mouth was dry, and it was not, so he spat on the boot toe of the nearest rider.

"Tell you what you do," Ashland said. "Take a piece of whang, and cross-tie his thumbs in front of him. Better pull him down first. And if you have to pistol-whup him again, tap him easy. I want him fit to holler."

They got hold of him again, and put the weight of their horses into dragging him from the saddle; and though they did not unseat him, the mule was pulled over, pinning his leg under it into the mud. Somebody swung a kick at his head, gashing his scalp, and sending his hat sailing. He grabbed a foot in both hands, twisted it almost a full turn, and felt the ankle break.

Rodger Ashland was laughing, but he was becoming exasperated too. "What a bunch of fighting men! That's two of you he's disabled. Will you learn to watch this rooster?"

Now he was skulled again, this time by a pistol barrel swung overhand, and he lay quiet for a time. When he began to come to he did not know where he was at first or how he had got there. Memory returned slowly, and a vacant space remained for a while, the minutes just before the blow staying blank the longest. He had been sitting on his mule. . . . He found that his thumbs had been lashed together with rawhide string that would cut bone sooner than it would pull free. His mule had not got up, but it had rolled off his leg, and Shep saw that his boots were gone. There were enough flapping boot soles in sight to explain that. They passed a loop of picket rope inside the thumb tie, and hauled him to his feet; he staggered, and fell face down in the mire, where he half strangled, but not for long. The bushwhackers flipped the picket rope over a pin-oak branch, and hoisted him upright; and there they stretched him with more weight on his thumbs than on his feet, bootless in the muck. The pain helped clear his head, and now he remembered that Pap was dead. He made a single convulsive effort to break free, but blood ran down his arm as the whang cut his left thumb to the bone, and he stood still after that.

"Call your brother in," Ashland said.

"Call him yourself." Shep's voice sounded unfamiliar to him, for it was forced through a tight throat.

"All right, Yancey," Rodger Ashland said, "take his whip, and cut the back off him."

Yancey picked up the whip, and ran it through his fingers as he walked around Shep. He flipped out the whip's full sixteen-foot length, so that it lay lightly on the surface of the mud, the snapper near Shep's feet. Then he stopped, and stood with eyes down, apparently in thought.

"Hit him, I said!"

"Ah'm thinkin' somethin'." Yancey kept looking Ashland in the eye, but only for a second or two at a time—glance and away, glance and away. "This here won't bring the little son of a bitch out of the woods. It'll bring him to the aidge of the woods. And it'll bring him shooting!"

"That's the theory," Rodge agreed. "What's the matter—aren't odds of twenty-eight to one good enough for you? He'll get off exactly one shot."

"Sure. And you know who'll git that one shot right through the haid? Me!" Yancey threw down the whip.

Rodger Ashland said nothing at all. He rode to the whip, and made a long stretch down from the saddle to pick it up. He cracked it once, sixteen feet straight up, then floated its length in lazy figure eights just off the ground. "Let's hear you yell, Daniels."

Shep had always known how to wake up a mule or slice an apple with the long whip, but he had never felt it cut into his own hide before. He could not see Ashland, but the whistle of the lash told him when it was coming, so that he supposed he was ready for it. It was the incredible bite the thing had that astonished him, snatching the wind from his lungs with a sound less like a grunt than a squeal. Somebody swore— "Right in my eye, by God!" Rodger Ashland's voice said, "Well, get back, you damned fool, if you don't want to get splashed." And somebody laughed, an idiot's giggle, as involuntary as the noise Shep himself had made.

"Louder, Daniels," Ashland said, and the whip whistled and bit.

Shep made his throat go slack, this time, so that the snatch of his breath was voiceless; it was a trick he had learned long ago. Toughest thing about this was not the pain itself, but knowing there could be no end to it until he hung senseless, past all reviving. Until then his job was to make no sound such as would bring Trapper back. He did not know how deep in the swamps his brother was, but he had a pretty good idea it wasn't anywhere near deep enough.

The lash sang, and sang again, striking with a wet splat, and Shep was silent. A thing that had happened to him five or six years before was helping now. He had broken his leg then, which wasn't much to face out, compared to what he was up against here, because you knew there had to be an end to it somewhere ahead, short of your death. Still, it had been bad enough—a compound fracture that had left his leg lumped and crooked, and more than an inch short; and though he had taught himself not to favor, people who got a look at it thought the mule that kicked him must have been trying for the record. It hadn't been that, of course; no Daniels ever got hurt around a mule.

What happened, he had run for the barn one night, when a mare was fixing to foal, and he fell over the woodpile. His father had laid him out on the kitchen floor, with his wrists strapped to the stove legs, for he was bleeding fit to ruin a bed tick where the bone stuck out. Trapper, twelve or thirteen then, was standing by to help how he could, until Pap noticed him turning green and sent him to do for the mare. The last thing Pap told him, before throwing his weight back on the ankle, was how to let his throat go slack. And seemingly it worked, for though his breath whistled in his windpipe, and the candlelight went dim, he did not cry out.

"You marveled me that night," Trapper admitted after. "I had my fingers stuck in my ears, out there in the barn, so's I wouldn't hear you holler. But you never let out a peep." And, "You know . . . Trapper . . ." Shep fumbled to explain it, "there wasn't nothin' to worry about, Trapper. A thing only hurts about so much; and then it don't hurt no more than that."

That remark of his own had come back to Shep sometimes, in the years between, and he had thought it was a good thing to have said. He was not remembering it now, or much else, in the few seconds of recovery between strokes of the black-snake, but perhaps the substance of it was in his mind some-where. And maybe as he lay on that kitchen floor not only his leg but his fiber had undergone a change that he owed to a woodpile and a foaling mare.

"Turn him around. I know how to make him yell."

They swiveled him to face their chief. The mud stumbled him, and his knees sagged, but the whang cut into his thumbs as they took his weight, and he straightened up. He saw that Rodge loomed over him much closer than he had supposed, yet without looking as tall in the saddle as he should have looked to a man afoot—perhaps because of the way Shep was stretched. Ashland's eyes were fixed on him with a sleepy gratification, making his face look puffed. And next he saw that all of them were looking at him with the same fixity, for-getting to watch the woods. Even the horses, their heavy heads no more than half raised, had every pair of ears pointed toward him.

Rodger Ashland let the whip lie quiet for a moment, with his eyes on Shep, while his face hardened and the pleasure in it went cold. It did not occur to Shep to wonder, at that time or ever, what was to be seen in his own face then. The mounted man flicked the whip into its backswing; for a moment it lay lightly on nothing, straight out behind him, before he sent it flowing toward its mark. And Shep did not understand at once what happened next.

It seemed at first as if the whip had cracked untimely, with a great explosive report that collapsed it in mid-reach and dropped it harmless in the slime. Rodger Ashland's arm jerked as if struck by a club, and he sat staring at his empty hand as if he were trying to move the fingers and could not. From his sleeve a sudden rivulet of blood ran down his hand, dripping fast from his fingers' ends. The whole illusion was as if the blacksnake handle had somehow blown up, like a three-dollar shotgun.

But most eyes had snapped to the swamp, where a telltale drift of black-powder smoke fogged the brier thicket in which a gun had fired. In another moment a broken volley answered from the road, cutting a hole through the canes of the briers and tearing the smoke marker into swirling rags. Behind the considerable billow of smoke in the road the bushwhackers scrabbled through the dozen motions necessary to charge the muzzle-loaders with which most were armed.

And now Rodger Ashland showed what it was he had that made these roughs obey him. With his left hand he whipped out one of the pair of pistols holstered on the saddle before him, but immediately put it back. "Here's your chance, Yancey." His tone was unexcited, yet carried an effortless lift of compulsion. "Go make sure he's dead."

Yancey headed his horse to the swamp with a haul that seemed to swing the animal's whole forehand by the bit. "Come on!" he yelled. "Let's git that man!" His spurs raked hard as he jumped his horse belly-deep into the flooded briers.

The men around him hesitated, slow to understand what was expected of them. Then half a dozen followed, raggedly, spreading out to flank him on either hand. For eight or ten jumps Yancey's animal fought the swamp, bursting through the hole in the brush from which the shot had come—but nothing was there. Yancey checked, turned his horse uncertainly this way and that, then round and round, searching the shallow water for a corpse and looking baffled.

Ten yards to the left the man called Elmer, the last of Yancey's support to get started, drove plunging and splashing into the thickets, sounding the long scream that was already called the rebel yell. Then the hidden weapon, or another, appeared in a new place, so close that its flash seemed to reach for the rider's face. The long yell stopped short and the horse stopped, reared, and fell backwards, pulled over by the death grip on the reins. The man was briefly lost to sight under the horse; then reappeared, unrecognizable within a shine of black slime, dragging by one stirrup as the animal floundered out of the swamp.

Rodger Ashland's orders crackled and snapped. "You, Tip! Bud! Close with that sniper. Rush him, you fools! You want to die one by one?"

A single rider swerved his wild-eyed brute toward the new drift of gunsmoke, but he never got there. A weapon of different voice—a pistol this time?—spoke from farther back, and this rider pitched off to land grotesquely in a mass of briers, his broken old boots sticking up and his face lost under the black water. His horse bolted back along the trace, making every horse there stir in an effort to follow.

Yancey came fast out of the swamp, and though he turned out to have an idea other than retreat, the half dozen who followed him wheeled their horses and splashed back onto the wagon track. Yancey rode straight to where Shep hung. He aimed Pap's pistol at Shep's head from a distance of four feet, and though his eyes were darting through the thickets, and the gun was shakily held, it was pointed well enough. And now the tied-back trigger took on a new meaning, for even if Yancey was shot and killed, the pistol would blow Shep's head off.

"Hold your fire in there!" Yancey was yelling. "Hold it, God damn you, or I'll blast his brains out!"

No answer came from the swamp but a buzz of argument started up in the road, while the night riders sat locked in uncertainty, looking from the unrevealing swamp to each other and quickly back again. Somewhere, deep in the tangles, the claybank bugled; and in a different place a crackling and thrashing in the brush began, and kept on, without seeming to go anyplace.

"You son of a bitch! What all you got hid in there?"

"That there—that there—" Shep was stuttering so that he could hardly speak. "That's Jayhawkers—that's Lane with his Jayhawkers," he managed to get out.

"By God, I knew it!" Yancey blazed up with such a fury that he could not yell at first, but only whimper, unheard until he got his voice up to a squall. "Jayhawkers! It's a Jayhawk ambuscade!" His yell loosened out with use, so that every bushwhacker in the band heard him before he was done. "Half of Kansas is in there! This son of a bitch has tolled us into ambush!" The gun swung away from Shep's head to throw a shot into the swamp.

And now Pap's pistol found a way, in some part, to avenge its owner. As Yancey cocked it, the modified hammer got away from him, prefiring on its own; and in the same instant Yancey's horse snorted and reared straight up. Shep could not see where the bullet had struck the animal, but a gush of blood jumped from its mouth as it whirled on its hind feet and bolted. Yancey cursed, and threw the pistol away, to saw the curb with both hands, but though he pulled the animal's head backwards into his lap, it disappeared around the bend of the trace, uncontrollable.

"It's a lie!" Ashland was shouting. "Get in there, you cowardly scuts, or I'll—"

Back beyond the bend in the trace a new burst of firing sounded, three shots, this time, not in unison, but tight together, following faster than a revolver could have been cocked or fanned. Who was back there? Nobody that Ashland's men knew about, certainly, for the fusillade set off a confused milling, and a great gabble of dispute arose there. Rodger Ashland was shouting above the confusion, and his voice was enormous. His right hand was entirely covered now with glistening red, but it held the reins, though loosely, like a dead hand. "Dismount! Get down off those crow baits! You sitting ducks, you can't fight critterback here! Get off, I say! Stand down—"

A few of those nearest him made a hesitant half start toward obeying, but nobody dismounted. Ashland's hold on them was fetching loose. Riders in the rear began splitting off, by singles and twos and threes, fading back the way they had come, while more began to edge their horses in the other direction: "On through—on through! Ain't no way back!"

Some, cowed by the sound of guns behind them on the trace, had already leaked away into the swamp behind, and here a fluky accident occurred. A hard-whipped horse set foot in a log-fall and went end-over with a broken leg. The fallen man clawed and wallowed to his feet in time to seize the bridle of the horse following next behind. Few saw him get possession of the horse in the only way possible, which was by killing its rider; but many heard the three shots he pistoled into the fellow while dragging him down. The instant assumption was that combat had broken out in yet another place, and a new yell went up: "They're on both sides!"

What Rodger Ashland had to say to them should have stripped the hide off a gator. He called them cowards, and trash, and dog dung; he even called them white niggers, and from there went on to every obscenity known to Missouri, but he could hold them no longer. A wild-eyed boy came rocketing through the confusion, knocking Ashland's horse to its knees as he blasted past. Ashland drew a pistol, but again put it away unfired. He sat for a moment cursing bitterly to himself, and Shep did not know just when he left. A buzz-bee from behind Shep passed close to his ear, deafening him for a moment, but without drawing blood. It might have been a left-hand shot thrown back by Rodger Ashland, but that was guesswork. Those on the run were firing wild into the wilderness, seeing enemies everywhere they looked. A ragged sound of skirmish firing, mostly from heavy-bore revolvers, built up and spread along the trace in both directions as the retreat strung out.

Trapper walked out of the woods, muddy to the eyes and very watchful. He was checking Shep's Colt to see what was left in it, and blowing powder fumes out of the barrel, as Shep had tried to teach him not to do. He cut the rope that stretched his brother by the thumbs, caught him as he fell, and sawed through the rawhide thumb bindings. A peculiar change, not often seen but easy to remember, came over Trapper Daniels' face when he was mad, tightening the skin so that his eyes were pulled into a slant yet at the same time drew closer together, until both seemed to look out of the same hole; and the rest of his face was all knots and bones. He was mad now, and looked something like an animal when it pins back its ears, showing such a streak of meanness as nobody would suspect any other time.

"Guess you oughter done a few dozen things like I told you first," he said.

Shep tried to get up, and went to all fours in the mud as Trapper let go of him. "I'll take that Spencer," he said, his voice unnatural.

"You'll take what?"

"I'm going to kill that son of a bitch!"

Trapper told his brother obscenely what he could do instead. "But I'll tell you one thang you ain't fixing to do—you ain't fixing to go off with my Spencer and hand it over to no Rodger Ashland. And another thang you ain't fixing to do, you ain't fixing to borry the only horse we got fit to raise a trot, and run the hell out of him, neither, nor hand him over to some bushwhacker, neither! By God, maybe someday you'll larn to fetch along your own fighting tools—and use 'em, too, in room of passing 'em out amongst the first murdering scum you come to!"

Shep heaved to his feet, with some notion of taking a swing at Trapper, but staggered, lost footing, and came down again. "Oh, hell," he mumbled, and gave up.

They shut up, then, and Trapper's hands were gentle as he bandaged his brother with axle grease and strips of his other shirt. He went off after that to pick up his claybank and the Jack of Diamonds. If he also made a quick survey of the several dead, looking for loot, Shep didn't feel like thinking about that. He crawled on his hands and knees, greatly bothered by his cut thumbs, looking for Pap's revolver. He knew exactly where it should be, but it wasn't there. He probed the mire some, supposing it must have been trodden out of sight, but he did not come on it.

It didn't matter. What he had mainly wanted was to hide it from his brother. He saw reason to think he had better not tell Trapper that their father was dead. Not yet.

✴ 21 ✴

For a while a certain amount of brush busting went on deep in the wilderness, slowly receding; and the firing in the trace ahead died out, as if the riders who had pressed on through were circling back to leave the way they had come. All through the dark twilight, and for an hour more after nightfall, random bursts of gunfire could be heard far to the rear, where the bushwhackers in the trace peppered away at those trying to rejoin them from the swamp.

The brothers plodded on for a mile or two more, until the trace came out upon higher ground. Here the harness mules, very willing in their work, but almost impossible to push beyond their strength, felt the firm ground under their feet and stopped, so they made camp. After they had simmered down, maybe Shep Daniels wanted to say he had been wrong and would probably be dead if Trapper had not disobeyed him. And maybe Trapper wanted to admit that it was the hurt done Shep, and his own fear for him, that had broken his temper. But they had always let their boyhood quarrels burn themselves out, uncelebrated by apologies, and the old ways came easier to them even yet.

Usually they rubbed down a dozen or so of the more poorly animals at the end of the day. Most work animals gave off a rank smell of old sweat, long dried and staled to a bitter dust, but the Daniels livestock more commonly had a buttery smell, something like fresh-ginned cotton. All the Daniels men had rock-muscled shoulders from the everlasting rubbing and grooming of the beasts that were their stock in trade. Tonight, though, they judged themselves justified in passing this up. Trapper boiled water and scrubbed the black powder fouling out of first his Spencer, then Shep's revolver, before he settled down. The wind had died, and a light snowfall was sifting through the bare trees, hushing the night. They sat late in the soft silence, bone weary, but unfriendly to sleep. Shep was stolidly enduring more kinds of discomfort than he had ever heard of before. He kept pushing them out of his mind, while he considered this self-determined stranger his brother had become.

Trapper appeared to have aged about ten years in one, and it wasn't in his expression, for he looked puzzled more than anything else. But he had thinned, in this hardest of all winters, losing the apple-cheeked look he had always kept in spite of his farmboy tan. In the light of their hidden fire his face showed deepened shadows that came and went, and sharpened highlights that did not, but seemed to stand out unchanged. He had cheekbones now, and a hard jaw line, and these caught the light; these, and the beginnings of a high hawk-beak, where only a snub nose had always been. The little boy who had been Shep's brother was gone, and nobody just like him would ever exist again.

"I sure don't know what got in 'em," Trapper said. "Of course, you got to allow for it, they been raising a right sorry pack of scrubs over here in the south end of Misery . . ."

"They fight, though. Always have. I never heard complaint they showed want of meanness."

"I know. What happened, you reckon, made 'em skedaddle thataway?"

"You surrounded 'em."

"For God's sake, Shep," Trapper said, "don't you ever tell this. The man don't live could believe it. I don't believe it myself. You let this out, and I'll be a laughing stock from hell to Paducah!"

Shep thought this was probably true. All that embattled firing at spooks and shadows, ending in total rout by one boy with a carbine, would never live in legend because they daren't tell it.

"When they began to pull out," Trapper said. "I first thought they must see something I couldn't. Like as if there really was other people in that swamp, on our side. But of course there wasn't. Only thing I can think of, they knew something—maybe got some word— Hey! What did you tell them bastards?"

"I told 'em you was the state of Kansas."

"Damn you, Shep, didn't you realize the powder smoke *showed* where every shot was coming from?"

"I didn't think," Shep brushed it off.

Trapper shrugged. "I guess we never will know what happened."

And that ended it for him. Someday they would know there had been no mystery. The war, that so few believed was almost upon them, would early prove that a rout of undisciplined men was a commonplace, needing no explanation. Trapper's exploit would be believable then, but no longer remarkable. Meanwhile Shep might beat his brains out on enigmas without any answers, but not Trapper. He propped himself up on one elbow and picked his teeth with a fatwood splinter, refusing to dwell on it.

They listened to the small hiss of snowflakes upon the bright embers and poked into minor puzzlements, almost visibly fencing off something both were leaving unsaid. Trapper told how he had left the Jack of Diamonds chained to a tupelo, fully expecting him to beller his head off. But, instead, the unguessable critter had just quietly loosed himself, and gone crashing around—adding to the confusion right nicely. "And I did too wire the latch-link," Trapper read this brother's mind. "He unwired it, was what he done." Shep didn't believe it. The Jack of Diamonds could chew through, untie, or unbuckle almost anything you put on him; he could unfasten a harness snap. But a latch-link—the boy never wired it, was what. However—Shep let it pass.

A nameless tension kept building up between them, relaxing when they talked, growing again whenever they fell silent. So Shep brought himself to say that, regardless of what lucky freak it had been that let them come off so much better than they had any right to expect, Trapper's part in it had been might fancy, any way you looked at it; and nothing could take that away from him.

Trapper allowed that beyond moving around some, like any hog hunter knew how to do, he couldn't see where he had done anything very smart. He had faked the sound of three guns firing at once by letting off the carbine with one hand and the Colt twice with the other, and he had believed that was real cute when he thought it up. But now he judged it a waste of powder. . . .

He spoke of these things listlessly, his mind on something else. Some kind of decision had become necessary to him, and stubbornness showed through his fatigue as he tried to come to grips with it inside himself. "You know . . . you realize . . . there's something has to be done different," he said at last.

"We'll be on the river, early on."

"Oh, sure; that part of the job has worked out all right. We'll lose a few more head. That mare that dropped the dead foal won't last the night. And some of the yearlings—whether they make it or not won't signify, they're so close to ruined. But we've saved what we can, and it's over. Or as good as over . . ."

He sat staring beyond the quiet snowfall at something that was not of this night or this place. When Shep said, "Well, what has to be different?" Trapper didn't seem to hear him until seconds later, then said, "What?"

Shep hoped Trapper was not thinking about the dead men back there. Especially not the one who had been dragged by the stirrup onto the trace—he did look so God-awful, with his eye-whites glaring out of a black mask of slime. Shep himself had seen more sudden death than Trapper had, probably, though never as much blood on the ground as there had been today. But Trapper, almost certainly, had never made any kind of attempt on a human life before, so was wide open to horrors of conscience, and maybe a full-out haunting, if he got to brooding about it. What Shep himself felt was a profound sense of shock, complicated by his own wounds and the stress of battle, but drawing the greatest part of its effect from the evidence that his father was dead. He didn't believe he dared tell Trapper before they were out of Missouri lest the boy go dead set on immediately hunting down Ashland

and his whole band. But now Trapper's thinking took an opposite turn that was just as dangerous.

"You'll have to load them yourself, I'm afraid," Trapper said. "I've got to go back and look for Pap."

"Why? That ain't what he wanted at all!"

"Something's gone wrong back there. You know Ashland couldn't have got past him in the trace. Pap must've never got into it."

"Then he's gone someplace else. He wouldn't just set there in Greenville. He's going to skin you alive one of these times if'n you don't start doing like he tells you!"

"So what he tells us is run for our lives at the first excuse. But that ain't what he does, and it ain't what I'm fixing to do. I'm going back there. For all we know, he's bushed up, somewhere, bad hurt, or something."

"Well, he ain't!"

"How do you know he ain't?"

That done it. The cows are in the buckwheat.

"Just take my word for it," Shep said. Up to here Shep had hoped that if he could only get Trapper onto a boat, as far as Cairo even, maybe he could fox him off onto some snipe hunt into eastern Tennessee, or someplace, leaving Shep free to do what he had to do. That hope was up the creek, without he found a way to get Trapper turned around.

"I don't think you'll have any trouble," Trapper said. "I'm right sorry to go back on you, with a heavy day's work ahead; you sure got a right not to feel up to it. But . . ."

Shep contended that this had nothing to do with it. It was the notion of following the trace back the way they had come that had no sense to it. He proposed that they stay together, and get the livestock to Cairo. They could remount themselves there, and Shep could rearm. From Cairo they could ride the river to Cape Girardeau, then take the good plank road to Jackson, from which they would have a fairly decent road right on down to Greenville.

"Even if you don't ride into a damn near certain ambush I'll be in Greenville before you are. And that's where we have to start looking, by asking people who seen him. You said yourself, Pap must never have come into the Black Mingo."

"Unless," Trapper said thoughtfully, "he come into the trace behind them; and caught up with them, and fought them . . ."

Shep shied off from that, it was so nearly what he himself believed had happened. Trouble was they thought too much alike. Or maybe they both thought like Pap, who had shaped their minds more than either one of them had any idea. The whole Greenville idea was a subterfuge anyway, a stop-gap measure for getting Trapper out of Missouri. He would have to find other ways to shake him off later. Shep was coming back to Missouri, but he meant to come back alone.

"Let's see how it looks in the morning," Trapper suggested, and Shep was glad to settle for that. They agreed to take turns on watch, lest some remnant of the night riders come on them, by accident perhaps, while trying to get out of the swamp by the river. "You go ahead and get some sleep," Trapper said. "I'll take the first watch, and wake you in a couple of hours."

Shep rolled himself in his blanket. Something about this arrangement made him uneasy, but he couldn't put a finger on what it was. Nor could he think about it for very long, he was so soon asleep.

✶ 22 ✶

TRAPPER DID NOT WAKE SHEP TO TAKE OVER THE WATCH IN TWO hours, or at all. Shep awoke in broad daylight, so stiff he could hardly sit up; but he got it done, and when he saw that Trapper's blankets were not where he had spread them he knew at once, even before looking for the claybank and the rest of his brother's equipment, that Trapper was gone.

He got their strongbox out of the wagon, on the theory that he might get an idea of the range of his brother's plans from the amount he had borrowed of their cash. He didn't have to count it to find out. On top lay Pap's missing pistol, carefully cleaned; and under this Shep found a receipt, and a note in Trapper's surprisingly good hand. The receipt was for two hundred dollars—considerably less than half the cash they carried, but enough to last Trapper for a long time.

I am sorry I can not do this your way [Trapper's note said]. I know Pap is dead, and I think you do too. Here is his pistol that you could not find because I already had it. I recognized it clean from the woods, so you sure must have knowed it. Good luck with the stock. I am going to track down Ashland and kill him.

Shep read it twice, then put it in the coals as he rebuilt the fire. A note like that could reappear sometime, as evidence against his brother, if it was in existence.

He wasted no time considering an effort to overtake the claybank. The Jack of Diamonds might have done it, but he had never been broken to the saddle and would only fight

132

himself to total exhaustion if Shep tried to put a quick break on him now. No other animal here would have any chance of closing ground. The Missouri wilderness had swallowed Trapper again, and this time it was not going to yield him up. Shep pushed the thirty-odd head that could still travel into the last of the trace, and surprised himself by reaching the Mississippi in a matter of hours. A beat-up little side-wheeler, called the *Kittiwake*, put ashore for him; by late afternoon he was loaded and on his way to Cairo.

Shep Daniels went alone to the forward rail of the hurricane, a tall, wound-stiffened figure, dressed like a scarecrow; and stood looking at the ugly water. The Mississippi was silted to the dirty yellow of a mashed banana, and running like the milltails of hell. It hustled great rushes of ice downchannel, the soiled slabs wheeling and tilting, lifting and falling back, in a blind and tortured resistance; and he watched that doomed struggle without seeing it.

He was thinking of his brother, and not in terms of concern. If Trapper got careless, he might run up on some pocket of bushwhackers; in which case, all the long work that had gone into raising Trapper, and all the big hopes that had been held for him, and everything he could have been, were all going to come to sudden nothing, under the swamp water. But this likelihood should decrease from day to day, and nothing could be done about it anyway. Trapper's chances of overtaking Rodger Ashland himself were remote. As Captain Handy—or one of those using the name—Rodge had been operating about as far from Ash Landing as he could get without leaving Missouri. Traveling critterback, by wretched roads or none, over rocky ranges, through forests and swollen rivers, it was a long five hundred miles away—farther than the moon, which at least could be seen from the Black Mingo. Rodge must have been out for months, to have wandered so far from home. To go back the way he had come would cost him at least eight weeks in the saddle, which he surely must be sick of by this time. But there were the rivers.

St. Louis was only a few days upstream, and from there the big steamboats of the Kansas City trade ran up the Missouri all the time—or would as soon as the Missouri was clear of ice. All Rodge had to do was to disperse his night riders, double back to the Mississippi, and hail a boat; he might already be afloat, and far up the river. The moment he set foot on deck, the trail Trapper followed would be broken off short, and Captain Handy would have vanished from the face of Missouri. What Trapper was about to accomplish in the wilderness wasn't much.

Yet the reprieve was only temporary. Trapper would follow Rodger Ashland forever, if he had to, but he wouldn't have to. Sooner or later he would look for him at Ash Landing, and find him there. It was the one worst place in the world to attempt any kind of action against Rodger. As a port, Ash Landing might be of small consequence in the western river trade; but it was imposing enough to make Tyler Ashland a dominating force, reaching far beyond the borders of his county. Trapper would have less chance than the proverbial one-legged man at a pants-kicking if he tangled with Rodger there.

Shep Daniels accepted, without any reservation of forlorn hope, that Pap was dead, but he did not feel it yet; that would come later. The empty sort of ache in his middle might have been partly a mourning for Pap, but mostly it was for Julie, lost to him beyond hope in the moment of Pap's death. For basically Trapper's purpose and his own were the same. The days when their home soil of Kentucky had been called "the dark and bloody ground" were not far behind. Most people could remember tales the old folks told about the first little groups of settlers who had forced their way into the Kentucky forests between warring Indian tribes. No military force from anyplace, nor any form of law, had helped those early pioneers. Very often one man alone, imposing justice as he saw it, was all the law there was. Kentuckians had been slow to delegate the enforcement of their personal rights to officials likely to be indifferent, incompetent, and far away. A similar want of law was to be found in Missouri now. No doubt entered Shep's head, now or ever, but what he was totally obligated to bring Rodger Ashland to justice, personally and by hand.

But to Shep, no bullet through the head, coming out of

noplace, would ever be sufficient comeuppance for Rodger Ashland. What he had wanted to do was to backtrack Rodge, find witnesses, and build up a total proof of wanton murder. He wanted to strip Rodge of all pretense that he fought for slavery or against it, or for the South or against it, or for any other justifying principle or cause. He didn't believe any court in Missouri would ever hang an Ashland, but he wanted to see Rodge disgraced, shamed; if not denied by his family, at least shunned by his class. He was only very dimly aware that it was because of Julie he wanted Ashland discredited. Though she was gone from his world, he still wanted her to know, someday, that the action he must take was just, and forced upon him.

Even after that was done—or proved impossible—they should have taken their time and closed on Rodge under conditions of their own choosing. All that was out of the question, now that Trapper was on the loose, glued like a kill-hound onto Rodger Ashland's trail. Trapper had committed Shep to immediate action, without room for maneuver or any choice of plan. Shep judged that his only bet, in favor of keeping his brother alive, was to get to Rodger Ashland first. Ice still locked the Missouri; the spring breakup seldom opened the Big Muddy to navigation before April, and sometimes not until May. Rodge would have to lay over in St. Louis. Catching him there would be Shep's last chance to deal with him on relatively neutral ground. *I've got to find him and kill him, ahead of Trapper. Anything else is the same as letting my brother die.*

Behind him he seemed to hear a door close where no door was, and the creaking of a great lock without a key.

Travel was slow in the last months of the winter weather. March was two and a half weeks gone before Shep landed at St. Louis. It made no difference. The Missouri River was still ice-locked; if Rodger Ashland had come this way he was here and would stay here until the Missouri opened or Shep found him. St. Louis had grown to a population of more than a hundred and fifty thousand, but nobody as prominent as an Ashland should be able to lose himself in it. Failing to find him registered at any of the hotels, Shep hunted up certain known connections of the Ashlands, who would surely have heard from him had he reached St. Louis. He learned nothing; apparently Rodger was not here. Not yet.

Every day Shep tramped the miles of waterfront, checking arrivals. Not much was going on there. By early summer three thousand boats at a time would tie up along the St. Louis levee, but just now the only craft ready and impatient to rush the season were thirty or forty "mountain boats" of the hazardous Far West fur trade, in which Jim Sam Delorme had found his beginnings. They didn't look like much, gaunt-lined, barren of wooden lace, weathered and peeling in the persistent rains. But they ran the highest pressures used in any trade, and their slaveless crews were the roughest river-men on earth. Every year they were first to challenge the winter-angry Missouri, their crack pilots taking fantastic chances to gain a few miles of mean water.

But not even these would try it yet. The Missouri was dis-gorging a glut of piling ice that shouldered one tied-up steam-boat clean out of the river and left it high and dry on top of the Columbia levee; where it sat, looking forlorn and foolish, for a long time.

During those days Shep remained curiously oblivious, as he realized afterwards, to the portents of that strangely omi-nous spring. Vast events were building pressures of deadly menace, not only to the nation but to his own immediate world. The Union had been hard hurt, even before the Danielses plunged into the wilderness, and the breakup had gone on while they were out of touch. Every military post in Texas had surrendered to the state; at New Orleans the rebels had seized the Mint and the Customhouse. The Confederacy had now adopted a constitution, setting up as a separate na-tion, with Jeff Davis of Mississippi as President; they already had a Congress of their own running full blast. Yet there had also been a dumbfounding upset. While Shep was lost in the swamp, proslavery Missouri had voted on her own secession—and had come out for preserving the Union. Such powerful slavery men as Pap Price, Colonel of Militia and former Governor; the furiously energetic Frank Blair; and Tyler Ashland himself had held fast against secession. A clean sweep ... On the 4th of March Lincoln took office as President, to the tune of an inaugural address that pleased nobody. The abolitionists, by far the noisiest element in the North, were incensed because the new President forswore interference with Southern slavery; and the South, while disbelieving that part, was enraged by Lincoln's idea that it was his job to preserve the Union. Next day the Confederate Congress replied by authorizing an army of 100,000 men. ...

Still the turbulent Missouri defied navigation; and still Rodger Ashland did not come. At first each day without word of Rodge seemed to Shep a reprieve; for at that time he was still hoping against hope that some legal means might develop for convicting Rodger Ashland of the crimes of Captain Handy. He could not believe that a vast public anger was not already long overdue to explode, forcing drastic military action against the bushwhackers—if not by the state, then by the Federal government. In St. Louis military action was certainly very much in evidence. Shep watched Frank Blair drilling his newly formed Home Guard on the St. Louis commons and for a while was able to hope he was seeing the emergence of a force to which Rodger Ashland could be delivered up.

He managed to talk briefly with Blair himself. Blair favored slavery, but believed it to be doomed; his great obsession was to save the Union, without which he did not think either North or South could survive as a nation of any account. Blair was acutely aware that Jackson, Missouri's secessionist Governor, was rallying his State Militia for open rebellion, in the teeth of the Union's victory at the polls; a quick military victory might easily sweep Missouri into the Confederacy. In this crisis the night riders seemed to Blair only a minor nuisance; the Home Guard was being readied to fight the rebels, and nothing other. Shep was invited to enlist. ...

Shep did not name the Ashlands to Frank Blair. Tyler Ashland had been Blair's close friend for a long time. Anything that was to be done about Rodger Ashland, *or* Captain Handy, Shep would have to do himself. He would find no help of any kind in St. Louis, or in this Missouri world.

I have to kill him. I have to kill him, no matter what comes after that. Every step he took, every hour that passed, was bringing him closer to that. Yet the days went by and March grew old; they were into the first weeks of April. Shep's certainty that Rodge would go back to Ash Landing by water now looked like a groundless guess; he might never have turned homeward at all. Or Trapper might have overtaken him in the swamp, in which case one of the two must have been dead these many weeks. *Which one? And where is the other?* Or, Rodge might even have gone home by the hard cross-country route. He might be there now if he had pushed hard enough. *How long will Trapper take to follow?*

Saturday, April 13. In Charleston Harbor, Fort Sumter fell to the bombardment of Beauregard's guns. No blood was shed; and these weren't even the first guns of rebellion. But now a different government was in the saddle in Washington. On Monday, April 15, President Lincoln called upon the states for 75,000 troops; and President Davis, for the Confederacy, called up 100,000 the next day. . . .

More important to Shep Daniels was Wednesday, April 17. On this day, an hour before daylight, the first mountain boat of the year backed out from the St. Louis levee to challenge the rampaging Missouri. Shep was aboard it; he had to be aboard it. Above all else, he had wished to avoid an encounter with Rodger Ashland upon his home ground. But a strong conviction was upon him that something deadly and irreversible was going to happen at Ash Landing, either with him or without him; he had to go there now.

Behind him he sensed the closing of another door; for he had no way to turn back.

⋆ 23 ⋆

SHEP DANIELS REACHED ASH LANDING ON THE SECOND OF MAY. Under the dark sky the little river town looked worn and shabby, but its waterfront was festive. All winter long Ash Landing slept as soundly as a hibernating woodchuck, but exploded into life at the first hooting of a boat whistle far off down the Missouri. Any steamboat, any time of year, drew a crowd, even when they were getting many landings a day. But the first boat of the year called out the whole town, for it brought here all the reawakenings of spring.

In the last days of this journey Shep Daniels had been very much aware that he was drawing near the place where Julie had been born, and which was at least supposed to be her home. At this time of the year she was far away; she never came home to Ash Landing from the convent school in New Orleans before June. This gave the crowded levee a feeling of emptiness for him, but he was grateful for it. He had no desire ever to face her again.

Now he slouched at the rail of the boiler deck, long-boned, awkward-looking, in old clothes that hung too loosely on his gaunted frame. He had two horses and a saddle mule with him, and he was waiting for the plank to clear before he led them off. In these minutes his glance briefly touched each face in the throngs within his view, recognizing most of them and classifying the rest, with attention to strangers who might be allied with Rodger Ashland in his activities as Captain Handy.

Then his eyes lifted to the upper gallery of the Delorme offices, and Julie was there, the last person in the world he was expecting to see. She waved at him, across the hundred feet of space between them, and he thought she looked serious-faced but glad to see him, as nearly as he could tell. He led his animals ashore in a state of shock.

Caleese was standing near the stage plank, watching him without looking directly at him. He beckoned to her, knowing that was what she was waiting for, lest she appear to accost him unbid. She came to him at once, all in black as always, but somehow not as tall as he remembered her. She moved with the stepless glide that had seemed spooky to him once; it did not seem spooky now. Her face showed no aging, but seemed sadder, and gentler than before. "Yes, sir," she said, and dipped her knees in a token curtsy.

"Is Rodger Ashland home? Or anywhere around?"

"Mr. Daniels, sir, I think not." Caleese spoke in the soft, measured cadences of the educated South; the words might have been spoken by a great lady, except that the low voice had a unique combination of dignity and humility in it, diffi-cult to imitate, yet impossible to forget. "I surmise Miss Julie may have heard something of him. But what I am sent to tell you—she wishes to see you, sir, as quickly as possible. It is about something very urgent, I believe."

"When and where, then?"

"Now. If you can be so kind, sir. She will wait there on the gallery, where she is." A look of pleading came into her eyes, puzzling him, as she repeated so softly he could hardly hear the words, "It is very . . . urgent."

He climbed the outside stairs of the Delorme offices to the toughest twenty minutes of his life.

Julie was looking wonderful—flushed by the open wind, and very slim-waisted, even in her winter coat. The upper gallery was a good place to meet, in a gossipy village, for they were in full view of everybody; and it was a good place to talk, because all that steamboat turmoil below gave them something to look at when they wanted to avoid each other's eyes. He had never been so ill at ease with her in his life. Yet at first there was no hint of anything ominous lying in wait, as Caleese had made him expect. Julie Delorme shook hands briskly and her tone was brightly chipper as they went through the meaningless forms of common greeting.

She entered a conventional complaint that he hadn't written to her, and he told her he had written to New Orleans, thinking she was there. She spoke of the rebel batteries that had been mounted at Baton Rouge and Vicksburg; some boats were getting through to the North, and others not. But anyway, she explained, Jim Sam had seen fit to snatch her home right after Lincoln's election, while he was sure he still could. . . .

He almost asked her if she had written to him at all, then remembered, with a feeling as if the stroke of a death bell had sounded in his head, that nothing like that was going to matter any more.

Most of the Delorme boats were tied up at Memphis, she rattled on. Her father was down there now, knocking heads together, and such like, she guessed; and she was right worried what would happen there—to the rebels, she meant, not Jim Sam. And what brought Shep here, by the way?

He told her it was a business trip, and she said she thought that was mighty insulting; he might at least have pretended he came to see her. And anyhow, Tyler Ashland was away, somewhere, and wasn't expected home for another week. Shep said he guessed he'd have to wait.

Suddenly all the empty chatter was over.

"I have to know the truth of something," Julie said. "It's a strange thing, but you seem to be just about the only human I can trust to come out with a straight answer." She paused there, and he waited.

"Shep, is Rodger Ashland Captain Handy?"

Nothing she could have said to him would have been less expected, but his horse-trading mask held firm. "How come you to ask that?"

"I think I'm going to marry him."

He hadn't expected that either, yet it was less surprising than the other, as if he had always known he would hear it sometime. "I see," he said, and for a moment weighed his choices. "I don't know if Captain Handy *is* any one man," he told her finally. "Could be he's only a name that any number of people use."

"Yes, of course, but does Rodger use it?"

In other circumstances he might have felt honor bound to tell her the truth, in her own protection—that, whatever name Rodger Ashland used, he was a night rider and a killer, like a hundred more; turning violence to profit as piously as possible, in the name of one or another political cause. Or, if that seemed vague, he could have said, "He and his men murdered my father. And he'll kill my brother next if I don't get to him first." She wouldn't have believed him, of course. Probably he would have been lucky if she hadn't turned him over to Tyler Ashland in the same hour.

But— *What she believes don't signify,* he reminded himself. *She stands in no danger of marrying him. On account of he'll be dead.*

"Julie, I can't answer that," he said finally; and he saw she took this to mean he didn't know. "What gave you the idea Rodge might be up to something like that?"

She drew back now, playing it down. "Oh—nothing really. Few scraps of rumors, cooked up in the Quarter, I suppose." The Quarter was what they called the slave cabins on any big place. "You know how those people love to talk. Among themselves, I mean—they hide everything from us, for fear of how we'll take it, I guess. But I have a—a kind of grapevine of my own."

She means Caleese, of course. Caleese knows about him, then. She's trying to make Julie know, without daring to tell her outright.

"Those people pass rumors across the country in the most mysterious way—sometimes hundreds of miles. But it doesn't mean anything."

"But what do they say?"

"Nothing," she said crossly. "Forget it now, will you?"

He had lost his chance to learn anything from her when he let her think he knew nothing himself. "Where is Rodge now?" he tried next.

She didn't know any more about that than he did. "Uncle

Ty has this Cavalry Club." Shep knew about Ashland's cavalry. It was meant to be State Militia, of a sort, but instead of being sworn in, it stood ready to go any way Tyler Ashland decided. Rodge had ridden south some while back, she said, supposedly rounding up recruits.

"Been lost ever since," Shep prompted.

"Oh, I hear from him. But you know how Missouri is in the winter. It's months since I've known just where he was. Oh, I'll straighten *him* out in a hurry when I'm his wife!"

Why did she have to keep harping on that marriage? It somehow gave him a feeling that she didn't really think it was going to happen. The arrangement had been predictable all the time; he had no reason to disbelieve it, except for Caleese. Caleese had favored Shep only negatively, yet today she had seemed to turn to him with something like a last-ditch appeal.

He said, "I suppose it was always in the cards that you'd marry Rodge someday."

"Well ... Our fathers are so tangled up together, financially, it does make a good deal of sense. Of course, my father never liked Rodger much. But Uncle Ty will bring Jim Sam around."

Julie moved closer to him, as if for shelter, and her shoulder touched his arm, so lightly that he wasn't sure she was aware of touching him at all.

"Julie, do you love this man?" Now, what had he asked that for? It was like hitting himself in the eye with a mule shoe. But she answered without hesitation.

"Of course! Or anyway, I will. No reason it should be hard to do. I've known him a long time, we've been raised much the same, we know the same people.... Do you realize, next month I'll be nineteen years old? Virtually an old maid! Rodge is a good match for me. I marvel I didn't marry him long ago."

"Why didn't you?"

"I swear, Shep, such fuddle-britches as you must grow only in Kentucky. It's impossible you don't know perfectly well. You kept cropping up again, that's all! But I've gotten over all that now."

"How did you get over it?" He sounded as if he were asking for a recipe, and maybe he was.

"I got tired of throwing myself at you, I guess. Poor Shep—I gave you a bad time, didn't I? Especially last summer, when I kept making you blush. Why did you think I said all those scandalous things—to tease you? I was trying to get close to you. Closer to you than anybody had ever been. Closer than anybody has ever been to me . . ."

Her extraordinary candor still carried some of the intimacy that had so unsettled him in the times of which she spoke; except that she had been moving nearer, then, and now she was moving away. Or was she?

"You'll never know what a fool I was," she told him. "I'd have run off with you to live in a mule barn any time you said."

She'd go with me now, he suddenly knew. *That's what she's telling me. All that nonsense about marrying Rodge is just a bluff, to build a fire under me; a girl is entitled to that much little thin shred of pretense.*

He had held motionless, so that she would stay where she was, but now, as she smiled at him, he looked down into her face. Julie Delorme's eyes were a golden brown on bright days, with gold-dust flecks in them. Under this swirling overcast they were almost a velvet black, yet he could see little sparks of laughter in them.

She's not the least bit worried about losing me off the hook, either. She's as sure of herself as an Ashland. More sure—as sure as Jim Sam. Doesn't believe she could lose me if she tried. And she's right, except for what I have to do. How do I look to her? Like a man made of stone? For that must be what I am. I never would have thought that stone could be hurt so bad.

They held each other's eyes steadily, and there was no shyness in it at first, for they were looking at, not into, each other's eyes. It could not stay like that; soon he would have to look away. What was he afraid to see? It was something like a small-boy time when he had tried to fly off the roof of the barn. Do all boys have to try that? Just before the earth rushed up, there had been an unforgettable moment of teetering fright as he overbalanced too far to turn back. It was something like that irrecoverable loss of balance that was scaring him now.

"If you hadn't had more sense than I had, that's where we'd be now. In a mule barn. But that's all past."

I wish to God it was. Why did you have to be here? I suppose I'll have to finish him virtually before your eyes. Drop him right in your lap. . . .

"I have to run now. You'll be at the Bishop House, I suppose. Maybe I'll ride with you tomorrow. If it works out, I'll send word."

She left him then. He moved his gloved hand to the place where Julie's gloved hand had rested on the railing, but there was no warmth there.

That night he lay awake a long time, intruded upon by fantasies of things that were never going to be. He resented this; he didn't believe in it for the same reason that he didn't believe in pounding his head with a pry bar. To put Julie out of his mind, he tried to plan the moves he must make against Rodger Ashland, and this was another futility. All must wait upon circumstance, including how he was to get out of Missouri afterward. Where was Trapper, and where was Rodge? He didn't even know that much.

Shortly after midnight he dressed, got his animals from the boarding stable, and rode south.

✷ 24 ✷

TRAPPER LAY FLAT ON HIS BELLY, HIS ELBOWS SINKING INTO A soppy bit of loam that happened to be in the wrong place, and studied the six men out in the open in front of him within forty yards. He liked to work in close, closer when he stalked men than when he stalked game, figuring he could count on human senses to be dull and weak compared with those of the wild critters. This time, though, he may have overdone it. His point of vantage, or disadvantage, as he saw it now, was much more poorly covered than it had appeared when he picked it out from a good distance. All that hid the most of him was a stand of lush grass, with a lacy-thin screen of hazel bush in front, through which he could look out at the meadow as through a window, whenever he lifted his head.

It was hard to believe the men making camp out there couldn't see him plainly if they looked in the right place. And, besides that, he had snaked his way into this position considerably previous. If he decided to fire he couldn't miss; but he couldn't get out of there alive, either, if he tried it before dark, and sundown was still three hours away. He thought, or perhaps imagined, that the men in the meadow seemed uncommonly alert, as if they sensed something hostile watching them. About the only thing in Trapper's favor was that their nervous eyes kept sweeping the forested hills, so drawn to great distances that they never thought to look into the grass almost at their feet.

He didn't recognize all of them, but two, at least, had been in the skirmish in the Black Mingo Swamp—the long-jawed turkey-neck called Yancey and the taller, even narrower slat of a man known as Hobe. A third man Trapper believed to be a small farmer named Hartog—friends pronounced it Wart Hog—and his presence with the night riders was a surprise. It might be a sorry one, for there was a bare possibility he could recognize Trapper, which the others almost certainly could not do. The three others were strangers, of whom Trapper knew nothing, except that the one man he wanted was not among them. Twice, in the two months that he had searched, and tracked, and questioned, Trapper had sighted Roger Ashland, a long way off; the first time with his right arm in a sling, where Trapper had put it, and the second time with his wounded arm in full use, the sling discarded. But Rodge kept disappearing again, and Trapper had not been able to close.

Presently he had found out why. Rodger Ashland, whom the night riders called Captain Handy, had one dodge that Trapper had to admit was pretty clever, the way Rodge handled it. He seemed to have about forty men in his command—maybe more. Hard to say, because since the Black Mingo he had never again brought together as many as had been there. He habitually split his riders into parties of as few as four, rarely as many as ten; and these small groups sifted over the country as timber cruisers, or transient drovers, or meat hunters, or whatever, where a larger number could never have passed themselves off as anything but a raiding force. Rodge continually shuffled and reshuffled these parties, sending them on different errands and by different ways, never riding with any one of them himself for very long, yet skillfully keeping track of most of them.

Apparently the bushwhackers themselves seldom knew where he was or where he would be; he appeared among them without notice, and left them the same way. Over and over Trapper had trailed and stalked a party of them, only to find his man no longer with them. He could have sniped off the half of them by this time, he supposed, and it had been a great temptation. But up to now, at least, he had held his fire. He had planted a lot of rumors among strangers that he was dead, and he was unwilling to give the night riders evidence that this was not so.

So the storms of March had passed, and the storms of April, and the upland roads dried out. He was high up in the Ozarks now, between the white water of the upper Gasconade and the Pine Fork country, with the spring coming on in Maytime fullness. The dogwood bloomed, and the hawthorn came out in clusters of flowers like white apple blossoms; honey locust, redbud, and white plum filled the woods with magic. On the little sloping farms between the woodlands, young plantings of fruit trees made half-acre spreads of unbelievably clean pink and white. And everywhere was the music of tumbling water. It was a land of forests, steeps, and deep gorges, great rocky outcrops, and swift streams; as beautiful a place as he had ever seen in his life, Trapper thought, if he had only had time to enjoy it.

But Rodger Ashland's tangled trails had already brought him more than two-thirds of his way home. Trapper had followed through evidences of enough misdoings to hang a hundred if he could have shown proof, or even found any authorities in Missouri strong enough and interested enough to act. But of course there were none, and now he had not seen Rodger Ashland for a long time. All Rodge had to do, to vanish Captain Handy from the face of the earth, was to ride off to Ash Landing and resume life as himself, a planter's son on the shores of the Missouri. Trapper hated to give up stalking Rodge here in the wild country that he loved, for he thought poorly of his own chances in the Ashlands' home stronghold of towns and cultivated plantations. Finally, though, he faced the fact that his man seemed to be gone from the wilderness; it was time for him to follow.

Reluctantly he had struck out to the northwest, for Ash Landing, going by way of Waynesville and the Potter farm. At least he would be able to pick up Brown Sugar, the little Morgan horse he had left resting at the Potters'. Like a horse Indian, his confidence much depended upon his belief in the horse he rode, and he still thought of the Morgan as the best rough-country traveler he had ever thrown a leg over. He would be happy to saddle Brown Sugar again.

He was only four miles short of Waynesville, and seven from the Potters, riding a little-used trail, when he sighted this one more armed party from a distant height, and pressed in too boldly, for a better look. He cussed himself a little for having got into this precarious pindown, where he could only wait for nightfall. At very best, his rashness was going to cost him another empty-bellied night in the woods, in room of a hot supper cooked by the Potter girls.

He tried his sights upon one after another of the night riders, aiming delicately between the eyes of each, as position offered. As he came to Yancey, the bushwhacker appeared to be looking at him steadily, straight in the eye, up his own carbine barrel. Trapper froze, and stopped fooling with his carbine after that. He rested his chin on the stock, and watched a gnat flying in and out of a jack-in-the-pulpit about six inches from his nose. . . .

Far back in the woods, Trapper's horse whinnied, where he had left it tied, and one of the grazing horses of the night riders answered. Hobe, who had been unhurriedly racking up wood for a cooking fire, allowed he had heard that same one horse before. Maybe four–five times in the last month.

That's a damned lie, Trapper silently answered him. *Ain't ridden him that long.* He had changed horses more than once since the claybank gave out on him in the muck of the Black Mingo. The gelding he rode now was a blaze-faced chestnut he called Spooks; about as good a horse as a man could want, under right conditions. Only thing, he was a flat-country horse, pretty long and flat-boned in the legs for mountain work; Trapper felt he had to place the chestnut's feet for him all the time. But Spooks could run like the devil, on decent going, and stay with it, too—a full-out miler, not a quarter-horse type.

Yancey told Hobe that maybe some could tell one horse voice from another, if they was different enough, but he misdoubted if Hobe could tell a horse from a mule, even was they in plain sight before his eyes. Hobe said, all right then, he never heard it, and Yancey said he didn't say that. . . .

Now something changed. One more man came out of the woods on the other side of the meadow, buckling his belt in visual explanation of why he had been out there all this time.

And this seventh man was Rodger Ashland, alias Captain Handy.

Trapper felt a shock of exultation, immediately followed by a pull-up like hitting the end of a rope. He could take Rodger Ashland into his sights, and finish him very easily, but only at the cost of his own life if he accepted this moment in which he was sure. He had to wait, and wait, and make a gamble of it still.

Rodger Ashland stood tall and straight, very lean in the hips from these months in the saddle. By comparison with his night riders he looked clean and trim, and very able. His eyes ran along the edge of the meadow where Trapper was, combing the nearest cover first and most carefully, then raising to a quicker survey of the wooded hills beyond.

"There's something out there," he said.

Yancey said, "Wull, I did think I seen something didn't rightly belong there, a while back. But I couldn't see it no more, when I looked hard. So I guessed it wasn't nothing."

"Did you go and look?"

"Wull, no, I never. Not yet, anyway—"

"Why not?"

"Wull, I guess I never seen no call to work up a lather over—"

"Four of you. You, and Hobe, and two more. Sprangle out, a good space apart, and skirmish a ways into those woods— say about four hundred yards."

Yancey started to answer, but changed his mind. First Hobe, then Yancey, then two more unwound themselves and hitched by easy stages to their feet. Rodger Ashland said nothing to speed them up. His way of handling them was to let them take their own pace, never demanding that they do anything with snap, or on the jump, or any faster than the situation required, so long as they obeyed. Thus he let them keep an illusion of independence that seemed to be necessary to their self-respect. With utmost leisure they inspected their rifles, verifying or replacing their priming; then walked irregularly toward the edge of the woods where Trapper lay, each in his own good time.

Trapper examined again, in his mind, the few yards of

ground behind him, between his position and the cover of the trees. He was calculating his chances of scuttling backward through the tall grass, and gaining the woods without being seen; and he judged it couldn't be done. He wasted no seconds in regrets. He had no plan for dealing with a thing like this, but what struck him as best to do he now did at once. He whistled sharply through his teeth, first, as a warning to them, lest somebody's snapshot in startlement bring him down. Then he stood up, his carbine in the crook of his elbow, and walked out into the ring of rifles.

"Drop that gun!" came Yancey's yell.

Trapper made no move to obey. He was feeling a deep, inner tremor of pure tension, but it did not show yet in his hands, nor in his voice, which he did not needlessly raise. His answer sounded weary, and disgusted. "Oh, hell, stop it, will you? I coulda picked you off very easy if that was what I come here for." By some instinct of protective coloration, he had dropped into the dragging inflections of downriver Arkansas, so that "hell" came out "Hey, El," and "easy" had three syllables. It wasn't too hard a speech to imitate; although, as he went farther with it, he sounded a little bit off, to himself, as if he might not be picking the right words.

Ashland spoke reasonably across the forty yards. "You looking for someone, bub?"

"I been awanting to see Captain Handy. So—I reckon I see him." He walked without hurry toward his enemy.

"Leave him be," Ashland said. "Come on in, boy."

"I am." He stopped five paces in front of Ashland, his carbine cradled loosely in front of him, while three or four of the night riders still inconspicuously ringed him at a safe distance. They stood there through a brief wrangle over who was who. Trapper said he was just passing through, when his horse spooked from some varmint he never got a look at— bobcat, most likely—and blowed up in a fit of the kettles, thrun him, and took out. That was his horse they must have heard whickering out there in the trees. He was minded to go catch him, in a minute.

"Threw you right there in that patch of grass, I see. Carbine already loaded and cocked in hand!"

"I grobe the carbine out of the boot to shoot the varmint. It was after that, I was throwed. I crawled in that patch of brush to see who I'd run onto, here. A man has to watch that kind of thing these days."

"He sure does," Ashland agreed. "Where you from, boy?"

Trapper said his name was Willie Hoxie, and he was up from Arkansas. His folks were sharecropping near a place called Possum Hatch.

"Where's that?"

"In Poinsettia County. Up a branch called Saddler's Creeyuck. It runs in the St. Francis."

Ashland glanced around him to see if anybody knew anything about such a place, but all faces remained blank. Yancey said, "Sounds a little bit like he's got that branch running along the spine of a hogback." And Trapper answered, "Don't mind that. If that's where it's clumb to, it'll run down again, without no help from you."

"I don't know how it is," Ashland said, "but it seems every time a drifter comes through Missouri he's from someplace nobody ever heard of before."

"Sure makes a man hard to backtrack, don't it?"

"What you up to, so far from home?"

"Well, they was this barn burned down . . ." Trapper put in here a fairly detailed lie about a misunderstanding having shaped up over how the barn took fire, leading around into more or less of an ambuscade. "Anyhow, in the upshot I kind of fetched loose at both ends; and I—"

Rodger Ashland's eyes were everywhere, and now he interrupted Trapper to speak to an undersized and buck-toothed boy in whose face he had detected some sign of dissatisfaction. "What's troubling you, Wash?"

"Sir?"

"You're from Arkansas. Does he sound like down home, to you?"

"Cap'n, I don't know. He talks some like the hills, and then again he talks more like the bottoms. I guess he sounds all right."

"There was this barn burned," Ashland prompted. "What then?"

"I come away from there, then."

Yancey had to get in his prod-pole. "On whose horse?"

"I was afoot for a good while, there at the first." Trapper was doing a good job of holding his temper, and now thought he saw a way of explaining himself that would drag in a few items they knew were so. "I worked up the shore of the Mississippi," he said, "and I come to this place where there'd been a big fight . . ." He spoke of three-four dead men, unburied in the swamp, and getting pretty high; and a great lot of trampled sign, like as if a big passel of cavalry had milled around; and the biggest sorrel jack he ever saw, running loose there, but too cute to catch. "But I did catch up a horse," he finished it, "saddle and all. Kind of lamed up, but I finally got him swapped off."

"How long ago was all this?"

"Oh, gosh—some while. Let's see—is this May already? It must have been nine-ten weeks back. Near the end of February, like, or early in March."

Ashland did not react, but some of the night riders looked at each other. Trapper did not know why they didn't believe him, but he knew they did not. Yancey said, "One of the Daniels boys, the young'un, was straw-topped like him, from what I heard. His own story puts him where they was."

"Don't talk so much," Ashland told Yancey. To Trapper he said, "Found that carbine, too, I suppose."

"This here? It come in the saddle boot. With the horse."

"Mind if I look at it?"

Here it comes. This thing can't last many seconds more.

"Sure you can look at it. Soon's I get time to unload. She has this one kind of bad point. She's partial to letting go at the half cock. Might be I better hang onto her, for now. Seeing's I'm more used to her."

"Half cock be damned," Ashland said. "Hand it over!" He moved toward Trapper.

Ashland's riders had eased forward by this time, and now Trapper allowed himself two long steps backward, bringing those at the side into the rail of his vision. "I believe I'd stop there was I you." He let the Spencer swing to cover Ashland's belt buckle, and Rodge stopped where he was.

"You, Wash," he said without taking his eyes off Ashland, "I can see you moving, there. Don't do that. Because if you move out of sight of my eye corner, I'll have to kill your captain."

"Stand still, all of you," Ashland said. "Let him simmer down. What's the matter with you, boy?"

"I figure you for Captain Handy," Trapper said. "But I don't know that's who you be."

"What if I am?"

"I'm more worried about what if you ain't." He stepped backward another two paces; he would be able to see any movement among them clearly now. "If I've tied into the wrong bunch, here, I'm still well-fixed to kill me one, maybe two Jayhawkers more." He thought of making them disarm, but he was afraid of bringing on a general movement, in which the turning of a weapon might go undetected until too late.

Rodger Ashland got out a gold toothpick, unfolded it, and idly picked his teeth. "Killed some Jayhawkers, have you?" he said pleasantly.

"Maybe." Trapper began walking backwards, stepping high, careful to make sure of the footing behind him. "I'm going out and catch up my horse," he said. "When I come back, I don't want to see nobody point no weapons, you hear? And I don't want nobody reaching for mine!"

"Let the man go get his horse," Ashland said reasonably. "I believe we'll have a right useful recruit here once he calms down. He'll catch onto our ways when he's been with us a while."

All watched him, but nobody made a false move as Trapper backed across the forty yards to cover, around the hazel bush in which he had hidden, through the deep grass, and between the first trees. As he passed the bole of a big beech, he sprang sideways, putting it between himself and his enemies; then turned and ran for it, while all hell broke loose behind him. A volley from the miscellany of guns back there clipped leaves beside him and ahead of him, but though they sounded like more than they were, he knew that not all had emptied their weapons.

"What the hell you shooting at?" Rodger Ashland was shouting. All but Hobe, Yancey, and Ashland himself had discharged their firearms. "Get in there after him—that's Trapper Daniels! Don't stop to reload now—you have to run him to a stand! And watch the trees—he'll try to get above you!"

In the woods Trapper stopped running, turned off, and crawled into a dogwood thicket so dense with blossoms that a man would have to comb every yard of it to find out what was there. In the heart of the dogwood he lay still, hoping the petals that were falling about him would come to earth in time; and almost at once the bushwhackers came through the trees. They moved slowly, but with surprising quiet, not liking this job much. Often they stopped to listen, though they must have known they would hear only each other. A couple of them went past so close that Trapper could see their boots through the lower stems of the dogwood.

Last of all, the boy called Wash came up to the edge of the thicket, and stopped, to stand reloading his heavy rifle musket. When he had set the cap, he came crashing through the dogwood, directly at Trapper; he passed within a yard, almost stepping on him, and it was Ashland's cagey forethought that saved Trapper then, for Wash was staring into the upper branches of the trees ahead.

After that the woods were quiet again, and Trapper lay listening, hearing a thousand small sounds but none of any use or meaning to him. Main thing noticeable was a Great-God bird, hollering somewhere far off in the woods. Great-God was the hill folks' name for a giant form of woodpecker, colored so brightly in black and white and red that almost anybody who saw one had to take a shot at it, so there weren't very many left. It had a strident, far-carrying call, something like "Cra-a-ake gawk!" But once you had thought of it as hollering "Great God!" you couldn't ever hear it as anything else. Trapper had to allow that the night riders could move mighty quiet, some of them as silent as he could, when they wanted to.

Now Spooks whinnied again, from where Trapper had tied him, and this was dangerous, as a guide to the bushwhackers; they would have the horse shortly. Trapper crawled out of the thicket and took a circuit through the woods, to get to the chestnut from the far side. His moccasins were quiet, as he possum-tracked through the undergrowth, but silence was less important, now that the woods were full of Ashland's men, and he moved as swiftly as he dared. It was a form of race, and Trapper didn't win it, though he got a tie. The man named Hartog was already at the chestnut's head, his fingers working loose the tie rope, as Trapper came in view.

Trapper brought the carbine to his shoulder. He could not aim too high, without endangering the horse; the only shot he had would break Hartog's back at about the belt line. And suddenly he couldn't do it.

"Just a minute, Wart Hog," he said.

Hartog made a wild grab at his rifle, where he had leaned it against the tree to which Spooks was tied; failed to get hold of it, and knocked it down. He made no further try for it, but whirled to face Trapper, his hands higher than his head and his eyes popping. "Don't you do it! Don't you do it, Trapper! I never told 'em who you was! I swear I never! Me and your Pap's been friends since—"

"Stand away from the horse," Trapper ordered him. "Not toward me—sideways! . . . Farther . . . Stop there." He went to the chestnut, loosed the lead rope, and mounted. "Soon as 'm out of sight, run for your life," he told Hartog, and jogged off into the trees. Moments later, when he glanced back, Hartog was gone from where he had left him.

A numbing shock, painless at first, and simultaneous with the crash of Hartog's rifle, collapsed him upon the neck of the chestnut. The horse went up in a great bound, but Trapper got him checked and turned back, in a rod or so. He didn't fully understand what had happened to him yet, but he knew he had dropped the carbine. He rode back, and found it, but as he tried to stretch for it his right arm wouldn't answer him; he fell heavily, but hung onto the reins, preventing the horse from bolting. He recovered the carbine, and got it into its saddle boot, and with great difficulty remounted.

He believed now that his right arm was broken, and the bullet, since it had not gone through him, must be lodged somewhere in the muscles of his shoulder. He was going to need help before too long, but what he needed now was distance, and in a hurry, worse than he needed the blood that already half covered him. With his left hand he pulled his right hand through his belt, with the hazy notion that this had to be done to hold his arm on. Then he put Spooks into a lope toward the trail by which he had come here.

⋆ 25 ⋆

"Hark'ee!" Caylin Potter said, and they all listened. "I thought I heard horses, far down. Beyond the road . . ."

The two Potter boys—Hick (for Hickson), eighteen, and Tom, seventeen—had gone down to the woods pasture to milk, their rifles slung on their backs, for since the night riders had been here they never left the house after sundown without their weapons. But the elder Potters and the two girls were having their after-supper setting spell. Between sundown and full dark they had some three hours of clear and gentle light, shading imperceptibly into twilight, then deepening dusk. After the supper chores had been cleaned up, they still had an hour and a half in which they could just sit, enjoying the quiet, and this had once been the nicest time of the day. They clung to it, never admitting to each other that this year the day's end brought unspoken forebodings of what the night might bring.

"You got ears like a woods owl," Caylin's father said.

"I don't hear it now," Caylin admitted.

Old Jim Potter was looking might grim. He was heavily built, and strong as a mass of oak knots, but helpless now, so that he had to be carried about in a chair that was half a litter for his game leg. He must have known by this time that his bullet-shattered thigh bone was never going to heal. Ma Potter certainly knew it; she was melting down into the resigned anonymity of an old, old woman, far beyond her actual years. She sat mending, forever mending, in the clear, long-lasting light, but now poised her needle to look a long time at her younger daughter. At sixteen Caylin was sun-darkened and wiry, but so thin she seemed frail. Her eyes were lively, yet had the odd haunted look that some people call fey. Ma Potter believe in signs like that.

Caylin said, "I wish the boys would come in."

"I don't look for 'em," her father said, "so long as they can see."

Neither did Caylin, actually. When the cows had been stripped, the boys would stand the milk pails in the creek to cool, and wet their fish lines, to see if the blue gills, which they called punkinseeds, happened to be biting. If they were, the boys wouldn't be back until full dark, when all the Potters went to their shuck ticks, to be up and at work again before the first sign of dawn.

"Saloney," Potter said. "Fetch me my rifle."

"Oh, now, Pa . . ." Ma said with a tremble in the words, then let it drop.

Saloney, a stongly built girl with a plain, big-featured face, went into the main room of the peeled-log house and brought out her father's long muzzle-loader. He looked at the cap, then replaced it from the cap-box in the butt.

"Things don't balance out like the preacher says they's supposed to," old Jim said, "don't seem like to me." Into his tone came a querulous note, never heard there until this year. He was brooding upon an unfairness of which he had spoken before. How trifling must have been each night rider's share of the Potter livestock; how great, beyond all mending, was the lifelong hurt to himself. . . . "Take like when a fox breaks a woodchuck's back, and carries him away. Which is the most? The misery of the chuck? Or the pleasuring of the fox? These things don't cipher out."

The little house clung half-stilted upon a stoney slope that climbed into wooded steeps behind. In front, the sagging gallery overhung a narrow belt of rich bottom land that curved between the foot of the mountain and the creek; here the young corn was beginning to sprout, and would come on abooming in the summer heat. The creek was their boundary; the hills and second-growth woods began again, beyond, but young mules could browse and flourish there. Saloney had been gazing down this slit in the world they called their valley, toward the Waynesville wagon track, her face empty, untroubled by any sign of thought. But now her eyes popped wide and wildcat sharp, as suddenly as if she had been struck.

"Look yander!"

On the Waynesville wagon track appeared a tall blaze-faced chestnut, galloping heavily; its hoofs thudded softly on the stoneless dirt of the bottoms. As they watched, it slanted out of the track, long before reaching the gate, and made a great winging jump over the work-laid rail fence, clearing the blackberry thickets massed in the corners. As it landed it stumbled, but recovered, reseating the half-thrown rider; then ran on toward the creek, trampling the young corn.

"That man's drunk!" Jim Potter said, and fumbled with his rifle lock, considering a warning shot.

He did look drunk, sagged low over the neck, and reeling in the saddle; as if he might be unconscious, riding by the reflexes in his legs alone. But now they saw that he was hatless, exposing a shock of pale hair. Caylin cried out, "That's Trapper! It's Trapper Daniels!"

At the cutbank of the creek the chestnut tried to check on stiff forelegs; and the rider fell hard, and lay quiet. He did not move again as the horse galloped over the cutbank, through a long screen of young willows at the edge of the water, and on across the creek into the woods.

Caylin was already bounding down the slope, her bare feet sure of the path. Her father was shouting something after her, but with an uncertainty that took no effect; he was not sure himself what his orders ought to be. Saloney hesitated, then followed her sister. Caylin cut straight across the hundreds of yards of plowed ground toward the fallen man, but Saloney split off, splashed through the creek, and dived into the woods. She could do no more for the man than Caylin could without her, but he appeared to be in flight, so her immediate practical thought was to catch and hide the horse.

Trapper was lying on his back in the grass between the edge of the plowed ground and the cutbank of the creek, barely recognizable to Caylin as she knelt beside him, panting. His face was wet, and the dead color of greenish clay; and he was much more than half covered with blood. Even when he opened his eyes they stared unnaturally, and their color was unfamiliar against the bloodshot whites. "Dark," he muttered thickly. Dry, cracking lips, dry tongue. "Dark ... Thought she'd ... never come."

Here Caylin began to cry, for it was not dark yet, or anywhere near it, and would not be for an hour. Trapper's lids lowered over his pupils, but did not close completely; he lay unseeing, with half-open eyes, so that he did not look asleep, but knocked out, or dead. She found the wound, and turned him on his face. He stirred and made some inarticulate sounds of protest; then said a few more words she understood. "Close. They're close. Close behind me ..." She spoke his name, and tried to tell him who she was, but he had blurred out again.

The bullet had entered the back of his arm, and hadn't torn its way out, anywhere, so must have ranged upward and stopped in his shoulder, which was monstrously swollen and discolored. Some stiffened rags had been used in more than one attempt to bind the wound, but these were now displaced, and he was bleeding again, not with a pulsing flow, but oozing swiftly. He remained insensible as she bound one of the clotted wads of rag tight upon the wound with the torn-off hem of her dress. Far down the road, before this was done, she heard the hoofs of ridden horses, trotting in a broken rhythm that made them impossible to count.

Caylin got hold of Trapper's left wrist with both hands, and began dragging him toward the cutbank on his face, getting her back into heaves that moved him a yard at a time. He cried out, and struggled feebly, but had not the strength to resist effectively. She was perspiring from her hard run, which had turned the mild night steaming hot, but the icy cold of Trapper's hand was a shock; she could sense no pulse nor life in it. From the edge of the bank she could see that gouts of red stained the grass where his weight had pressed it down. She left him a moment, to throw a few handfuls of dirt upon the worst of the blood marks, and kicked at the bent grass, hoping to confuse the shape of the imprint.

But the beat of hoofs sounded very near, and she dared take no more time there. Jumping down into the long thicket of willows at the edge of the stream, she pulled him after her over the four-foot drop, easing him down as gently as she could. He remained quiet, unrevived by immersion in the foot of water that was running between the stems of the young willows. His head was propped in the mud at the margin, but if he was pulled deeper by the current he would drown. Through a moment's panic, she looked for a way to secure him without disturbing his wounded arm. A single sharp rock stuck up through silt and running water; she braced her knee upon this, to tie rooted willow switches across his chest. The rock cut into her knee, but she dared not take time to change her position until she was certain he was secure.

All this while the trotting hoofs had come on and on, somehow getting no closer; but now three riders came in sight upon the Waynesville wagon track. She saw them through the leaves, before she crouched down in the running water beside Trapper and became as still as a nesting snipe. She thought they were hidden well enough, by the overhang and the leaves, if nobody parted the willows.

Trapper said distinctly, "Is it getting light?" and moved in what appeared to be an effort to sit up.

Caylin leaned over him to hiss into his ear. "Shush! Lie still—don't make a sound—"

The three riders pulled up at the Potter gate for the space of time it took to study the ground, in the still-clear dusk. They were Yancey, Hobe, and Rodger Ashland himself, though Caylin knew neither their names nor their faces, then; but later, when she found them out, she knew which had been which, and what each had said.

Yancey said, "He never turned in here," and Hobe said, "Nothing did. Not today." Ashland grunted, and cantered ahead to the shallow ford, where the track went through the creek. It didn't take him long to read the mud at the edge of the water.

"Nope! He didn't come through here, either," Ashland said, and when Yancey cussed, "Don't get yourself all worked up," Rodge told him. "We'll find him."

The three riders turned back at a walk, Ashland working one side of the road, Hobe and Yancey the other; and of course Ashland discovered immediately where the chestnut had slanted off. "Tallyho," he remarked, and put his horse over the work fence in the tracks of the chestnut. He hand-galloped across the young corn, following very easily the trail of Trapper's horse, but swerving downstream to pass the end of the long willow thicket, instead of blundering through it as the chestnut had done. All three riders stopped their horses knee-deep in the creek to let them drink, the two woolhat bushwhackers giving Ashland the upstream position.

"Now, look'ee yar," Yancey said to Ashland. "I'll fight any man on this yarth, but I ain't ahonin', nor yet awhettin', to quarter no breshwoods in the dark."

"Just stay behind me," Ashland said. "I think you'll be safe enough."

The two coldblood horses had plunged their noses into the water to their eyes, but Ashland's horse, drinking with dainty lips, suddenly snorted, tossed its head, and pawed in protest.

Rodger Ashland leaned low to look at the water. "Blood, by God!"

Now Caylin saw the thin red threads that floated off from where Trapper lay, holding together in a ribbon that went winding between the willow stems, traveling quickly with the stream. Trapper must be bleeding dreadfully; Ashland was fully a hundred feet below. Or had been. He was walking his horse slowly along the lip of the bank, bending to part the willows with his carbine.

Caylin half stood up, and with all her strength stamped upon the rock that had cut her knee. She thought she must have cut the flesh to the bone, but no blood came yet. Half frantic, she twice more drove her foot down upon the edged stone; and suddenly the blood spurted, faster than she had needed, or had meant. Immediately she slunk crouching, careful not to splash, to the upper end of the willow rift, thirty feet upstream.

Rodger Ashland had come almost to the stained imprint in the grass that showed where Trapper had been lying; she dared not let him linger there. She stood up, blubbering out loud, and hopped on her unhurt foot into ankle-deep shallows. There she stood with the bleeding foot held in her two hands, so that her skirt was hiked up almost to her waist, while Rodger Ashland stared. "Hell," he shouted at the others, "it's nothing but a gal with a cut foot!" He brought his horse abreast of her, and his two men cantered up to stop alongside him.

Ashland said courteously, "Are you in need of help, mam?" Then sharply to Yancey, "Stay on your damned horse!"

She was all right, Caylin told him, but went on bawling, while through her fingers ran a red stream. Yancey settled into his saddle again.

"Stop sniveling a minute," Ashland said to Caylin. "A chestnut horse with a blazed face crossed over into these woods a short while back. How long ago?"

"Just now. About fifteen minutes."

"Did you notice anything about the rider?"

"They warn't no rider. It was a empty horse.'

"I trust that brings you peace of mind," Ashland said to Yancey.

"Wull—I don't mind a horse hunt, if that's all it is."

"To hell with the horse. I want the man."

"He's fell, summers," Hobe said. "That's what he done."

"Evidently. But he's between here and Waynesville. Not far from the road either. If we don't pick him up on the ride back, we'll track him very easily in the morning." He jogged off toward the gate.

"Them's right pretty laigs you got there, gal," Yancey called back over his shoulder. "You don't need to be bleedin' 'em any whiter than they be. Go git patched up, because maybe I'll be back. To do a little plowin' at the forks of the creek!"

"Get on up there and open the gate," Ashland ordered him. "And mind you close it after us this time. I'm sick of telling you."

Soon after they disappeared, Caylin's brothers came running down the creek, through the dusk that was deepening at last, Tom racing lightly, and big square-built Hick pounding after him, some way behind.

✶ 26 ✶

SHEP DANIELS RODE SOUTHWARD, USING HIS MULE TO CARRY HIS bedroll and his sacks of shelled corn, and spelling off his horses under saddle. His intention was to go as far south as Waynesville if he had to, remembering Trapper's determination to pick up the Morgan he had left resting there. Failing to cut Trapper's trail before, Shep felt sure he could pick it up at the Potters', where the horse was; hoping meantime that whatever news he got there would not be too old for use.

He could have made Waynesville in four or five days by making a direct ride there, but he was afraid that both Rodger Ashland and Trapper were already nearer Ash Landing. He dared not let them get much to the north of him, lest Trapper close with Rodge before Shep could get to either one of them. So now he had to keep swinging back and forth across Missouri in great zigzags, making inquiries on all the roads. The going was firm now, and he made high mileages, but the farther south he got the more the roads from Ash Landing fanned out and the more his way to Waynesville widened; until he was covering most of the country from the Pomme de Terre to the Gasconade.

Sometimes he knew he was recognized by people who shied clear of him and made fast time leaving his vicinity. Carrying messages? Maybe, some of them. Not necessarily. Sometimes he was able to verify that he was followed, though apparently by men more interested in watching him than closing with him. His strong pace and constant changes of direction shook these off, but he rode long

165

hours, never letting his most trusted friends know where he next would sleep.

Less often, now, Shep Daniels found himself wondering what Pap would do in his place. The loss of Pap had left an unexpected hole in Shep's world. Since early in his teens Shep had preferred to operate on his lone, whenever he could manage it, finding it easier to hear about his mistakes after a job was done, rather than move by move as he went. All through that period he had been wary of asking Pap's advice, lest he be prevented from going ahead in his own way. And yet, even while he was doing his best to get out from under his father's domination, he must have leaned on Pap more than he supposed; for at first whenever it came home to him that Pap would never again advise him, Shep had felt an unseemly childlike sensation of being lost and alone. By an effort of will he could turn his back on that emptiness, and this was becoming easier every time he denied it. The last of Pap, the image he had left in the minds of his sons, was already fading away.

Pap had turned dour in these last years since Ma died. The father for whom Shep grieved had not really been lost in the swamp at all, for he had not been in existence for a long time. The times Shep truly grieved for Pap were those in which he remembered small meaningless things that Pap had done for them long ago; and these were somehow the very tools of heartbreak. Like, there was once a rabbit, made of a knotted napkin, that peeped over the table edge to snap at pieces of bread. ("Don't play with the food!" Pap always scolded the rabbit.)

Why did those simple things Pap had done to amuse them when they were babies made Shep feel such a sharpening of grief? They had a bite as if with the teeth of remorse. He hadn't thought of those small fooleries for a long time, and certainly he was not missing them now. Pap had kept on with the more childish of them for too long, until his young sons had become bored, and even their pretense of attention failed. Shep remembered the time that Pap had finally noticed this. He had started to make a shadow picture on the kitchen wall, then had faltered, and let his hand fall, looking strangely sheepish. When he remembered that, Shep knew why the memory hurt. Pap had tried to do a gentle, loving thing for them, and they had shamed him. It was the unatonable guilt of that small-boy cruelty that made the memory scald worse than tears.

Shep was aware that great ominous things were happening as he rode, events all-important to America and the world, yet he had a hard time feeling that they had anything to do with himself. Virginia joined the seceding states; North Carolina would follow. Kentucky and Missouri refused to obey Lincoln's call for troops; Tennessee was boiling with rebel enthusiasm. Union troops were poised to enter Virginia.

Atrocities increased in number and savagery. At Friar's Point, Mississippi, a man accused of abolitionism was hanged without trial, and his body sent down the river in a barrel; while public announcement was made that any Northern man caught there would be better off in hell than in Friar's Point.

Shep Daniels himself observed, from a great distance and late at night, a drunken orgy upon a hilltop, centered around the burning alive of several human figures. He went no nearer to find out who was burning whom, but got the hell out of there.

And it was in Missouri that the most vital action occurred. On Monday, May 6, a brigade of some six hundred Missouri Militia camped outside St. Louis, under orders from Missouri's secessionist Governor, Claiborne Jackson. The Governor's plan, known to pretty much everybody, was to storm and seize the Federal Arsenal; but on Friday, Nathaniel Lyon marched out with six or seven thousand Federal Volunteers, forced the surrender of the entire militia, and marched it through St. Louis for imprisonment. A mob of yelling, stone-throwing secessionists massed to block the march; several shots were fired into the troops. A captain went down with a bullet in his leg, and as he fell gave the order to fire. Two or three companies obeyed. Twenty-two people were killed, including women and children, and scores more were wounded.

On Saturday the rioters again gathered, this time to dispute the passage of a large body of recruits, enlisted that day in Frank Blair's Unionist Home Guard. A fourteen-year-old boy fired a pistol into the ranks of the Guard, and six more died in the ensuing embroilment. Twenty-eight dead in two days. . . .

It was a turning point in Missouri. A great wave of reaction against the Federals swept the state. Most influential military man in Missouri was Sterling Price—ex-Governor, a brigadier in the Mexican War; though pro-Southern and pro-slavery, he had ruggedly and effectively opposed Missouri's secession. But now, angered by Lyon's attack upon the militia, he offered his services to Missouri and was given command of state troops. The whole strength of the disunionist militia was promptly called out, to be readied for war. Above a dozen county courthouses the Confederate flag went up, appearing, at first, in a somewhat variable assortment of designs, for want of exact information as to just what it was. But the spirit of the thing was there. The illusion was that all Missouri was springing to arms.

This was no small to-do in a backwater. In size, resources, and manpower, Missouri was more important than Kentucky, and could probably swallow up the combined forces of Arkansas and Tennessee. Shep Daniels could not wholly understand all this. He resented the firing upon pro-Southerners in St. Louis, but the popular reaction seemed to be less one of anger than of enthusiasm for war. Over and over people had said that war was the last thing they wanted; yet now they rose up cheering, the first minute they could tell themselves they were being forced. When a Yankee reconnaissance platoon totally disappeared in the wilderness, somewhere west of Cape Girardeau, the citizenry welcomed this as a gay event, a happy stroke of fortune for the South. . . .

Closer to Shep than any phase of the threatening war was the land itself through which he traveled. Spring was turning into summer unseasonably, partly because Shep was riding south to meet it. In the tiny villages through which he passed the smells of leaf mold and opening buds were giving way to the heavy yet glowing smell of lilacs, even when he couldn't see where it was coming from. By the doorsteps of little paintless houses, the syringe bushes, as the Danielses called syringa, were masses of white, and the snowball bushes were beginning to come out, the big round heads blossoming in shades of pink and lavender first, which would later turn pure white in the summer's heat. All these things were common-place. Shep had never known a spring without them all, yet he noticed them more this year, and they meant more to him than they ever had before. Maybe somewhere in the back of his mind was an awareness that he might be seeing summer come for the last time, but if this was true he did not know it. Getting himself killed was no part of his intention, and his acknowledgement that it was possible took the form of mea-sures to prevent it. He rode with unrelaxing caution, never letting himself forget that the loveliness of a flowering thicket could be full of sudden death. Yet, for a long time, he was unable to feel any deadliness, in this newborn world.

Then, late in May, as Shep Daniels approached the Potter place, this was abruptly changed. He came at it from the north to avoid Waynesville, beyond, until he could learn something about what was happening there; and so passed the homestead of the Potters' nearest neighbor, first, some miles out, and with a range of hills between. In the open gate lay the decomposing carcass of a farm dog, evidently dead for some days. He saw that the house was still standing, far back from the wagon track, but he did not go up there. The fact that the dead dog still lay in the road was sufficient evidence that he would find nobody there alive.

Shep pushed on in dread, filled with a black foreboding. The embarrassment of Caylin's attachment for him had kept him away from the Potter place whenever he had been able to pass it by, yet he had thought of these people for a long time as the salt of the earth. Pap had done so much for the Potters, wouldn't you have thought they would have ended up by hating him? That was the way it usually worked out, if you trusted people too much, or helped them more than you had to; but not with the Potters. Every one of them had re-mained totally loyal to anyone named Daniels.

He reached the Potter place at high noon. Here there was no dead animal, but there was another left-open gate, and the same unnatural quiet, without cooking smoke, or movement, or any sound that people make. Shep rode up to the peeled-

log cabin. All the doors and shutters stood open, but nobody
answered his hail. He tied his animals to the sagging gallery,
and walked through the house, learning very little; nothing
appeared to be either in present use or out of place, and nothing told him any fragment of a story of what had happened
here.

He went on through the lean-to, and hunted around behind
the house for some kind of sign, without knowing what he
was looking for, very well. And now Saloney Potter came
running out of the woods on the slope above, threw herself
into his arms, and began to cry.

✦ 27 ✦

STUMBLING, BROKEN FRAGMENTS OF SENTENCES, MIXED-UP PIE-
ces of events, without order or connection . . . Saloney's story
couldn't be put together, at first, into any kind of an account
of what happened.

Caylin was dead, and so was Pa Potter; that much of it
came out at once. But Saloney was so overwrought, so
shaken in mind, that she had lost all track of time, and was
temporarily unable to place events within five days. Day before yesterday . . . or maybe it was a week . . . The things she
was talking about finally turned out to have happened four
days before.

Caylin and their father had been killed by Yankees, in uniform, Saloney told Shep. But she knew their names, and who
they were. *Now, how can that be?* Shep thought. *She's talking
wild.* He did not pursue that vein at once, but asked about
where her mother was, and her brothers. Ma Potter, she told
him, was with "the relations," so stunned by the tragedy that
she had lost all touch with earth, for now; she just sat, staring
at nothing, never speaking, nor answering anyone. She had to
be fed, dressed and undressed, and all things done for her.
Nothing physical seemed to be wrong with her, but she was
alive only as a vegetable is alive.

Hick and Tom hadn't even been there. Weeks ago they had
gone to Jefferson City to enlist, in answer to the Governor's
call for men. No word had come from them since, and
Saloney knew of no way to reach them or find them, until she
could leave her mother and go to the capital herself. In the

midst of all this confusion of mind, the next statement she interjected caught Shep by surprise.

"Trapper had left, too, by that time. Just a day or two before." Then she made a strange qualification, obscure in meaning. "If," she said, "he ever really left at all."

"How long was he here?"

"Oh, many weeks. He almost died."

She was calmer now, in the comfort of Shep's arms; he made some coffee for her, and gave her time to collect herself. Even then, he could get no connected story from her, but had to put it together for himself out of misplaced chunks. How Trapper had come there remained unclear for a while. After that part of the story finally came out, and he had placed it in the beginning, where it belonged, he began to understand the sequence of events. She explained to him what Caylin had done to save Trapper, after he was unconscious and helpless.

"I kind of thought it was for you, she done all that, more than for Trapper. Caylin always was mighty smitten with you, Shep." He didn't want to think too much about that.

After hiding the chestnut horse as well as she could, Saloney had doubled back, thinking maybe she could toll the riders away, somehow, if that was needful; so she got a look at the three men, and heard the names of Hobe and Yancey. Nobody had spoken the name of the man giving the orders, but Trapper was able to tell them, later, who that had to be. And his name was Rodger Ashland, the son of some big planter, up on the Missouri.

Shep saw no reason for surprise. This was exactly the sort of thing he had foreseen when Trapper took to the wilderness after Rodge. Trapper's success in the Black Mingo, when he had dispersed Ashland's night riders by hand, would be the death of him someday. If it hadn't already. Trapper knew perfectly well that the swamp skirmish had been a bunch of unlikely flukes in the blind confusion of the tangles, but he would be bound to *feel* that he could do it again. Apparently Trapper had found Rodger with his band, and tried to molest them; whereupon they had wounded him, and run him to earth. It was only another big stretch of luck, and a costly one this time, that they had lost him.

"And that was how both Caylin and me knew who they was, when they came back."

"They came back?"

"Twice. The first time was in the next few days, and they seemed right friendly that time. And it was a good thing, because they only asked questions, and never bothered to search the house. And all the while them three was here, Trapper was lying in the lean-to, more dead than alive. . . ."

Pa Potter had got the bullet out of Trapper's shoulder joint, but he like to died anyway. His hands and feet seemed frozen at first, and when that was over they swelled, and his heart labored, and what with his loss of blood they like to lost him. And next he went into a fever, in which he raved out of his head, and hollered for his ma, and for Pap, but for Shep oftener than any other. It was only God's mercy that Trapper didn't come to while Ashland was there, and start yelling, out of his mind.

Later the wound went into a proud flesh that Pa Potter said smelled a whole lot like gangrene. Pa would have taken the arm off then, for lack of anybody else to do it, but the trouble was so high into the shoulder he didn't know any way.

And yet Trapper had pulled out of it, though it took a long time. As soon as he was clear in his mind, he had begun worrying that he would bring trouble down on the Potters, sooner or later. He hadn't meant to stop on the place to start with, but only to get on through into the woods, so that he would be near help, when he crawled out later. He was so fearful of pulling them into the same trouble he was in, he wouldn't even tell them what it was. And he claimed not to know where Shep was, or Pap Daniels, or anybody. Whatever kind of deadfall he had got himself into, he was full set on facing his way out of it alone. Finally he decided he was ready to travel, long before it was true, and nothing they could say or do could stop him. He was very weak, and his shoulder was a long way from mended properly, but off he went, riding the Morgan he called Brown Sugar, and leading his other horse.

And two days after he was out of there, Ashland and his

two roughs were back. Pa Potter had always said they would be. But nobody else had believed they would have kept on looking for Trapper, all these weeks.

Shep didn't explain it, but he didn't believe it either. Trapper wasn't important enough to Rodge, or dangerous enough, to justify so much trouble. More probably, Shep thought, Rodge had only happened to pass that way again, while following other errands, and had taken another look around, so long as he was in the neighborhood. Shep had an idea of his own, now, of what Rodge Ashland's reasons were for building up his band of night riders. He couldn't be sure of it yet; but he thought maybe he would know later if he had been right.

Pa Potter had told Caylin and Saloney what they must do if Ashland and his men came there again. Whether Trapper had told him something, or he was playing a hunch of his own, he thought Ashland would be in deadly earnest next time he came. "They'll be sure in their minds he's been here, when they come again," Pa had said. "They won't believe us, that he's long gone. They'll do us any hurt they need to, to make us tell where he's at."

So the girls were to go out into the edge of the woods behind the house, as soon as the three riders appeared, and wait there, listening. If Pa yelled, "Run!" they were to take to the woods, not together, but one around the hill one way, and the other the opposite, and never stop running till they dropped. And the way it worked out, when the three night riders did come again, the girls were so startled they did exactly as Pa said.

This time the three came in their full uniforms, the blue uniforms of Yankee soldiers. Ashland had the shoulder boards of a Yankee captain; Saloney got a better look at those, later.

Shep Daniels was puzzled. He had no firm reason for disbelieving that the Ashlands would not end up as Federal soldiers; so long as Tyler Ashland stood fast as a Unionist, it was more likely than not. And Frank Blair, who was hand in glove with Nathaniel Lyon, would see to it that they were made officers at once. But he couldn't imagine Rodger Ashland putting himself under any form of discipline before he had to.

More likely the uniforms Saloney had seen had merely suggested the United States Army. Lots of small places, all over the country, but especially in the South, had uniformed social clubs with names like the Pottsville Rifles or the Boone County Light Horse. Woolhats like Hobe and Yancey would never be able to get into one of those, but the thing was that anybody could contrive himself any kind of uniform he felt like. Since the St. Louis riots, the back-country people were ready to believe any evil of the Northerners, and anything resembling a Yankee uniform would do to throw Missourians wide off the track. Shep recalled the episode of the missing Yankee patrol, but shrugged it off. The whole thing was an oddity, but whatever it signified was unclear.

Because Pa Potter had sent them to the edge of the woods, Saloney and Caylin had not heard what was said when Ashland rode up to the front of the house. But they had heard Pa holler, "Run!" in a great voice, and they ran. Behind them they heard a shot fired.... Twice, as she told what more there was of her story, Saloney broke down, and Shep had to wait for her to quiet. One of these times was when she spoke of that shot, for that was when Pa must have died, about half his head blown away. He made a dreadful corpse.

Right after the shot, the three riders came thundering around the house and took after the two girls, their horses crashing and bounding through the brush under the trees. Ashland himself followed Saloney, while the two others went after Caylin. Ashland overtook Saloney before she knew what was happening to her. He grabbed her by the slack of the dress, swinging her feet clear of the ground, while he demanded to know where Trapper was. Then a rifle let off in the woods, and Ashland dropped her. He sat for a moment feeling his shoulder, and blood showed on his fingers, where his left shoulder board, with the captain's bars on it, was cut in two. Unhappily, he was only creased; his arm was seemingly numbed for a moment, but not disabled.

That single shot from the woods was Saloney's reason for believing that maybe Trapper had not left the neighborhood when he pretended to, but had perhaps doubled back, in hopes of a shot at his enemy. Of course, lots of people were willing to take a shot at a Yankee uniform; but Saloney knew of nobody who was likely to have been in those particular woods, at that time.

Ashland began cussing through his teeth, then spurred his horse into the thickets, charging the hidden rifle; and Saloney ducked off in a different direction, and hid out. She listened to a lot of crashing around in the woods, that lasted for some while, and finally dwindled into the distance. But she saw nothing more happen, and she never saw Ashland again. A long time later she heard horses, and saw Hobe and Yancey ride out of the woods, and take the road to Waynesville. And Saloney went looking for Caylin. . . .

This was the other point at which Saloney went to pieces.

She found Caylin's body, after a horrible hour of mystification and doubt, in which she passed within a yard of it four times, without knowing. Caylin had been "harmed," by which Saloney meant raped, and choked to death.

Saloney showed Shep the graves of Pa and Caylin. "She loved you," Saloney said, quiet now, almost in a state of lassitude. "She loved you very much. I used to admire you, because you knowed, all right, yet never laid hands on her, or took her into the woods. But now—I don't know. Maybe you should of."

Shep said, "Maybe. I don't know. I never do seem to know what's right to do, in a case like that."

Before he left, Shep carved headboards for two graves; and he found out he didn't know how to spell Caylin's name—or what her name rightly was, for that matter. Saloney showed it to him in the family Bible. The girl's name had been Caroline. Caylin was a pet name, taken from the way she herself had said it when she was a tiny girl.

When he had saddled, he asked Saloney, as he supposed he had to, if there was anything he could do for her.

She said shyly, "Do you think—maybe—I could come with—" She faltered, and searched his face, and of course found her answer there. "No," she changed it. "No. I'll be all right." She still stood, looking after him, when he waved to her from the bend in the road that took him out of sight.

★ 28 ★

TRAPPER DANIELS ARRIVED IN POOR CONDITION AT ASH LAND-ing. It had been his bullet that cut in two Rodger Ashland's Yankee shoulder board in Potter's woods, and the kick of the 56-caliber had almost torn his wounded shoulder off, spoiling the shot, and making a second try impossible. He knew that Rodger had pursued him, quite closely at first, and for two days Trapper had simply outridden him, while he pulled himself together. After that he had tried to set up an ambush, but had somehow failed of it, and had become convinced that Rodge had got ahead of him. He was still painfully weak, and tired so easily he hardly knew himself, but he had ridden hard, in hopes of overtaking Ashland before he gained the sanctuary of his father's plantation; and when he reached Ash Landing, in a state of pain and exhaustion, Rodge wasn't even there yet. For all Trapper knew for the next three days, Rodge wasn't coming home at all.

What was at Ash Landing ahead of him was the news of the murder of Caylin Potter and her father. He managed to steal a Jeffersonville newspaper that carried an account of the crime, received by telegraph from Rolla by way of St. Louis; and what he lacked in strength was instantly more than made up for by a great upsurge of angry determination. He decided to bush up for a week, in the woods and hills near the Ashland plantation, resting himself and his horses and giving his shoulder a chance to mend, if it was going to. After that, if Rodger Ashland had not appeared, he would have to head south again, healed or not and rested or not, and begin his weary search all over.

His shoulder bothered him all the time. Something was very wrong inside it, in the neighborhood of the joint. A long time would pass before the shoulder was sound enough to fire from, if indeed it would ever be able to take the recoil again. Meantime he had to fire left-handed, and the switch-over was more difficult than he could ever possibly have imagined. His whole right arm was half useless, unable even to hold the carbine barrel, so that he had to use a rest—something he hadn't done since he was six years old. He had always fired with both eyes open, but now he had to squint his dominant right eye shut in order to get an aiming with his left, and this made the target seem dimly lighted and of uncertain range.

And next he found out what a delicate skill had been developed in his right trigger finger by lifelong use. He had not realized before that he never had held a rifle perfectly still as he fired, but had timed his touch on the hair trigger as the muzzle made a microscopic swing across the target, invisible except through the sights. His left hand couldn't do that at all. But he would have to make do as best he could with what he had. He practiced with empty carbine by the hour, teaching himself a whole new way to shoot.

He kept a daily surveillance upon the Ashland Great House, from far off across the fields by day and from nearby at night. Somewhere out among the stables, two couples of bloodhounds made frequent mournful noises, practicing their singing lessons; a rash of runaways among the slaves had persuaded many planters to put in kennels of tracking dogs. They didn't worry Trapper much. In some situations, as when Trapper had lain close hid at Benjamins', and again the day he was wounded, they could make quick finds, but once he was mounted he judged the dogs would not be hard to outrun.

It was on the fourth day of his waiting that he saw Rodger Ashland come home. It was time to move in for the kill, and this time he would have to make deadly sure; for he understood now, in a way he had never understood before he was wounded, that his next try might very easily be the last in his life.

✲ 29 ✲

Partly, no doubt, it was the nature of the crime at Waynesville that made news of it more incendiary than the vague and belated reports of a hundred other deeds of violence. Word-of-mouth news always did travel at speeds hard to account for; it might not outrun the telegraph or the steam cars, where these things were, but could outtravel a man on a good horse, nobody knew just how. But here was the rape and murder of a young girl, a killing so lurid that word of it raced to every corner of Missouri overnight.

Strangely missing from the accounts was the sister's identification of the guilty men. Evidently Saloney had been prevailed upon to shut her mouth, in fear of reprisals. In want of identification, the blue uniforms, already in disfavor since the St. Louis riots, became the focus of mass incitement.

This was one atrocity that would not drift into limbo for lack of culprits. Nobody effectively questioned the validity of the uniforms, or the right of the culprits to wear them; the Damnyankees stood exposed in their true colors to the public eye. The lagging enlistments in Governor Jackson's secessionist militia swelled immediately, and a new wave of war enthusiasm swept Missouri. . . .

To Tyler Ashland, secession of the South from the nation was a preposterous concept, in itself a contradiction of terms. The South *was* the nation, and the statesmen of the South were the statesmen of the nation. They had run it for a long time, and if they did not panic at the results of their own asininity, they would keep on running it. They had not been beaten by an Illinois mudsill named Abe Lincoln. *He* wasn't

179

any sort of a power—a vague, weak species of abolitionist, pushed forward in compromise by confused Northern factions, mainly because he was completely unknown. If the damn-fool South had not split itself three ways, Douglas would have been swept in by a million votes. The silly kick-away of the election was exasperating, but nothing had actually happened. Men like the Blairs would handle Lincoln like men handling a boy. Meanwhile, the Union was a going concern; the thing now was to keep it that way, so those Deep South hotheads would have something to come back to when they regained their senses. . . .

As for the Waynesville murders, Tyler was furious. He didn't believe there were, or ever had been, any Yankee troops within three hundred miles of Waynesville, and saw no national importance in it if there were. Catch them and hang them—that was the appropriate measure. But as a reason for war—! His most eloquent cussing fell short of his opinions.

Rodger Ashland returned to the Great House to find his father in a fuming mood. There never was any prodigal-son kind of celebration when Rodge came home. His mother, of course, would never lose the maternal affection compelled by the undecorated fact that he was her son, however much she might disapprove of the way he shaped his life. Diligence Delorme Ashland had a famed graciousness as a hostess, and a stately sort of beauty in that role. But in the absence of guests she was a silent, inconspicuous woman, with a look of dark severity in repose. Upon Rodger's return she had clasped him to her and cried softly on his shoulder for a little while. But, "You'd better not keep your father waiting," was almost all she said. Father and son had not been much more eloquent, though they had gone through those politenesses that serve better as a cover for feelings than an expression of them—the brisk handshake, the crisp smiles; the "I trust I find you well, sir," and the "You had a tolerable journey, I hope?"—culminating shortly in the invitation to a whiskey, as soon as Rodge had scrubbed up and changed. . . .

They presently sat on a side gallery, over glasses of whisky and water in poses simulating easy relaxation; but though both were known as hard and convivial drinkers, they barely sipped their liquor. Father and son looked considerably alike, both tall and spare, dark of hair and eyes. Rodger was shaved to a deep-tanned shininess, and his fresh linen was hard-starched; he had never looked better in his life. Yet his father's age and whiskers made less difference between them than the expression each assumed. Tyler's attitude of friendliness veiled a look of eagles, while his son presented an air of frank and open charm hard to disbelieve.

Neither was deceived. They had known each other so long, so well, they could almost literally read each other's minds. With each thing either one of them said went thoughts unspoken, yet nearly as clear to the other as if they had been voiced aloud.

"You are looking well, son." A faint wonderment in that seemed to imply that Tyler did not understand how his boy could look so good, yet act so stupidly.

"You, too, father; never saw you looking better." Perfunctory words, useless even to postpone the imminent clash of issues.

Tyler said with an effort of heartiness, "Well, I should think you might as well tell me where you've been all this time. When you weren't fooling around aboard the *Royal Oaks*, I mean. Good God, haven't you even closed in on that girl yet? I expected an announcement long ago."

Rodger portrayed a mildly concerned surprise. "You haven't been getting my letters?"

"Oh, I've had letters, all right. Nearly every week. Had a little difficulty matching them off with known events, that's all."

"I seldom see reliable reports of anything, sir, nowadays."

"I grant the truth of that. But you haven't answered my question."

"You've always encouraged me to travel, sir."

This was true, and partially disarmed Tyler, for a moment. "Thought you might learn something about the river trade. I certainly never intended for you to go raking out the back ovens of red hell all over Missouri, fit to get yourself hanged. Damnation! Do you realize, sir, it's over two hundred years since an Ashland was hanged?"

"It occurred to me, sir, that only a small part of our state is on the rivers," Rodger said. "I thought I'd take a look around the rest of Missouri."

"Looking for what?"

"Horses, first. If it comes to full-scale cavalry actions, we'll need a lot of horses."

"Assuming the 'if,' that is an astute conjecture." He hadn't meant that to sound so sarcastic. It was part of the effect Rodge always had on him.

"Unfortunately, the horse supply in the back country is of very disappointing quality."

"I could have told you that," his father said.

"But I found something else we're going to need. Except in a few centers, there's no law at all down there—nothing but chaos—"

"I should have thought we had chaos enough," Tyler said.

Rodger's quick smile acknowledged the interjection. "It's a matter of disunity. We have great numbers of potential fighting men, all over the state, out of touch with the towns and plantations. Those people can't read; they live within a world of their own, and taking orders comes hard to them. They'll never be parade troops, not in this life. But they can ride, and they can shoot. Given leaders, they can fight like very devils. I've proved this for myself."

"I have a clipping," Tyler Ashland said. "Something about some farmers repulsing a considerable body of Jayhawkers, at a place called Redstone. Were you there?"

"Yes, sir."

"Why?"

"Sir, I was blooding my hounds. Those people are subject to panic, until they have had experience under fire. You need at least one veteran to the squad. I can call up almost a hundred who have seen some sort of action. And enough raw volunteers, for, say, a brigade."

"I see."

But he didn't see. He didn't comprehend this at all. He believed the boy incapable of making up such a complicated lie. Yet, when he considered the possibility that Rodger had finally sprouted some seed of ability, he couldn't conceive of that either.

"I remind you, sir," Tyler said, "that Missouri is not at war! What do you propose to do with this—this—this weird brigade?"

"Governor Jackson has called for fifty thousand men. That's a force hard to come by—whether for him or to stop him. I propose to put my brigade at your disposal. Where it fights is up to you."

"What reason have you for assuming that I mean to fight *either* for him or against him?"

"I think there's going to be a fight."

The question had been stupid, Tyler Ashland recognized, and not the answer. Nobody had to know him well, but only to have heard him at all, to know that if there was a fight in dead earnest he would be in it.

"You apparently have no convictions at all in this matter. Why have you taken all this upon yourself? What did you lack, and what did you hope to gain?"

"Sir," Rodger Ashland said, "I wanted to please you."

Tyler looked acutely at his son for some moments. Incredibly, preposterously, he could not get around the conclusion that the boy was telling the truth; and Tyler suddenly had to avert his eyes. Diligence had reminded him many times, too many times, that this boy was what he himself had made. He was acutely aware that he had often shown great want of judgment in the raising of this second son. David Ashland, his first-born son, had developed with great promise, so preoccupying Tyler's attention that only Rodger's persistent waywardness ever caught his father's notice.

When David died, riding beside his father in a Kansas raid, the younger son had been thrust forward as an unacceptable and resented substitute, an unwelcome stranger in boots he never could fill. Tyler Ashland had been emotionally misled into alternating fits of undue severity and remorseful over-indulgence. Had Rodger been a horse, Tyler would have known better, but he had never thought connectedly about it, in the years that mattered.

And there had been another, relatively minor scarring, that

he seldom remembered because he didn't want to remember it; yet it typified the kind of thing that accounted for his periods of laxity. Rodger must have been something less than two—he was still sleeping in a crib—when for a time he fell victim to a fear of the dark. Every night he climbed out of his crib and came paddling down the long halls to wherever the family was, regardless of how many people were being entertained there; and kept reappearing, no matter how many times he was put back. Tyler gave orders that this must stop, and it did stop, until the dreadful night when Tyler discovered that a black nurse had taken to sitting beside the crib, crooning softly, through the early hours of dark.

Tyler Ashland was incensed. He conceived that the child was being spoiled, and worse than spoiled. He always had been full of Spartan ideas, expecting a great deal of himself and of everybody else; and now he brought himself to suppose that such pamperings were prejudicial to the boy's future fortitude. He chased away the nurse, blew out the candles, and locked the boy's room.

When he discovered his imprisonment, Rodger pattered upon the door with baby hands, calling the names of those to whom he looked for rescue. "Mama, Davey, Mammy, Daddy!" he shouted, with confidence at first, then with doubt, and finally in panic. Hi brother, then six, had tried to let him out, and had got locked into his own room. Diligence had tried to go to him, but Tyler had stopped her, with a sternness she dared not defy. Tyler was sick of his decision by this time, but had esteemed that to relent would be to fail of his duty by a cowardice of his own—an unthinkable weakness.

The child's wheel of names had come to a stop upon that of his father: "Daddy, Daddy, Daddy, Daddy, help, help, help, help, help, Daddy, Daddy . . ." The tiring cries had gone on and on. And it was Diligence who had driven home for him this ordeal, too. She had wept at first, while she assailed him with protests and appeals, but tears always irritated Tyler, so now she faced him dry-eyed. "All your life," she told him, "all your life, and in the hour of your death, you are going to hear that little voice . . ."

Rodger Ashland drank off a finger of whisky and water. "Will you accept my brigade, sir?"

"I shall be honored," Tyler answered, "to accept your brigade." For this one moment father and son were nearer together than they had ever been in their lives. It would have been a good time for Rodger to shut up. But—

"I've always felt that your Cavalry Club would make a fine cadre of officers," he went on. "I remember you sitting your horse in front of them, at the Battle of Clover Prairie. Just before you sent me to the rear, on the pretext—I mean, to take a message to somebody, I remember how you were smiling as you looked over the enemy; and you were quoting Shakespeare to yourself. Macbeth, wasn't it? 'Charge, Ashland, charge! On, Grover, on!' . . ." It had been the wrong thing to bring up. Rodger saw his father's face turn gray, and seem to age. "Are you all right, father?"

"Of course." Tyler Ashland's words at Clover Prairie sounded puerile to him now. A battle? He was ashamed to hear it called that. They had charged a muddle of dismounted farmers, who had cut big holes in his line of horsemen with the single volley they had fired before they took to their heels. A number of plow hands had been pistoled in the back as they ran, and there were men who jumped down to ransack the bodies. But none of that mattered now, for it was at Clover Prairie that David died.

Rodger said, "Ever since that day I've wanted above all things to prove myself. To you, sir, I mean. You know, somehow, I've always felt you held it against me that it was Davey died there, and not me."

"I blame nobody but myself," his father said. He didn't want to talk about it. "These men of yours. How are they to be paid?"

"They find their own pay, sir."

"They what?"

"I'd say they've done very well for themselves, so far."

"And their weapons, and horses—they get those in the same way?"

"Of course."

"I see . . . I see." The moment in which they had drawn

nearer each other had gone dead. "I wish to caution you about something. A man assumes a heavy responsibility when he organizes irregular troops. It can be a wicked thing to forge a weapon you cannot control."

"I don't see what you mean, sir."

"What Yankee troops were those, in the neighborhood of Waynesville?"

"I don't know, sir. Until the murders, I hadn't heard of any in that part of Missouri. The news overtook me at Tuscumbia," he added. "On the Osage."

"Yes," Tyler said, going testy again. "I am aware that Tuscumbia is on the Osage. How many of your men can you account for at the time of the murders?"

"None, under my immediate orders. I've told you, I was on my way home then."

"And how many of them were in the vicinity of Waynesville?"

"Sir," Rodger said, and the maturity went out of his poise as he stiffened. "If you are asking if I had any connection, directly or indirectly, with what happened at Waynesville—I decline to hear the question!"

"I must tell you this," Tyler said. "Under my command there will be no looting, no corpse robbing, no form of the disorders you saw in Kansas. I recognize nothing whatsoever as 'spoils of war.' "

Rodger was thunderstruck. "Are you serious, sir?"

"I promise you that any men of mine caught looting will be shot, and any officer condoning it will be hanged."

Rodger got up, and stood at the gallery railing with his back turned, to hide the angry flush he felt rise into his face.

"I suggest you count your men again," Tyler Ashland said. "You may find that you cannot raise a brigade, or a hundred, that would be acceptable to me. You may even find that you have none at all."

"In that case, of course," Rodger said, without turning, "I shall put them to such service of the South as I can find for them."

"I am sorry," Tyler said. "I ask you to believe that I am truly sorry. But your cadre sounds like a band of common night riders to me. If I find out that that is what they are, I shall move against them without hesitation, wherever they are found."

"I'm sorry too, sir."

"I suggest that we speak of this no more, during your stay here." His tone was as dull as his empty words, but some of the starch had gone out of it, as though dampened by a final loss of hope. Both knew Rodge would not be here long.

"As you wish, sir."

Through the stillness of the afternoon, at meaningless intervals, a bloodhound out in the kennels kept voicing a single far-carrying note, monotonously musical, ludicrously sad. "Damnation!" said Tyler Ashland. His furious resentment, stirred by almost every circumstance he could think of, had to explode in some direction. "Why can't that infernal sobpumping bitch ever say anything but 'Bloop!'"

★ 30 ★

As he had kept watch on the house before, so Trapper now studied Rodger Ashland's daily movements. In a few days he knew which rooms Rodge occupied. The Ashland Great House was extensive, in a wandering sort of way, said to be capable of sleeping forty guests. The broad lawns, largely free of shrubbery that might shelter skulkers, were as good as a moat. The house could not be approached, even from the stables or the slave quarters, without crossing great open expanses.

Because it had been built a piece at a time, it was mostly on one galleried main floor. But all windows were shuttered at night, and every shutter was decorated with a curly tracery of wrought iron, so that in effect the whole house was secured at night by iron bars. Most slaveholders declared their chattels to be inflexibly happy and loyal, but a good many of their houses could be turned into forts, nevertheless.

Only one part of the house was of two stories, and this was the main entrance hall, extended upward in another afterthought, to provide a more imposing façade. The hall had a grand staircase, dividing at a huge landing to give glorified access to practically nothing; a couple of narrow rooms on each side served as tokens for the great second-floor wings that had never been built. But of course, Rodger Ashland lived up there, in the most inaccessible quarters in the house, from whatever angle.

Mornings, Rodger Ashland often rode down through the village to the waterfront, never for a moment out of sight of dozens of people. Every day at two in the evening, as they called the afternoon, he rode through the upper edge of the town to the Other Great Houses, where Julie Delorme joined him. They rode for at least an hour, and often for two, but seldom twice by the same lanes and trails. Sometimes they rode woodland paths where Trapper could have picked off Rodger Ashland very easily, while the two were in single file, if he had been in the right place, which of course he was not. Usually they turned off cross country somewhere, to jump the worm fences, so that he never could tell where they would be.

Julie Delorme handled her horses beautifully, Trapper thought, not discommoded in the least by the sidesaddle she rode, or the voluminous skirt that went with it. He could see why Shep thought so highly of her. And he could see, too, why Rodger was lingering here, instead of getting into a fight with his father, and making off into the wilderness again, as Trapper had led himself to hope. Twice in a week Rodger had dinner at the Delormes', and went calling there evenings besides. But Trapper had little confidence in his marksmanship any more, even in the best of light, and none whatever in the dark. He never did find a chance he could be sure of, without certain immediate capture.

He watched patiently, hunting for ways to make himself a chance, and meantime made what arrangements he could for his own escape. Six miles from Ash Landing a disused path turned off from the river road, leading up a rivulet called Hog Creek. The path ended at a tumbledown shanty once used by a man who had raised pigs there; it had a ruined horse shelter with a manger in it, and a paddock with the fence fallen down. Trapper never stayed here overnight, or indeed twice in any one place; but he repaired the fence, and left Brown Sugar here when he rode Spooks to Ash Landing.

Nearest place to the Ashlands' where he could safely hide Spooks, while he scouted on foot, was a mile from the house; no other place he could find was any better than that, unless he could intercept Rodger in one of the woodland trails. If he did bring Rodger down, and could get his horse, he would have a chance. There were fast horses in the Ashland stables, but it would take at least a little time to fetch them out, and find out from the bloodhounds which way he had gone. If he could manage to give Spooks about a mile start, or even a half— even a quarter—maybe his horses could run their hearts out, on level going, and at the six-mile distance to Hog Creek. There he would change to Brown Sugar, and he was confident that the blown horses of the pursuit would never catch the Morgan in the rough going of the hills and woods. Not a very good plan, nor a sure one, but at least it gave him something to try.

He was becoming impatient now, what with his seemingly permanent fatigue, and recurrent pain. He wanted to get his execution of Rodger Ashland over with, and get back to Paducah, where he could crawl into his own bed, unslept in for so long; and there bury himself in sleep for the rest of his life. And he had a nagging suspicion that his time was running out. Julie Delorme herself was a danger, for one thing. He had never seen two people spend as much time together as Julie spent with Rodge, without they turned up married pretty soon; it could happen any time. Whereupon they would be off on a honeymoon—maybe for a couple of years, maybe in Europe—out of his reach for certain.

What he had hoped for was a chance at Rodger Ashland that would allow him at least a possibility of escape without identification. He had never imagined how hard this would be at Ash Landing, with Rodger always surrounded by his numberless people. After all, when he had skirmished with Rodger's night riders in the Black Mingo, he had left them with nothing but a circumstantial case against the state of Kansas. But his luck was out, now; he never got any fluky opportunities any more. If he could have got away unrecognized, it might have helped his brother as well as himself. Maybe Shep would still have had his chance with Julie Delorme; which of course he never would have as the brother of her cousin's murderer. But in the end he had to give it up.

To be sure of his mission, Trapper accepted, he would have to step out into the open road in front of Rodger's horse, in broad daylight, and in full view of witnesses; perhaps within sight of the Ashland house, or Delorme's.

Kill him with a heart-shot that could not be missed, at

powder-flash range; and then simply ride for it, while all Missouri turned out to shoot on sight, by name or by description. And that is what would have happened, except that the day Trapper decided upon it, Rodger did not ride. Trapper watched Julie start off early, and alone. Tomorrow, then; tomorrow. . . . He rode Spooks by devious ways back to Hog Creek.

There were fresh hoofprints in the Hog Creek path. He hid Spooks in the brush, and spied out the makeshift paddock where he had left his Morgan. Somebody was there, all right; and it was Julie Delorme. She sat on the top rail of the paddock in her vast sidesaddle skirt, her horse tied nearby, and she was whittling a stick. Yes, whittling a stick, by God, and obviously waiting there for him. And he knew instantly, with a great sinking of heart, that he was through at Ash Landing. Even if he laid low until she left, and moved his horses as soon as she was gone, the bloodhounds would be on the trail of the Morgan before dark. So he stood clear of the bushes, and walked toward her, shifting the carbine to lift his hat with his left hand. "Evenin', mam."

"You're Trapper Daniels," she said. "I saw you at Jefferson City."

To give himself time to think, he climbed slowly up the fence, and sat near her, but not too near, on the top rail. It was the closest he had ever been to her, and he saw how perfect her skin was, with only the shading of biscuity tan that girls have when they try to stay in the shade but can't quite manage it. The sun was striking her eyes, yet they did not flinch, or squint, but seemed luminous, as if they had a light of their own; he could see the golden flecks in the golden brown.

"You've hurt your arm," she said.

"It's nothing, mam."

"I knew it was you, hiding out here."

"How did you find out?"

"I have a grapevine."

Trapper knew nothing about Caleese, but the general idea was plain. He said, "I happened to be passing through here, mam."

"You've been here a sight longer than it takes to pass through. You're wanted for something, and you're hiding out—isn't that true?"

"Yes, mam."

"Why here?"

"Well, I kind of hoped to find my brother."

"Here? Why?"

"Because you're here. You have him eating his heart out, mam. Though he surely must know, you'll likely marry Rodger Ashland, about any time now."

"No," she said. "No; I'll never marry anybody while Shep Daniels is alive."

"Can I tell him that?"

She shrugged. "He knows it well enough, I should think. Your brother is the worst fool in the world, Trapper."

"Yes, mam."

"He was here, you know, some weeks ago. I talked to him."

"He walked right in here? Openly?"

"Why not?" She let it pass, as a stupidity. "But he wasn't here to see me. He left me a note at the Bishop House, saying he was going to look for you; and by morning he was gone."

"Well, then, he'll sure enough be back."

"I guess you must have done something pretty bad."

"Well, no—it wasn't anything I done. But I saw something, at Waynesville, mam." He saw she didn't believe him, so he told her enough more to back himself up, without really telling anything. No names, no descriptions. He did tell her that there had been no Yankee at Waynesville, but only some falsely uniformed bushwhackers, whom he knew for what they were because he had run into them before. Julie Delorme didn't seem especially surprised at this, but she was fascinated to have stumbled on virtually an eyewitness. She had some questions to ask, but none that pinned him too closely.

He explained he had been stopping by the Potters', and had "just happened" to be out in the woods when he heard shooting, and rode back. He admitted he would recognize the three men he saw there. They seemed, he said vaguely, to be trying to find out something, or something. The old man was down—dead, as he heard later—by the time Trapper came in gun range.

And he told her he had thrun a shot at the one wearing Yankee Captain's insignia. Almost a good shot, but not quite. Cut his right shoulder board span in two—drew blood, even—but must have only scratched him. This bushwhacker had then run him to hell—"excuse me, mam"—out of the country. Might be looking for him yet. Must have been the other two who murdered the younger girl.

"You could testify against them if they were ever tried. But, what with the uniforms . . . nobody like that ever does get caught, in Missouri. Not officially, anyway."

"No, mam. But they do catch up with people who know too much, sometimes. Like me."

"My name's Julie, Trapper. You're virtually my brother-in-law. Or would be, if anything ever worked out to make any sense. We've got to get you out of these woods. Get you rested, and scrubbed up, and into some decent clothes. There's an empty cottage, on our place, where an overseer used to live. We can put you up in that. Nobody would dare come after you, there. And later—"

Her offered reminded him of the condition he was in, and he was glad he had approached her from the downwind side. Caylin had patched his clothes, and made him new moccasins, but that was a good many long, long rides behind. He knew he could not have been more shabby, with about two inches of reddish beard, and as filthy as a bear. He tried to smile as he said, "All this dirt is just a disguise, mam—Julie."

"I know it is. Last time I saw you you looked like a scrubbed baby. . . . Later, when you're rested, we'll put you on a boat, for wherever you want to go, so long as it's north of Cairo. The Mississippi's under blockade, south of the Ohio." As for money—she could let him take whatever he needed, if he was in want.

He told her he had plenty of money. "I don't believe Shep would want you mixed up in this, Julie. If you'll promise not to say anything to anybody—"

She looked disappointed, but she didn't argue. She had an

exaggerated idea of the protection she could afford him, but she obviously hadn't expected him to believe in it.

"I couldn't ever do anything to hurt Shep Daniels' blood kin," she said. "But you'll have to promise me something, too. Promise you won't hurt somebody while you're around Ash Landing."

"Hurt somebody, Julie?"

"Like supposing, maybe the man who's hunting you—or the man you're hunting—which is it, Trapper?"

He started to answer that he hadn't said it was either one, but he saw no benefit in that, the way she seemed to see through him. He mumbled that he guessed it worked two ways. A little of each, or call it both.

"Whoever it is, he's either here or you expect him here. Otherwise you wouldn't be hiding out so tightly—isn't that true? If I say nothing, and you are killed, or kill somebody—I'd feel I was guilty of it myself."

"Julie, that's exactly like making me give a cottonmouth first bite!"

"Then stay away from the cottonmouth."

He had to promise in the end. She didn't threaten him, but he knew that if she breathed a word about his being in these woods, even without naming him, there would be a posse here, with the Ashland bloodhounds, inside of a couple of hours. He had his fingers crossed as he promised her, but he knew that wasn't going to do him any good. As much as anybody could have done it, she had tied his hands.

★ 31 ★

Saturday, June 15, 1861, was Julie's nineteenth birthday, and for weeks her father had been trying to complete arrangements for the huge birthday party he always gave her. Julie had had some big parties before, but now that she was ageing, as she saw it, into the realm of old maids, Jim Sam was desirous of consoling her with such a party as would go down in history. It must be aboard the *Royal Oaks*, of course. The Delorme flagship was lying idle at St. Louis on account of the blockade, but now she was painted and refurbished throughout, and her enormous crew recalled, preparatory for a sojourn at Ash Landing.

But the politics of Missouri and of the nation were giving him the fight of his life to get on with it; whole armies were being raised to interfere with his plans. Jim Sam swore he was going ahead anyway. He had always given Julie a birthday party before, hadn't he? He sure had. Neither lunatic abolitionists nor punkinhead secessionists were going to stop him this time.

But now General Price came off the fence. Pap Price was probably the most influential man of any military background in Missouri; he had served as a brigadier in the Mexican War and had been Governor of the state. Like Shelby, Ashland, and Frank Blair, he was entirely proslavery, yet, up to here, had stood staunchly for the Union. It was the St. Louis riots that reversed his position overnight. Suddenly he joined Governor Jackson, and immediately began preparing the secessionist militia for action. By the end of May, Price and Jackson had some 4,000 men at Jefferson City. Sudden war seemed certain in Missouri. It began to look as though there might not be an able-bodied male within a hundred miles of Ash Landing on the 15th of June, and that any party attempted could only end up as a hen party, a cross between a sitting-up to await news and a wake. Party off. The *Royal Oaks* drew her fires, and stayed where she was.

Julie had written to her father, urging him to call the whole thing off. With war hanging over them, seemingly off again, on again, for reasons to which she hadn't even a clue, she couldn't think of anything that should interest people less than the birth date of a little featherhead without the brains even to understand what was happening. But now—a reprieve. Price agreed to a truce with the Federals and ordered the secessionist troops to disperse to their homes. The *Royal Oaks* came boiling up the Missouri. Party on, Jim Sam decreed, in spite of all hell and a falling river.

Or was it? The rebel volunteers refused to disperse, and the order that they do so was rescinded. All up and down the Lower Mississippi the rebel cadres of regiments, divisions, whole armies, were building: 6,000 rebel troops were reported at Fort Hawks, and 4,500 more at Fort Wright, both near Memphis, Tennessee; 1,800 were readying at Courant, Mississippi. Ten companies of rebel troops were on their way from New Orleans to Fort Smith, in Arkansas, where 1,500 were already assembled at Mound City. General McCulloch was understood to be mustering an army in northwestern Arkansas to invade Missouri. It was a great popular uprising, all over the whole South.

Unexpectedly, another popular counteruprising had sprung up in the prairie states of the Upper Mississippi Valley. Six regiments had volunteered for the Union in the little new state of Iowa, where the governor had despaired of raising one. Illinois was over quota, and more than half of Indiana's volunteers had been turned away for want of arms. Cairo was being fortified at the mouth of the Ohio; a battery of huge thirty-two-pounders was emplaced there, and more were on the way. General Lyon sent a full Union regiment of Missouri Volunteers to occupy and fortify Bird's Point, across the Mississippi from Cairo, the only point on the Missouri shore from which Cairo could be attacked. The war was marching like a storm.

But—one more flicker of hope. There were still dreamers who thoughts that Missouri could take a spectator's position while the North and the South fought out their differences. These optimists arranged a truce conference for Tuesday, June 11, four days before Julie's birthday. Party definitely to be held. The *Royal Oaks* resumed her upstream run.

On Tuesday, Governor Claiborne Jackson and General Price went to St. Louis under safe-conduct from Federal General Lyon, and met with Blair and Lyon at the Planter's House. The single meeting lasted for sometime, but blew up in the end, with the inflexible and hot-tempered Lyon giving promise of immediate war. Jackson and Price entrained for Jefferson City within the hour, burning the railroad bridges across the Gasconade and the Osage behind them as they went; and by that time General Lyon's troops were already on the move. Generals Sweeny and Sigel were sent southwest with 3,000 men, to cut off Jackson and Price if they tried to join forces with McCulloch in Arkansas. Lyon himself prepared to advance upon the capital.

The *Royal Oaks* turned back, and anchored below Jefferson City at Bonnet's Mill.

At the capital, Jackson issued a proclamation, asserting that the first duty of every Missourian was to his state and calling for the enrollment of 50,000 men to drive the United States troops out of Missouri. He then fell back upon Boonville, ninety miles to the west.

On Friday, June 14—the day before Julie's birthday— General Lyon disembarked with 2,000 men at Jefferson City, to find the Governor fled and the capital undefended. Retreating before the Yankee steamboats, the *Royal Oaks* was already upstream of Jefferson City, and this time stopped only for news and fuel. But it was too late. It never did get home for Julie's birthday party, such as it was; and the war was already only a few hours by riverboat from Ash Landing.

Something had already happened there, under pressure of these events, significant enough to dictate the future of Ash Landing. Tyler Ashland had made up his mind.

He had been a pro-Southern Unionist of so firm a mind as no secessionist could argue down, but he had been badly shaken by the events in St. Louis. He discounted the riots that had made such a massive impression throughout the state, noting wryly that the "peaceful citizens" fired upon had just happened to be firing into the troops at the time. But he saw the arrest of the legally assembled state militia as an outrage against the state.

At about that time Frank Blair had written Ashland offering him a commission as colonel of United States Volunteers. Ashland's reply temperately withheld decision, but demanded to know who was this Lyon, who presumed to make himself dictator over Missouri? He had been captain of the St. Louis Arsenal Guard, the last Tyler knew. How came he so suddenly to be commanding general of all Federal troops in Missouri, defying the Constitution at behest of a Yankee minority? He heard no more from Frank Blair, who, as Tyler knew perfectly well, had personally obtained Lyon's promotion.

Then General Lyon moved upon the capital of Missouri, and Tyler Ashland had had enough. An oratorical diatribe could have been expected to accompany Ashland's decision, but there was none. "I won't have it," he said quietly. "I don't propose to stand hitched for this kind of nonsense at all." Somewhere deep beneath the soft-spoken words could be sensed a breaking of rocks, and a grinding of gravel. "Sterling Price will fight, and so will I," he added. He immediately sent messengers on good horses to muster the Cavalry Club.

Mrs. Ashland, with a coterie of servants, was sent upstream to Lexington, to stay with friends; she departed promptly, and without objection, perhaps glad to get away from the perpetual tension between her husband and their son. A great deal of this evacuation of families was going on among the planters, as Julie Delorme knew by a last-minute flood of regrets from her intended guests. Julie herself had been exposed to her aunt Dil's strenuous persuasions. But though an elderly relative, called Cousin Celeste, was in theoretical charge at the Delorme house, nobody at Ash Landing, in the absence of Jim Sam, could tell Julie what to do.

Tyler Ashland's Cavalry Club, called to muster on over-night notice, proved not entirely capable of such sudden assembly. The enrollment, as reconstituted after suspension of the Kansas effort, showed a force of about a hundred and fifty men, theoretically the skeleton of a full regiment, or perhaps a small brigade. But enlistments of strength had been deferred, pending possible hostilities, in order to maintain the exclusiveness upon which depended the organization's prestige. This same exclusiveness made impossible any serious discipline, and attempted drills had always broken down into purely social occasions, featuring horse racing, cockfighting, and poker. The members furnished their own horses, arms, and equipment, and the uniform consisted of nothing but a white armband, bordered in red, with a blue star. Probably very few of their number had ever really expected the outbreak of war, or that the Cavalry Club, as such, would take any part if it happened. During Saturday, June 15, about fifty straggled in to report at the Ashland Great House, a good many bringing along their body servants. About as many again sent word that they would be along later; but a third of their number would never make it at all.

Late in the afternoon Tyler Ashland called for a formation on the lawn in front of the house. He already had some experience with forces of this type, and thought he knew how they had to be handled.

He informally got them mounted, and placed his guidon. "Now get yourselves in line!" he bawled at them. "No, not over there! Right dress on the guidon!" He continued his instruction at the top of his lungs. "When I yell 'Atten-SHUN!' I don't want you to scare me to death by falling silent. You will gradually die down, continuing thereafter in lower tones. Atten-SHUN!"

They quieted, within moderation. "For the present," Ashland addressed them, "I do not propose to dishonor the traditional commands by the type of execution I can expect of you." He chose to ignore that half of them were smoking cigars. "The guidon is about to turn right. I want you to get yourselves into single file and follow him. This, and all other movements, will of course be executed with your usual laughing and scratching. Don't turn your horse until the man on your right makes room, and if anybody steps on your horse's heels, crack the son of a bitch over the head with your carbine. Move off Ben."

Almost immediately he put them in line again, at horse-length intervals. Only one other maneuver was to be attempted, so he halted them for final instructions. "Try to remember," he told them, "the command 'Ho!' does not mean 'Whoa.' It is what we call the command of execution. If I yell 'Everybody turn around and ride the other way,' don't do it. Wait until I say 'Ho!' *Then* do it. And muddle back into a herd as best you can." He finished by promising them an exhibition of fine pistolry, in which he would personally shoot the cigar from the mouth of the first hero who forged to the front.

He then led them into a charge at the canter, reversed them twice, and halted. Through all this, considering their want of practice, their alignment and maintenance of intervals had been amazing; their good horsemanship was, of course, the secret of that. Every man of them could place his horse with precision as easily as he could walk. More easily, if there had been drinking. Tyler Ashland held them silent in line while he congratulated them, with only a modicum of sarcasm. He judged they were as ready for battle as they were likely to be, until a few of them got their heads shot off. He even saw hope they might do fairly well. In conclusion, he named four or five for succession to command—Rodger's name was not among them—in case of untoward event; announced embarkation for one hour before daylight, promising to see that they were partially awakened for this purpose; and dismissed.

Servants ran out to take the horses, and everybody went into the house for a drink.

Julie Delorme had expected to see the Ashland grounds covered with rows of white tents, but of course the Cavalry Club had nothing like that. "The Regiment," as they were beginning to call themselves, were all quartered, without undue doubling up, in the Ashland Great House. She was also disappointed in their come-as-you-are attire, which displayed all types of formal and informal riding garb, including a number of beaver stovepipes and a scattering of fox-hunting high hats. She considered that their general effect, as a military organization, was on the comic side. Yet she looked at them with pleased eyes, for it was not a military unit that she was seeing; she was seeing the most fabulous stag line ever known at Ash Landing. With the men in hand, enough young ladies could be counted on at short notice to make up quite a party, in a spontaneous kind of way. Her party would not be the great river-riding ball that her father had intended, but it would be well spoken of, anyway, as a patriotic send-off for Ash Landing's first contingent of troops.

She was also going to have an uninvited guest whom she didn't know about yet; for that night Shep Daniels got back to Ash Landing.

✶ 32 ✶

SHEP DANIELS HAD RIDDEN LONG HOURS TO REACH ASH LANDING well after dark on Saturday night. He knew that this was Julie's birthday, but though it was his reason for coming here, there was nothing he could contribute to it, however much he might wish he could.

He had picked up the news that Lyon had already occupied the capital, and he accepted the fact that Missouri was irreversibly at war. Rodger Ashland would of course get into it among the first; he had been preparing for it, in his own way, for a long time. Probably he could bring into it his own battalion; although, oddly, Shep still could not guess on which side. Once absorbed into either army, Rodger would become suddenly more difficult to get at, delaying his own man hunt enough so that Trapper might beat him to their target yet.

But he saw a good chance to hope that Rodge would be at Ash Landing tonight. Julie would have a birthday party. He believed Rodger Ashland would come home for that, and if he did, a chance must be made to close accounts with him, once and for all, and without another siege of weary tracking.

Even before he reached the Bishop House with his tired animals, Shep was able to see that the party was at the house on the bluffs and not upon the river. He checked in, and had cold cuts and a tub of hot water sent up. Questioning the servants who brought them, Shep learned for the first time that Tyler Ashland had declared for the South against the Union and verified that Rodger Ashland was here. He had been seen to drill with his father's cavalry, which would embark for Boonville in the morning. And Shep knew, then, what he had already suspected—that whatever move he was to make must be made tonight.

He had more baggage now than he had known he needed a year ago, when he had taken his first boiled shirts aboard that little *Tealwing*. His wardrobe included a proper tailcoat, and the stuff that went with it, all of it disused since his last days on the *Royal Oaks*, but in decent enough shape after a valet had pressed the suit. He no longer had to pull down the legs of his only black pants over the tops of scuffed work boots. So now he scrubbed and shaved, and dressed with unhurried care.

He had no intention of bringing on a fight in the Other Great House, or anywhere else upon the Delorme grounds. He judged that Rodger Ashland, too, would avoid this, particularly if Shep appeared there unarmed. What he expected was that Rodge would very happily meet him halfway, on terms to be arranged, upon neutral ground. Yet, to walk unarmed into the presence of his enemy had a feeling of foolhardiness in it that he could not quite justify in his own mind. In the end he shoulder-holstered his father's pistol under the tailcoat, which had been recut to accommodate it; and along about midnight he went to Julie Delorme's party.

He went on foot, to spare his tired horses, strolling slowly up the hill, methodically savoring the cigar that had come with his supper. At the steps of the Delorme mansion he threw the cigar away and walked without hindrance through the open doors, crossing the threshold of Julie's home for the first time in his life. He had correctly imagined Ash Landing's Other Great House as impressive, but now he found it overpowering. The house itself was of a luxury that exposed the gaudy *Royal Oaks* as a sham. There were lashings of flowers, great banks and pyramids of candles, a fortune in silverware; and the prismatic crystal pendants of the enormous chandeliers seemed carved of diamonds. Two of the three great high-ceilinged rooms were filled with dancers, and in another an enormous buffet supper was laid out, its vast variety recalling the menus of the steamboats. Two borrowed Negro orchestras were brightly costumed, one in red, the other in green and gold. And even the guests were impressively decorative.

This is what I was trying to take her away from, he thought. *To give her what in its place?* Reminding himself of that somehow took part of the weight of finality off what he was determined to do. He wandered through the great rooms, skirting the dancers and watching for Rodger Ashland. All Shep had to do, he supposed, was to let himself be seen. Rodge had already proved, long ago in the Black Mingo, that he knew it had to be one of them or the other. It was unlikely that he would let morning come, and his embarkation, without taking this chance to bring on a finish. Sure of himself, he would walk to meet it with a cold-blooded pleasure that Shep envied but could not share.

Equally sure of himself, Shep awaited the next move stoically, glad to be done with hunting and following, but in no hurry to make himself known. He leaned against the wall for a time, and from the shadows watched Julie whirling through the dances, all aglow, and lovely enough to crack the crystal of the chandeliers, yet with differences from his memory of her aboard the *Royal Oaks*. Caleese had not used gauze in the pale gown she wore this time, so that she was a flesh-and-blood girl instead of something made of mist; but there were other changes he could not have named. Then she danced with Rodger Ashland, and Shep was suddenly willing to bring his errand to an end. He stepped forward, and tapped his enemy's shoulder. "If you please," he said. Watching Rodger, he never did know what came into Julie's face as she saw him there.

Rodger's reaction showed less in his face than in the fact that he broke the beat and for a moment stood motionless. "Sorry. I think not," he said, and would have danced Julie away. But—

"Sorry—I think yes," Julie said, and turned her back on Ashland to dance with Shep. Rodge bowed slightly and left the floor.

"I thank you. I do thank you," Shep said with humility. "How long have you been at Ash Landing?"

He told her he had come in tonight. "Of course I knew this was your birthday," he added, in evasion.

"That's not why you came. I know why you came, and I want a promise from you—I *must* have a promise from you. I want you to promise me you will not fight Rodger Ashland tonight."

To gain time, he said, "In this house? Of course not."

"Not in this house, nor any place else, before his regiment moves out. He knows you are here to kill him if you can, and he is entirely frank in his intention to kill you. But he has already given me his word he will not fight you here, or now, unless you force it. Rodge will abide by that; he has almost all the faults there are, but breaking his word is not one of them."

He could not imagine how she had drawn Rodger Ashland, or anybody else, into so bloodthirsty a discussion, and he told her so.

"I stumbled onto the right questions to ask. Though I had to guess at them, partly. Have you seen your brother?"

"Not for a long time. But—"

"Don't you know where he is?"

"I don't even know if he's alive."

"Well, he is—and he's here."

At this point Shep was tapped by a handsome and beautifully groomed young man, confident of his rights and inclined to dispute the matter when Shep refused to yield, but Julie said, "Later, Jeremy," and the stag-liner backed away.

"Your brother is here," Julie picked up the thread at once, speaking rapidly, in anticipation of further interruptions. "Oh, not in this house. Hiding in the woods. But I found him and talked to him. He claims he's hiding out from somebody who means to kill him, because of something he knows or saw. I wanted to help him get out of Missouri—put him on a boat, lend him whatever he needed—I even promised him virtually safe-conduct aboard our own boats. But he wouldn't hear of it. Just mumbled something about waiting for you."

"What made him think I was coming here?"

"He said he knew you'd come because I was here. But that didn't make any sense. I've been here all the time, and you haven't come. All of a sudden I knew he was waiting for something else."

"It doesn't sound like Trapper to telling you lies," Shep said.

"Does it sound like him to be hiding in the brush for fear of his life?"

Shep had to admit that that did not sound like his brother either.

"Shep, he's in *very* poor shape. He's been wounded— badly, I think—and he doesn't seem to be mending. He looks like a starved little boy. But there's something in his eyes as hard as the flat side of a knife. He's not the hunted animal— he's the hunter himself."

He's talked his head off. That much is plain. How much more did he tell her that she shouldn't know?

He had guided her near to the orchestra, where they were less likely to be overhead, yet, by sometimes dancing improperly close, they could hear each other. The orchestra now went into the flourishes which indicated that its number was coming to an end; but, close by as they were, Julie was able to signal the musicians to continue.

"That was all I could get out of him," Julie said, as if she had read the question in his mind. "But it was enough to fall together into a hunch. So I asked Rodge outright why he was feuding with you Daniels boys. And he answered me straight out, without the least hesitation . . ."

A middle-aged member of the Regiment, slightly paunched and with the ruddy face of senior authority, now attempted to cut in. Shep turned to him, intending to refuse with courtesy, but the sheet lightning of his annoyance must have jumped into his face, for he was surprised to see the old gentleman start backwards and retire of his own accord.

"Rodge is like his father," Julie said. "They have both killed men before—mostly under the code duello, but sometimes not. They don't boast of it, but they don't conceal it either. Rodge would have told me before if I had happened to ask."

"Well, what does he say we're feuding about?"

"He says you think he killed your father."

That wasn't all of it, of course. Close enough, though. He let it stand without remark.

"All I ask is a truce for this one night," Julie said. "Let Rodge move out with his regiment tomorrow. After that—it can all be worked out some way. Do you want Trapper to die out there in the woods?"

It was as good an argument as any, and doubtless she had a thousand more, but the one that counted had not been spoken, and need not be, for it stood out plainly, unsaid. If was simply that she had a hundred ways to stop him, if she did not get her way. She could set the whole Regiment upon him, if she wanted to, with hardly more than a word. *I did not foresee it,* he thought. *It's all in the open now; or will be soon.* He hoped that was a good place for it to be.

"Very well," he said slowly. "I'll hold off if he will, for this one night."

Immediately he was tapped again, and this time let her go.

★ 33 ★

As he moved to leave the house, Rodger Ashland barred his way, not conspicuously but in all casualness, as if it were an accidental encounter. Shep could have walked around him if he had chosen to, but he did not. "You looking for me?" Shep asked.

Rodger said, "Not particularly." And now they talked for a few moments, voices low, faces without any show of expression such as would have been likely to catch the eye of an unalerted observer. They might have been discussing an appointment to look at a horse. "I suppose," Rodger Ashland said without much hope, "Her Royal Highness got to you, too?"

"I made the same promise she tells me you gave her."

"One does, doesn't one?" Rodger said with sour dryness, and he shrugged. "No way out of it. Refusing her would only have brought on a great hue and cry, coming to nothing. I don't know who has done all this talking—maybe you— maybe your brother—it doesn't matter. Our quarrel will be county property before morning."

By common consent they strolled slowly, aimlessly, side by side through the peopled rooms, to handicap eavesdroppers, while staying in full sight of everybody at all times. Rodger Ashland pleasantly acknowledged his friends here and there, ignoring those who wished to stop and chat with him. But it seemed to Shep that a number inconspicuously avoided running into Ashland.

"It is reduced to a matter of time and place," Rodge said. "Suddenly too many people know too much. Bushwhack me now, and the whole county will turn out to string up you and your brother both, without the slightest question."

He's right, of course. But that won't stop Trapper. He's probably lying out there some place with his sights sulphured, this very minute. My time's getting mighty short.

"Tomorrow," Rodger Ashland said, still maintaining that strangely casual effect of talking about a horse trade, "tomorrow we're going downstream to run the Damnyankees back where they came from. . . . Good evening, Judge Cameron. You're looking extremely well, sir. I trust you'll join me in a brandy—later. . . . We mean to hit them as they move on Boonville; probably day after tomorrow. It's imperative that I take part in this first engagement. Can't expect it to last long enough to give a man a second chance. I'll have no time for you until that's done."

Still hopes to impress his old man, Shep translated this.

"But I give you my oath, you'll get your fight, and a bellyful of it, just as soon as they're whipped. Stay at Ash Landing if you want to. I'll pass the word you're not to be molested. I'll come for you in a space of days. Or go where you like, for that matter—I'll come for you anyway, and I'll find you—never doubt it!"

"Or, better yet," Shep suggested, "I'll come to Boonville and find you. Quicker that way."

"That's not acceptable at all. A shot in the back is just a little bit too easy in that kind of fighting, for one thing."

"Are you forcing me, sir?" Shep seized on this.

"I am not!"

"Well, it sounds a whole lot like it to me!"

"In that case, I withdraw it. I was trapped into a stupid promise but, by God, all the mudsills out of hell won't stop me from keeping it! Instead, let me put it this way. . . . Oh, good evening, Miss—I mean, Mrs. Copeland. Your pardon, mam. For a moment I mistook you for your daughter. . . ."

Oh, for God's sake . . .

"Let me put it this way. If you are found skulking around Boonville, I'll have you arrested on sight."

"On what charges?"

"If you doubt that I can arrange a hanging for you, you'll just have to try me, that's all."

"We'll see," Shep said.

"What does that mean?"

"Let's leave it like this: If I don't show up at Boonville, you can figure I stayed away."

He forced himself to grin, and bow slightly; and he walked out of the house.

⋆ **34** ⋆

Shep Daniels walked back to the Bishop House in a state of considerable puzzlement. Some of the wheels and springs that governed Rodger Ashland were of course plain to be seen, but in other ways he was still an enigma. Within his own family, Rodge had been embittered by being born second-best in his father's esteem. His early rebellions against this position had endeared him to nobody. Apparently he had never loved anybody he ought to have loved. When his brother David died, Rodge was inspired only to jealousy by his father's grief.

Against this background, Shep supposed Rodge had largely misinterpreted his grave experiences in the Kansas actions, into which he had ridden under his father's command. Almost certainly he had misunderstood his father's grim but righteously intended purposes in those raids. Tyler Ashland had fought what he believed to be a wicked injustice, shielding itself behind a screen of false law; he had called up military violence to shatter and destroy the deadly hypocrisy of that law. Now came this conscienceless and not especially intelligent boy, with his father's brittle fighting-cock pugnacity, but with little else his father had; taken into these actions at the age of fifteen, less to participate than to see and learn. What Rodge had seen had seen the lawless bloodletting, the looting, the merciless attacks. The justice and the injustice must never have touched his mind.

That was the night rider of the back country and the wilderness. Shep thought it likely that Rodger had expected his father's admiration for a career of cruelties that had served

211

only to "blood his hounds," and so forge himself a weapon that could cut deep.

But what about this other Rodger Ashland, the gentleman of honor, who, among his own people, supposedly lived by so sensitive a code? Shep believed that the code honestly existed; he believed that Tyler Ashland, within human limits, lived by it as well as he could. Tyler detested Shep, and spared no unpleasantness to make this plain, yet Shep would have believed his word above another man's oath. Rodger had the graces, the polish that went with his father's code. Probably the manners and mannerisms that identified a gentleman were not too hard to sustain if you were born and raised to them. But the solidity of principle upon which the code of honor had been built—Shep did not believe Rodger Ashland capable of comprehending it. He could not and dared not believe in Rodger's word or in his promised performance in any respect. A flawless wariness, an unbroken vigilance, was still his best hope. . . .

Thinking about the measures of caution he must perfect, he walked flat-footed into what could have been a death trap, just as well as not. He climbed the dark outside stairs of the Bishop House, dissimulating that he was analyzing every shadow within range of sight. He groped blind through the unlighted upper hall and found his door. Not good, this hallway darkness up here. He dug up his key, let himself in, and locked the door behind him before he struck a light. But, as his lucifer flared, he saw he was not alone.

Trapper was sitting cross-legged on Shep's bed, fully clothed, but with a blanket muddled around him; he looked as though he had been asleep. His Spencer was across his knees, and his left hand was easing the hammer off full cock.

"You look like you tried to crawl out of hell through a knothole," Shep said. "And got dragged back."

"I feel a little bit that way," Trapper admitted. "Though better than I did before I borrowed your soap." He had appropriated Shep's secondhand bath water to scrub up. He had borrowed Shep's razor, and the kinky reddish beard Julie had noticed was gone. He had found an old worn-out pair of his brother's butternut work pants and a shirt, and though they fitted him a little late in places, they were clean.

"You haven't asked me how I go in," Trapper said.

"I can think of a lot of ways. Don't see it matters which you used. A man inside a room can be got at, but only at the cost of at least one life. The man coming into a room has no chance."

"I guess the best thing is to stay out of rooms," Trapper said. "I've been doing that for quite some time."

"Is your shoulder ever going to mend?"

"Shep, I don't know. I sure can't shoot like I used to, I can tell you that. I don't dare risk a shot unless I'm right on top of my mark. And I haven't been able to make that kind of a chance."

"What the hell did you tell Julie Delorme?"

Trapper explained that he had had to tell Julie something, else she would have reported his presence and he would have been through. When he had repeated everything he could remember having said to her, Shep couldn't find much fault with it; though he could understand now how everything had suddenly come to the surface as it had. Julie had been smart enough, or intuitive enough, to fit Trapper's situation into things she already knew about Rodger Ashland, and about Shep; guided to her guesses more by what didn't fit together than by what did. Thus she had stumbled upon the direct question that had opened Rodger up. And Rodger, probably led to believe Julie knew more than she had even surmised, had faced the issue with short, blunt answers, brash but forthright—and down came the cobhouse. So actually it was Rodger himself who had done the talking he blamed others for having done. . . .

Doesn't signify too much, Shep decided. *No feud lies hidden very long.*

As for Trapper's promise to Julie to hurt no one while he was there, lest the onus of murder fall upon herself—Trapper was unable to make up his mind whether he should consider himself bound by it or not. "I swear, Shep," he put it, "I'm thrown completely ass over crop, trying to figure if she's tied my hands, or what should I rightly do." The dilemma had sapped his resolution, to a degree that lately he had just been nosing around, and nosing around, not really trying to make an opportunity but just marking time, and hoping Shep would come.

Yet he had found out something. Five of Rodger Ashland's night riders were in the neighborhood, mighty careful not to show themselves, the same as he was himself, but he knew where they were. There was the ruin of an old log cabin, far back against the hills behind the plantation, dating from before the Ashlands came. It had been on one of the pieces Tyler Ashland's father had bought when he first laid out Ash Landing, but its fields had proved disappointing and had been allowed to go back to woodlot. At this disintegrating cabin, Rodger Ashland's five men were bushed up. Every day one or more of the slaves carried out there big buckets of food cooked at the house; Trapper had seen some of these people bashed around by the bushwhackers for failing to steal liquor for them.

Only two of the five in the woods were known to Trapper, these being Hobe and Yancey, who seemed to have made themselves Rodger's top lieutenants. All were better mounted than he had ever known them to be before; so Trapper thought, and Shep agreed, that the five must be standing by as couriers, to fetch the rest of Captain Handy's band to rendezvous when Rodger should need them. Since Rodger had been home he appeared to have been acting about as was to be expected of a gentleman of his father's class. Was he considering a return to the life into which he had been born, or not? Set to do one thing or the other, seemingly. Maybe Julie would decide it. She had told Trapper that she would never marry Rodge; with uncommon restraint, Trapper held back from tormenting Shep by naming the reason she had given. The very nature of their errand here would put Shep out of her world, in any case.

Trapper placed no great confidence in the stability of Julie's decision. She might turn around and marry Rodge any minute, for all he knew. "I like women," Trapper said, "and I admire them—mostly—and all. But I'll be switched if I can tell what they're liable to do. I know just one thing about 'em, for dead certain: It ain't true they're all alike. They ain't—not even any two of 'em. They're all different, every dang one, and there can't ever be any rule fitted onto 'em. And every time you think you know for sure what ways one of 'em can be counted on—why, she changes."

"These bushwhackers—do they act like they're going to Boonville?"

Trapper had seen no sign of it. Fighting in lines, with plenty people shooting back at you, wasn't rightly their style, regardless of what Rodge expected he could make of them. Trapper looked for Rodge himself back from Boonville pretty quick; couldn't imagine him serving under his old man for very long.

"Tell you what I want you to do," Shep said. "I want you to live on for a while in this room. I'll speak to the landlord, so you'll be brought everything you want. I've already fixed it so you won't be bothered here at Ash Landing." *I hope I've fixed it. The whole town will know he's here. I see no help for that.* "Although, was I you, I believe I'd be kind of careful how I was seen to come and go."

"Don't worry about that!"

"And speaking of taking care, maybe you better sleep with your gun in your hand for now."

"I always do," Trapper told him. And Shep had one of those twinges Trapper could still give him, that the wide-eyed little brother he remembered should have turned into a hurt and hunted animal, with nothing bit a deadly vengeance in his heart in place of any hope.

"About once a night, any time you think best, I'd like to have you take a look at Rodger's bushwhackers—just keep an eye on them and see if they change in numbers, or anything. I expect I'll be back pretty quick. Or else I'll get word to you someway."

"Where you going to be?"

"Boonville."

"And after that? . . . No. That's a stupid question. Neither one of us will know what we're fixing to do. Until after Boonville."

"Now let's see that shoulder."

It didn't look good. The healed-over wound had abscessed, deep inside. Shep thought he detected a grating, in there, as of the disjuncture of a broken bone, but the swelling was so dreadfully sensitive he could not make sure. He would have to lance it. *Now, should I feed him first, and work on him just before I leave?* It was already pretty well on toward morning; a first graying in the east could be looked for within the hour, and Shep wanted to take the Boonville road just as soon as he knew Rodger Ashland was sure enough on his way. *God knows he needs feeding. But if I feed him first, and then work on him too soon, he'll just toss it up. Have to open the shoulder first. Start on it now, and trust he has enough sense to get himself fed right tomorrow. . . .*

★ 35 ★

As it turned out, Shep Daniels had a good deal more time than he thought he had. "The Regiment" proved in no shape to embark in the blackness before dawn, as Tyler Ashland had intended. It was half past eight before any attempt could be made to put the horses aboard a small side-wheeler called the *Little Ben*, which would take them to Boonville.

From a great distance Shep watched their muddled attempts to get started, beset by unaccountable delays. At the last minute, as the horses were being led down the stage plank, a sad, pitiful little incident occurred, delaying the start a full hour more. At the distance from which he watched Shep couldn't tell what was happening; there was a lot of shouting, and some firing, and hard running of horses, and he had the impression that a man had been killed. But, "Oh, no," the landlord of the Bishop House told him later. "Nothing serious happened. I believe one of the Ashland niggers got shot—stealing a horse, I heard. But nobody was hurt, or anything."

It was Rodger Ashland's body servant who had been killed. He had had a formal name, such as Nebediah, or something, but Rodge had always called him Roughhaid. He had been assigned to wait on Rodge hand and foot, since they had both been about ten years old, and while they were boys Rodge had been fond of him, as much as he was fond of anybody. But after the Kansas raids, when Rodger Ashland began his prolonged absences, Tyler Ashland had refused to let Roughhaid accompany his son, and Rodger had found the boy's services more unsatisfactory every time he returned.

217

While Rodge was away, Roughhaid took over the carpenter shop; he loved working in wood, and showed a deft and delicate talent with it. There was always plenty of stuff to be mended, but what Roughhaid like to make was musical instruments, sometimes banjos and gittars, but mostly fiddles. He always had a few under the bench, to work on when nobody was looking, and he taught himself to make them beautifully. In the course of time the Ashland slave quarters came alive with more discordant practicing—and more real music, too—than those of any other plantation.

Rodger Ashland was at first annoyed, then constantly infuriated, because Roughhaid was never on hand when wanted. He found out why, of course, and caught Roughhaid finishing a fiddle. It wouldn't have been like Rodger to wonder how many loving hours of patience had gone into Roughhaid's fiddle. He smashed it to lightwood splinters, and when Roughhaid wept, as uncontrollably as a little child, Rodge whipped him for that, and had him replaced in the carpenter shop.

Roughhaid had become a good body servant after that, always hovering inconspicuously, so attentive and willing that, although Rodger continued to dislike him, Tyler Ashland had believed him of unquestionable loyalty, one of the chattels sure to stay with the family even if the Yankees swooped down and turned him free.

He was wrong. As the cavalry horses were led aboard, Roughhaid loitered to the rear, pretending to examine the feet of Rodger's horse. Suddenly he mounted, and cantered down the levee toward the blacksmith shop, half a block away. The shop wasn't even open, but Roughhaid disappeared around the side of it, as if he had entered it. He was next seen a quarter of a mile down the road at the end of the town, riding Rodger's horse at a brisk walk, apparently trying to get around the bend of the road unnoticed before he was missed at the stage plank.

Rodger Ashland let out a yell that Roughhaid must have heard clearly at the distance, though he pretended not to. "You, Roughhaid! Come back here!" Roughhaid proceeded

evenly, as if he had not heard. "Here, somebody, quick!
Where's a horse? Somebody stop that boy!"

Three or four who had not gone aboard immediately took
out after Roughhaid with a yell; and Roughhaid, exploding
Rodger's horse into a dead run, disappeared around the bend.
He might have got clear, and lost himself, but beyond the turn
in the road he ran into half a dozen riders of the Regiment,
who had gone off to exercise their horses and were just now
coming back. Roughhaid turned square off the road, trying
for the woods, but a pistol shot dropped him from the saddle.
He struggled up and tried to run, but five more bullets found
him, and laid him stone-dead in the roadside grass.

An effort to find the horse dragged out for some time.
Rodge wanted to send for the bloodhounds, but his father, at
the end of patience, ordered him aboard. There were other
horses, and other saddles. "All my equipment is in my saddlebags and my bedroll," Rodger objected. "Even my good
pistols are on that saddle!" But his father would not hold the
boat.

The Regiment saw no tragedy in this episode. Rodger had
been laughably discommoded by the loss of his equipment,
and Tyler Ashland had lost an expensive chattel, which was
a joke on Ashland. But nothing much had really happened, in
the view of the members. They were mistaken. A strange and
deadly accident had happened to the Ashlands when
Roughhaid fell. A freak accident, naturally, as Trapper Daniels would have pointed out, since no other kind ever happened.

By late afternoon Rodger's horse had been brought in,
somewhat scratched up from having tripped on the reins, but
not otherwise damaged. The saddle was still missing, rolled
off by the horse or knocked off by the trees; and Julie
Delorme, since she was out riding anyway, joined in the
search for it. It wasn't too hard to find, once you took time
to back-trail the animal. Julie was close at hand when it was
located. The saddlebags were intact, but carbine and pistols
were lost, or more likely stolen, and might never be recovered. Rodger's bedroll, scuffed off and partly broken open,
was found by a half-grown Negro boy, not far away.

"I'll take that," Julie said.

"Mam?"

"I say, I'll keep that for him!"

The boy passed the bedroll up to her. A blue sleeve was dangling from one end of the tube of loosened blankets. Anybody might have a blue coat. Most people did have one. But three gilt buttons at the cuff made this one unusual. She stuffed the sleeve out of sight into the blankets before she draped the roll over her pommel, and rode home.

⋆ 36 ⋆

WATCHING TYLER ASHLAND'S REGIMENT DEPART, SHEP DANIELS was watching his enemies. But when they were gone he was glad that he, as well as they, would have a chance to strike a blow for the South, in this first pitched battle in the West. After all his lifelong hard riding and practiced use of firearms, it seemed to him that he ought to be fighting if anybody was.

He had no self-interest in the politics of this war. Slavery had meant little to him, one way or the other. In general, it seemed to him that the employment of slaves was a hard way to run a farm, but he did not know how a big plantation could be run otherwise. He thought the South was hurt by being unable to make anything that an illiterate and unwilling Negro could not make or do. But he didn't know what must be done for the slaves if they were freed. In their present state they had a greater security than any small cropper ever knew. It wasn't a type of security he wanted himself, and presumably they didn't want it either. But if five million were suddenly turned loose, he could imagine the most of them wandering the roads, starving and marauding, until they died.

There were other things he didn't like about the way the South was run. He resented the unbreachable wall with which the aristocracy had surrounded itself. He felt pity, touched with contempt, for the little woolhat croppers who revered the aristocrats, hat in hand, never noticing that the plantation system had crowded them onto stony hillsides and thrown their struggle for survival into competition with unpaid labor. . . . But he had no solution for these things. . . .

He knew nothing about the constitutional rights or wrongs

221

of secession, except that the division of sentiment followed the same geographical line as that between slavery and abolition. It was a line hard to respect, for it was a fence of dollar signs, cutting irregularly across states, counties, families, even religious denominations. Below the dollar line, soil and climate made slavery profitable, whereas above the line it was not. Just how the country was supposed to operate with its main system of transportation cut in two, though unclear, was not his responsibility.

The business he had been raised in had never demanded much thought as to whether he was a Southerner, or a Northerner, or simply an American. But now that you had to be one thing or another, there was never a moment's question in his mind as to which he was. He was a Southerner born, and a Southerner raised, and all his people had called themselves Southerners. The hundreds and hundreds of people he had known and worked with, from Potters to Delormes, were Southern, and all the great area of country he had ranged over was the South. Even the parts of Indiana and Illinois that he knew had been peopled by Southern pioneers.

And the one thing he did know for damned sure was that an army of strangers was shooting its way up the Missouri, committed to imposing the will of outsiders upon the South by force of arms. There could be only one answer to that, ever. Soon after the departure of the Regiment, he was on the Boonville road, riding Trapper's Morgan—name contracted by this time to Brownie, from Brown Sugar—as the best-conditioned horse they had between them. He was elated by the joyous thrust with which the strong-quartered little horse stepped out, and looked forward happily to a head-on smash with the Yankee columns—the only form of remonstrance the invader could be expected to understand.

It wasn't going to work out the way he imagined it. Not on Monday's battlefield, but in the quiet hours of that bewitched Sunday, while Brownie sailed along the river road, and the Regiment rode the broad Missouri, an unaccountable madness swept over unmolested Boonville; and wave after wave of confusion, vacillation, and ruinous panic of command overwhelmed Missouri's hopes. Parallels may perhaps be found in some later seizures in the armies of the North; but the beat of it does not exist in the annals of any war. With no shot fired, nor any military confrontation, not only Boonville but the whole Missouri River was lost to the South before Sunday's sun went down.

Early on Sunday morning some of Governor Claiborne Jackson's downriver pickets came in with the word that seven huge troop transports were coming up the river, massed with men. The Governor consulted with General Price. The militia at hand could not hope to withstand any such force as that described; to resist seemed a commitment to useless slaughter. The Governor issued an order for immediate disbanding of the state troops, all to return to their homes. General Price himself, relieved of duty, boarded one of the many packets being herded up the river, and went home to Lexington, a long way up the Missouri.

The rebel volunteers were outraged, and made it known they had no intention of following any such orders. They had come to fight, and they proposed to do it; though Colonel Marmaduke, in command of most of them, now resigned in disgust, and detachments began to wander away.

A few hours passed; the seven troop-carrying steamboats did not appear. No such flotilla was on the river at all, and the whole report was in error. When this became plain, Governor Jackson reversed himself, and ordered the troops to take position for a fight, with a Mr. Little nominated to command. But the damage was irretrievable. On Sunday morning the militia on hand could have overwhelmed Lyon's two thousand, and driven him into the river; after which they could have gone southward, with high hearts and captured cannon, doubtless snowballing in numbers, to destroy Sweeny and Sigel as well. By Sunday night the volunteers had dwindled to less than a third of their morning strength; the outcome was foreseeable, the opportunity gone.

★ 37 ★

SHEP DANIELS, SINGING TO BROWNIE AS THEY SWUNG DOWN THE
Boonville road, didn't know about all this. Even if he had, he
would probably have been among those who stayed to march
out next day, to make what fight they could. What prevented
him from taking part in the fiasco of Boonville was the interference of Jim Sam Delorme.

The encounter with Jim Sam was entirely unexpected to
Shep Daniels. Nobody at Ash Landing knew just where the
Royal Oaks was. Julie would have bet a horse that her father
would get home for her birthday, and all she knew about it
was that he had not appeared. Not a mile of telegraph was
working above Jeffersonville, and everything below was in
Federal hands. Jim Sam himself could not have said with any
certainty at any time what he was about to do, because he
couldn't find out the immediate intentions of the Federal
troops. It was Saturday night, and Julie's party was already in
progress many hours away, before he was entirely convinced
that General Lyon was not stopping at Jeffersonville, the capital, but was coming right on, determined to close with
Claiborne Jackson and Sterling Price or chase them clean out
of the state. Jim Sam Delorme was not easily stampeded by
rumors or swayed by the fears of other men. But now, suddenly, he saw that this time he had perhaps ignored warnings
he would have done better to believe; for he had run the
Royal Oaks into a trap.

On that Saturday night he touched only briefly at the
Boonville levee, then hastily backed out, after repelling as
many as he could of a great swarm of noncombatant fugitives

224

who wanted to be anywhere else but where they were and fought in a panic to get aboard. He could not get away from them, he found, merely by anchoring in midstream, either; a lot of them paddled out on anything that would float, or even swam for it. What he wanted now was a chance to break past or through the Federal army, and get back to the Mississippi, in an all-out try to get the *Royal Oaks* past the Union batteries and into the lower river and the South. How this was to be done depended first of all on the outcome of the Missourians' stand at Boonville; for the moment he could only wait and see. So all night long, while Julie was partying, the *Royal Oaks* loafed up and down the open water above Boonville, waiting for what the next day would bring.

On Sunday morning Jim Sam Delorme nosed his way down past Boonville, unhurriedly feeling his way, to find out what was really on the river, or beside it, to keep him from going where he wanted to go. Wherever the river road came within sight of the water it was clogged with the high-piled wagons of refugee families moving west from the capital, trying to get some of their possessions out of reach of the Yanks.

On toward noon a haggard party of horsemen hailed the *Royal Oaks* from the shore, and Jim Sam, recognizing some of them, picked them up. They were the captain, two pilots, and second mate of a Missouri packet commonly called the *Katy*. The Yankees were commandeering everything on the river, right and left, Jim Sam learned from these people. They were coming to Boonville, all right, and they were coming now. The *Katy*, undesirous of this form of "charter," had made a run for it, and had got a stack knocked off with a cannonball; those people weren't fooling any more.

Jim Sam turned around and went upriver again, resuming his wait-and-see patrolling above Boonville. Late in the day, a little above Boonville, he saw a familiar figure resting his horse on a bluff, almost eye to eye with the pilothouse of the *Royal Oaks*. "You, Shep!" Jim Sam bawled, in a voice that echoed up and down the river. "Shep Daniels! Come aboard, here! Want to talk to you!" Ringing of bells, thrashing of paddle wheels, a great blasphemous yelling of the mates, and the stage plank lurched and bumped to a steep contact with the shore. Not even the deck hands could do anything right under the conjures of that bemused day.

The *Royal Oaks* was a mess. A great number of people milled about the upper decks, a few of them cronies or acquaintances of Jim Sam or his officers, but most of them unauthorized, having come aboard by storm. The boat's officers had put ashore as many of the unwelcome as they could, here and there, but it was a hopeless job; several hundred had eluded all efforts to be shed of them. They wandered all over the boat, helping themselves to anything that could be eaten, pocketing small objects, tracking clods of mud, and strewing an unaccountable quantity of miscellaneous trash. Four or five times in a space of hours, one party or another of them had drawn up petitions which they had sent by committee to Jim Sam, demanding peremptorily that he hold course upstream, or downstream, or set out a meal, or peacefully surrender, or what not; but this pastime had lost favor after Jim Sam took to throwing the spokesmen bodily down the pilothouse stairs.

Far more ominous than any amount of this inconvenience was the defection of a large portion of the crew. Jim Sam had been forced to tie up at a woodyard to take on fuel, and here a general break for freedom caught him curiously unprepared. Later he considered his own lack of precautions unpardonable; he could not excuse himself merely on grounds that nothing like it had ever happened to him before. The outbreak itself actually lasted only minutes. A huge rouster, trotting off to freedom, could not resist patting himself on the back, with a jubilant shout of farewell to the *Royal Oaks*. "Dis back, 'e lift no mo'!" Somebody on the promenade deck let go at the runaway with a pistol, missing him, but bringing on a regular shooting gallery of small arms fire upon the fleeing Negroes. A considerable number of those who had not reached safety in the woods stopped where they were, and threw themselves to the ground; the outbreak died away. Not a single casualty had occurred, but in the brief moments of the bolt Jim Sam had lost half his rousters, deck hands, and firemen.

No military order and no Federal pronouncement of any kind had authorized the freeing of chattels or the harboring of the runaways that were already hunting for refuge behind the Yankee lines. But the spontaneous assumption that was spreading up the Missouri through the slave population was that once a slave could get the Yankee troops between himself and his masters he would be forever free.

Most surprising was the runaway of about a dozen of the upper-deck stewards and waiters. These had always appeared proud of their jobs, which carried a good many perquisites and privileges. They constituted a kind of special aristocracy among their lesser brethren; yet they had seemed as eager as any for the chance to go free. Soon even those who remained gave up all pretense of keeping the great packet in any kind of order. When a bunch of drunks who had looted the bar became afflicted with cases of the toss-ups, the upper-deck help retreated to a huddle on the main deck, cotton-eyed and bewildered.

Shep Daniels found a relatively quiet place for Brownie on the tail fan, and climbed to the pilothouse, carrying his carbine and most of his gear lest it be stolen off his animal. "This barge looks like a whorehouse in distress," he told Jim Sam.

Captain Delorme acknowledged this with a brief snarl of blasphemy, then put it out of his mind. He had a lot of questions to ask. He hadn't been getting any word from Julie at all and he demanded, with a brusqueness in proportion to his embarrassment, to know whether Shep had been hearing from her.

"I believe she was expecting you home for her party last night," Shep said.

Captain Jim Sam Delorme was so completely nonplused that for once he was struck silent. He stood glaring at Shep for so long that Shep almost asked if he had something wrong. Instead, he filled in with a few matter-of-fact statements about the presence of the Regiment, that had made the party a success; the profusion of flowers, the two bands; the present whereabouts and intentions of Ashland's Regiment. . . . Jim Sam turned his glare from Shep to the river, and they stood silent while the captain turned purple, then pale, then red gain, looking very much as though mixed emotions might explode him in any number of directions. He put Shep in mind of a steam boiler, when the engineer has hung a wrench on the safety valve and his hat on the gauge, and nobody knows when the whole thing is going to let go and blow out a whole section, from keel to pilothouse.

"What the devil is she doing at Ash Landing?" Jim Sam asked at last.

Jim Sam had explicitly ordered his daughter to Lexington with her aunt Dil. And that damned Tyler Ashland—he was supposed to see that she got there safely, and Jim Sam felt he had a right to assume it would be done. But Tyler had not even acknowledged his instructions—not yet, not no, not go to hell—nothing. By God, if his damned brother-in-law saw no reason for so much as replying to reasonable requests, there were ways to show him he did have reasons! Find Ash Landing jerked out from under him like a carpet one of these days. If he was looking for a fight he would get it—and not by the damn-fool code duello either. Take his silly pistol away from him, by God, and tie it around his neck in a knot, for a necktie. He'd look good in it.

He had lost sight of the likelihood that most of his own messages had miscarried. He couldn't have expected any answers in any case, because nobody knew where he was; he hadn't known where he would be from hour to hour himself. The confusions of that bewitched Sunday had finally befogged even Jim Sam Delorme.

Abruptly he changed the subject. "Where are you trying to go? And what for?"

Shep said he judged he would find a place for himself, turning the Yankees back from Boonville. When Jim Sam wanted to know why he hadn't attached himself to Ashland's regiment, Shep avoided a great mass of explanations by simply reminding him that the Regiment was really the Cavalry Club and did not admit mudsills to membership.

"Stop calling yourself a mudsill," Delorme ordered him. "You're a Southron Mounted Sharpshooter. Which means you use your horse to get where you're going, and then show enough sense to hide him out and fight on foot. This war isn't going to be won by any little passel of gentry on horseback. It's going to be fought out by hand." Jim Sam took little stock in cavalry anyway. Horse never lived that could be taught to get behind a tree. To expose him to a line of modern rifle muskets was nothing but a waste of horseflesh, accomplishing nothing. . . .

"You think you want to fight, do you? All right, you got a job fighting. Beginning no later than tomorrow. Soon as the troops are engaged, to take up the attention of their field guns, I'm going to run their damned blockade!"

Somebody was going to have to go back and get Julie and Caleese. Maybe fetch them around the Union Army, if things went badly, and bring them either to the *Royal Oaks* some place below or to her mother's people at Natchez. But maybe the Missouri River would be fee water again by then.

"Tomorrow," Jim Sam deferred his decision. "We'll know tomorrow . . ."

★ 38 ★

ONLY THIRTEEN HUNDRED, OF WHAT HAD BEEN MORE THAN FOUR thousand rebel volunteers twenty-four hours before, were present Monday morning when Lyon landed his two thousand Federals in a woodyard five miles below Boonville. Those who remained were farmer boy mostly, undrilled, ununiformed, and armed with the squirrel rifles and shotguns they had brought from home. Their principal officers were long gone, and Governor Jackson had taken position in the extreme outskirts on the opposite side of Boonville, with a full company of militia as his personal bodyguard. But the young Missourians marched out to meet Lyon anyway.

While the hostile columns approached each other, head on, upon the same road, Tyler Ashland rode forward alone to scout the enemy and made a pretty fair guess as to where the battle would be fought. Returning to his troopers, he galloped them a long way around, by woodland lanes and pathless crosscuts, and took position in some woods on what he hoped would be the Federal flank.

The opposed columns now sighted each other, and the Federals briskly countermarched, seeking room for deployment. They found it in a wheatfield immediately to their rear, and Ashland saw that he had not contrived himself much of an opportunity. He was on the Federal flank, all right, but at a distance of some three furlongs—call it between a quarter and a half mile of open ground.

Almost at once the militia appeared. They had mistaken the Federal maneuver for a retreat, rushed in pursuit, and now debouched into the open to find the enemy in line of battle.

Tyler Ashland had been watching a Federal battery unlimber on the nearer flank of the enemy, and now, as it prepared to fire, he led his line of horsemen yelling out of the woods. The cannoneers frantically manhandled their pieces into position to meet the attacking cavalry, whereupon Ashland turned his line wrong side out and scampered for the woods, pursued by a short-ranged blask of canister.

Now the Federal rifle muskets let go with a crashing though somewhat drawn-out volley, scaring the horses, and the whole enemy line disappeared in a great billow of black-powder smoke. When this had cleared, the Federal battery was seen to be trained on the militia again, so Ashland once more charged a little way out of the woods, forcing the Federal cannoneers—how they must have been sweating!—to change direction to the flank; and another round of canister fell short behind the horsemen as they retreated. For a few minutes a desultory firing at will continued on both sides, but the state troops had already been broken and routed. Very shortly thereafter, Lyon's bugles sounded the cease fire.

Nineteen men had been killed, on the two sides. The Federals marched on into Boonville, encountering no further resistance. A number of militiamen who surrendered were questioned and sent home, on their promise to stay there. And that was about all there was to the Battle of Boonville. It hadn't amounted to much. But the whole Missouri River had been handed over to the Union, along with the vital transportation systems of the entire state. The Governor's state troops had been dissolved clean out of existence in a matter of minutes. Missouri had been cut in two, its northern half isolated, and effective secession had been made impossible.

Tyler Ashland's short-rostered Regiment withdrew quietly and rode back to its transport above the town, circuitously but unhindered. Tyler didn't have much to say, beyond the statement that he always had said that Claiborne Jackson was a damned fool, and a hypocrite as well, and nothing any different should have been expected of him. He pointed with pride to the accomplishments of his own half a hundred, who had totally diverted the enemy artillery without loss of a man. But the state would have to fight for her life now—he could tell them that much—and there were dark days ahead of Missouri. He then withdrew into an unapproachable silence, from which nobody cared to summon him.

But it was Rodger who walked the decks with clamped jaws, his eyes fire-shot. During the brief action he had three times approached his father, once to urge a full-out charge on the Federal flank, and twice to ask for a handful of men with which to take the enemy battery. All three times he was sent back to the ranks, the third time with such a hide-peeling explosion of blasphemy as he should remember. He considered that they had twice charged, and twice been routed in the face of the enemy, and he let it be known that he had never in his life seen such childish futility. He was promptly reminded by the riders nearest him that he was a probationer at best, and would do well to shut his mouth and keep it that way; and thereafter he nothing more to say to anybody.

★ 39 ★

Jim Sam Delorme had been among the strongest of the Unionists, a resident of the Mississippi and Missouri Rivers, rather than any one state. To him, as to Shep Daniels and Tyler Ashland, the vast drainage basin of the Mississippi was America, all of it that mattered.

He never had believed there would be any general freeing of slaves by anybody. His own activities would not be affected; plenty of labor would be available for running his boats, in any case. If the slaves had been allowed to learn anything about the world at large, they would have had enough sense to sit tight, even when freed, where they know how to get fed; but they hadn't been let to learn anything at all. Millions of them would simply cut and run for it, intent only on putting this land of unpaid toil as far behind them as they could. There would be a dreadful period of famine and suffering, and it would last for a long time.

And when it came to cutting in two the vital transportation system of the nation—Jim Sam truly believed that the whole Upper Mississippi Valley, including the great Northwest, would wither and die, like a tree chopped through the trunk, if secession ever prevailed. What the brave but fool-hardy secessionists couldn't seem to see was that the prairie-state Yankees not only outnumbered them, but were of the same frontier-tested stock as themselves, no more likely to save themselves by yielding to the Confederacy than their pioneer forefathers had been likely to join the Indians. They would fight for their lives, and to the end of resource; driven back, so they would forever come on again.

So there you had three unthinkable disasters—secession, abolition, and war—all of them so ruinous that they couldn't be allowed to happen. War was an impossibility.

When the South blockaded the Mississippi, he was astonished and appalled and mistook this act for a bluff conceived in madness, sure to be swiftly reconsidered. But when Lyon marched, with his uniformed Federal troops, and drove Missouri's volunteers out of their own capital, that was war itself, and the old horse-alligator was the last man in Missouri to stand hitched of it. The two sides were going to let it happen; it had already begun, and neither knew how to back off under fire.

Under his resentment of coercion perhaps lay a deep dread, amounting to a panic—the riverman's instinctive aversion to a landlocked entrapment, cutting him off from the sea, and thus from all the world. Even if the Yankees did not commandeer his finest packet or force him to run her aground someplace far up the Missouri, out of their reach, he could imagine his boat rotting away in idleness, throughout what might prove to be years of war. And there anger came into it, the strongest influence of all. Perhaps he himself knew that plain belly-anger, more than any line of reasoning, turned him irrevocably to the South.

"We got in a fight," he explained it all, long afterwards. It was as simple to him as that, for a million words of recriminations failed to turn up for him any useful purpose to be served. "We fought about we got in a fight, nothing more. . . ."

The very few—mostly his own officers aboard the *Royal Oaks*—who knew of his intention of driving the great packet through the Yankees to Southern waters, very much doubted that it could be done. The great boat was too vulnerable to knockout by cannon fire. The huge steam boilers made an unmissable target, and the pilothouse was another. Emplacements of heavy batteries might already be operative at Cape Girardeau, and elsewhere. There were no real Union gunboats, yet, but swiftly mobile horse artillery was inescapable; and a floating battery, called "the fighting dry dock," said to be building at Cairo, was towable, and might turn up anywhere.

But Jim Sam was looking backward, to his early days in the rugged fur trade, when he had made supposedly impossible obstacles his steppingstones to fortune. He planned to strengthen his boat as he went along. Bales of hemp and cotton to shield the boilers, first. Main deck rudder controls, to replace the pilothouse if that went. An increasing force of Southern sharpshooters which he expected to pick up as he went along, to dampen the ardor of the enemy horse artillery. A bracing of heavy timbers in the bows for ramming anything that stood in his path. And as for the Fighting Dry Dock, if he came on it, he proposed to lash a coal barge alongside for protection, grapple and board the floating battery, and acquire some guns of his own. "We'll get through, all right," he declared, with a whole lot more confidence than anybody else had in the whole thing.

Discounting all the rumors he could, Jim Sam still had adequate reasons to believe that the Missouri volunteers were heavily outweighed, undrilled, and badly armed. Still, if they had the sense to take cover in the woods and fight with the skills they had learned as meat hunters, and if a little bit of initial success should give them confidence, maybe the fact that they were defending their own land would brace them to a stand beyond their strength. The Union troops had had some drill, and their ranks were full of stubborn squarehead Dutchmen from St. Louis; yet these were no veterans either, but unblooded green troops, as capable of panic as any others if anything went wrong. Jim Sam couldn't fool himself into thinking what he wanted to think, that the Missouri volunteers had a fifty-fifty chance, but maybe they had something near it. "Anything can happen in a brawl like this one," was his hopeful conclusion. "Nothing to do but wait and see."

What he wanted most was that the Yankees would somehow be broken and driven, and kept on the run long enough so that the could go back to Ash Landing to get Julie. With enough luck the Yankees might even be chased back through Jeffersonville without another stand, and all the way to St. Louis to reorganize, refit, consult with Washington, clear two thousand miles of red tape and a million words of debate; and thus let him get well down the Mississippi before they pulled themselves together to impede anybody. But he didn't see much hope of all that. It was habitual self-reliance that made him feel Julie to be safer with him aboard a blockade-running packet than entrusted to anybody else on earth.

Yet, as between Julie's position and that of the *Royal Oaks*, the great packet was for the moment the more vulnerable in the event of a Yankee win. In spite of his outburst of impatience with his "damned brother-in-law," he supposed Tyler Ashland would see that Julie was under as stern protection as was to be had. He would run the Boonville blockade at the moment most advantageous to the boat, as the battle itself must decide.

Along toward the middle of Monday morning the people aboard the *Royal Oaks* heard the beginnings of the Battle of Boonville. This was about on schedule, as predicted, except that it began much farther downstream than Jim Sam had expected. He had been loafing up and down about two miles above Boonville, which put the *Royal Oaks* some seven miles upstream of the woodyard where Lyon's troops actually landed. At this distance the rifle fire came upriver only as a whisper; not even the single great crashing Union volley would have been clearly recognizable for what it was, had it not been bracketed by the heavier detonations of the cannon fire that Ashland had drawn by his two feints from the woods.

After that, almost immediately, even the random musketry dwindled and died; the *Royal Oaks* could not hear the bugles that blew the cease fire, nor anything else thereafter. No cheering, no chorusing rebel yells—nothing. Jim Sam at first supposed that a fluke of the wind had cut him off from the sounds of battle. He turned downstream, closing on Boonville, and as the silence continued he became more and more mystified.

Now a great riotous expostulation began among the packet's uninvited passengers. Jim Sam answered this by passing the word that they were all going downstream to join in the battle. He then placed his officers where they could prevent, at pistol point, any further desertions from among his crew, turned inshore, and dropped his plank. Shep Daniels rushed down to the tail fan, where he prevented the theft of Brownie by knocking a couple of panicky horse thieves into the water; then watched the refugee passengers abandon ship, in a head-long stampede that jostled a dozen or so more of them over-board before they made the levee. A few of the well-armed, of unknown principles, stayed aboard—to see the excitement, apparently. But the steamboatmen Jim Sam had picked up had seen all the boat seizures they wanted to, and went ashore with the rest.

Jim Sam nosed cautiously downstream past Boonville, forced now to accept the unlikelihood that the battle was ac-tually over with in this matter of minutes, decided by not much more than a single round. At first he hopefully assumed that the Missourians had put the Federals instantaneously to rout; he could not imagine the rebel volunteers having been beaten in such short order. He had supposed that a disaster to the Missourians must take the form of a drawn-out, stub-bornly contested retreat, in which the increasingly disorgan-ized state troops fell back upon Boonville slowly, fighting from tree to tree. But presently a thin straggle of militiamen began to appear along the shore, plodding rearward, plainly in a state of dispersal past all rallying. Jim Sam was forced to concede that the Missourians had so disintegrated that there wasn't even a pursuit, so far as he could make out.

In actuality, Lyon had sent out a couple of companies to round up prisoners for questioning. They had brought in a few, whom Lyon, upon talking to them, disgustedly classified as nothing but a bunch of deluded young boys. He exacted a promise from them to stop all this nonsense, and go on home and get to work; then turned them loose again, without wast-ing time in so much as a lecture.

Once Jim Sam got this course of events through his head, he saw his danger. Since he was engaging in no pursuit, Lyon would doubtless countermarch to his boats and continue up-stream to the occupation of Boonville. If the Federal troops got this done with sufficient dispatch—and Lyon did seem to be notably brisk of movement—the *Royal Oaks* would meet the leading Federal transport in midstream, bristling with rifles, of such a fire power as would leave nothing alive aboard the unprepared *Royal Oaks*.

He was left with two alternatives. He could retreat above Boonville, a long way above, if he needed to, and wait until Lyon was disembarked and settled ashore again. Then, at the deepest and darkest hour of the night, he could drift lightless down the Missouri, with a high head of steam but silent paddles. . . . The Yankee field guns would doubtless be emplaced to command the river, by that time. But maybe, if he rode the current as far as he could until challenged, then hit it with everything his engines had, he could charge past the battery before the artillerists could pull themselves together.

Or he could make a dash for it now, hoping to get past the Federals while they were unwatchful, and preoccupied with their loading. Jim Sam Delorme went through the mental motions of weighing the several chances; but, since he was who he was, there never was much room for doubt as to what his decision would be. It was his habit to carry a few tons of lard, for bringing up a sudden great pressure of steam, and he now ordered the lard barrels into the fire alley. He cleared the pilothouse of everyone but Shep Daniels and his two master pilots, Ham Bridgman and Joe Caruthers; both pilots were good shots, and armed with repeating rifles. Jim Sam himself would take the wheel as they came into the critical stretch of their run.

For a few minutes now Jim Sam scribbled out a note to Julie. "You'll have to get this back to her by saddle," he told Shep. "That's a good horse you've got there; you'll make it, all right. I expect you'll find she has plenty of people taking care of her—but you make sure of it—you hear?"

"Yes, sir."

"Sorry if it takes you out of your way."

It would not take Shep out of his way. Ashland's horsemen would fall back on Ash Landing, and Rodger Ashland should be with them for at least a little while more; or even if he weren't, Shep would have to go back anyway, on account of Trapper. Evidently Jim Sam Delorme still knew nothing definite about the climaxing Ashland-Daniels feud. Shep noticed with mixed reactions Jim Sam's clear assumption that Shep would do anything possible for Julie, without obligation or hope of reward, or any least question whatsoever.

The big packet was roaring downsteam now, broadsiding the turns, pushing the river out of her way in heavy waves that ran up the shore line. The *Royal Oaks* was ordinarily a quiet-running boat, but now she was beginning to shake all over, bringing out a thousand unaccustomed rattlings of complaint. Jim Sam shouted down the speaking tube for more steam, and took the wheel.

Now they opened a quarter-mile reach of straight river, and the Union transports were suddenly in view at the lower end. For a space of minutes it looked as if Jim Sam had indeed taken the jump on his opponents and would win his trick. Only a few figures were visible aboard the transports; a field gun was being eased down the stage plank of the nearest steamboat. A company or so of soldiers lounged about the woodyard ashore, but they were not in ranks or ready for action. Troops and steamboatmen alike seemed to be staring in a stupor of disbelief. Apparently no standing orders, no preparation of any kind had been set up to deal with the unexpected rush of the huge packet.

Except one. Out from the shadow of the transports steamed a preposterous token of a war vessel, unarmored and insignificant. A ferryboat was all it was, with a single field gun secured by breechings on its forecastle, but an improvised jack-staff had been raised upon the bow guards, and from this streamed an enormous flag, bearing the stars and stripes of the United States, to make it a ship of war. It held straight up the channel, challenging the towering mass of the *Royal Oaks*, closing fast now, within the furlong. From Jim Sam's pilothouse the cannoneers of the single fieldpiece could be seen to load, and ram a roundshot home. The gunpointer primed, then stood by with a lighted punk. The vessels were within the hundred yards.

"Joe," Jim Sam ordered, "kill that gunpointer!"

"I can't get a line on him!" came Caruther's answer; and Ham Bridgman said, "It's the flag! That big bedsheet of a flag—it's blanking us off!"

"You, Shep—bring down that flag!"

Shep Daniels lifted on his toes to damp the tremor of the deck and fired immediately. It seemed a snap shot, scarcely aimed, but got off by reflex of hand and eye, and for an instant it appeared to have missed. But the jackstaff was cut half in two, and behind it a man fell to the bullet's ricochet. Slowly the staff toppled, and fell across the guards, the colors trailing in the muddy water.

Instantly both Joe Caruthers and Ham Bridgman fired, and the body of the gunpointer jerked twice as he went down. A strange, sick feeling swept through Shep. It was his first blow against the Union, the Federal government of the United States. *I fired on the flag. No turning back now, ever. Not until one side or the other is fought clean into the ground—if I live to see it....*

Jim Sam blew a terrific warning blast of his whistle, its deep roar echoing far up and down the Missouri, then leaned out of his pilothouse to bawl at the makeshift gunboat. His bellowings were not louder than the whistle, as some claimed; but even over the laboring of the engines and the thrash of the paddle wheels he could be heard for a mile. "Give way, you damned fishbox! Give way, I say! Give way or I ram!"

These were the tactics that had won him fortune, in the young, wild days of the Upper Missouri, and the old ways came back to him easily in this extremity that was not his alone, but a crisis for Missouri and for the nation. But the old days were gone, and nothing worked for him as it used to do. The idiotic armed ferryboat came dog-paddling straight on, while its commander shouted through his megaphone, the words half intelligible, but his meanings clear: "Lay to, I say! Or by God I'll fire—"

"Try it!" Jim Sam answered; and at fifty feet the fieldpiece let go a round shot through the packet's monster boilers. The black-powder smoke that welled up to hide the fighting ferryboat was as nothing compared to the explosion of steam that instantly engulfed the *Royal Oaks*. It seemed to come up through the solid deck plankings, penetrating everywhere with its lung-killing strangle; and from the heart of the steam came a dreadful screaming of scalded men.

The dying steamboat ran on by momentum alone, crushing through the other vessel as through a melon crate; the ferry-boat sent up its own explosion of steam as the weight of its machinery plunged the fireboxes under water. The *Royal Oaks* plowed on through the debris, then lost way, and drifted dead in the current.

★ 40 ★

TYLER ASHLAND TOOK HIS TIME ABOUT GETTING AWAY FROM Boonville. He put out vedettes, to watch the Yankees, and held his horsemen aboard the *Little Ben*, at her moorings well upstream. He was praying for the appearance of rumored reinforcements under General Price, such as might yet sweep the Missourians into a victorious rally; so there they stayed through Monday night, all day Tuesday, and much of Tuesday night. By that time Governor Jackson had fled to the southwest, with a few remnants of his volunteers straggling after. Not even a token command of any kind remained in the Boonville area, so the *Little Ben* cast off at last.

It was a party of greatly subdued gentlemen who disembarked Wednesday noon at Ash Landing. They would listen to anything Tyler Ashland cared to propose, but they didn't feel committed to him any further. On the *Little Ben* many a low-voiced group had discussed how best to oppose the invasion, but nothing now afoot promised the immediate defense urgently needed by their own counties. They were silent and sober-faced as Ashland dismissed them, and Rodger, staying in the saddle, rode off toward the rear of the plantation without a word to anybody. Most, though, dismounted for refreshment, as if by habit; and no sooner set foot to the ground than they were blasted by news more shocking than the defeat at Boonville.

Only half a dozen servants ran out to help with the horses, but these were able to explain, in a white-eyed babble, what had happened. On Sunday night, following the departure of the Regiment, a great epidemic of runaways had swept Ash

Landing. Two-thirds of the Ashland labor force, many of the house servants, and almost all the slaves from the Delormes' had run off, along with most of the body servants left behind by the Regiment. The bloodhounds were dead in their kennels and nobody knew where the overseers and their assistants were; maybe they, with some volunteer posses from the village, were attempting pursuit. For many hours armed villagers had guarded the two Great Houses, but threat of damage had died down, and they had gone home at daylight. Food supplies had been looted and some mules taken; but the liquor cellars had not been broken into and no good horses were missing.

It was a mass exodus such as no one present had ever heard of in the history of Missouri, and the specter instantly raised in everyone's mind was that of a universal slave uprising. This was a possibility almost tacitly derided and rejected, being considered improper to mention; yet it survived, dormantly, a vague nightmarish dread, deep beneath the surface of many Southern minds. Most members of the Regiment dispersed at once to their homes, the speed of each limited only by the distance he must ride without change of horses; and a dreadful fear that was not for himself rode with every one of them.

Actually the Ash Landing exodus proved localized, an inevitable and recurring by-product of every Yankee advance. Long before any Federal revision of chattel status was declared, the slaves began seizing every chance to put Yankee troops between themselves and their masters.

Upon Julie Delorme had fallen the one greatest disillusionment of all. Nobody ever did seem able to tell which slaves were most likely to gamble for freedom, and which, from timorousness or loyalty, would be most likely to remain. But as the Ash Landing story slowly unfolded it became plain that a single slave had incited this mass flight, planned it and timed it, divided the runaways into groups, and dictated in which direction each should go; and finally, departing last of all and alone, somehow managed never to be heard of again.

This leader was Tia Caleese.

Julie was left almost alone. The impact of events had

driven Cousin Celeste a long stride forward into senility, so that a great deal of weeping and hand-wringing and the frequent repetition of questions many times answered were all of her contribution.

And where was Jim Sam Delorme? Somewhere down the river, of course, but the gentlemen of the returning Regiment had landed and re-embarked so high above Boonville that they had not even seen the *Royal Oaks*, and could only say she was nowhere between Boonville and Ash Landing. The telegraph lines were stone-dead—not only the branch wire to Ash Landing but the main line along the railroad. The railroad itself was inactive for want of bridges, and the river traffic from below Ash Landing was limited to the trickle of small craft that had kept leaking away from Boonville, for a day or so, following the Federal victory.

These latter brought sparse, conflicting reports, none of them reassuring. Apparently the *Royal Oaks* was no longer at Boonville. You could hear any explanation you wanted to of what had become of her. She had steamed downriver, trying for Memphis. She was on the bottom, with loss of all hands. She had been commandeered by the Yankees. She had blown up and burned. She was being converted into a Yankee gunboat. Jim Sam was a prisoner. He had gone to St. Louis to protest. He was dead . . .

Mystified, sick with apprehension, Julie Delorme tried to find Shep Daniels, but could learn nothing of his whereabouts. She made up her mind to drive a team downriver, with such escort as she could find, or none. But first she had an errand she must complete; and she rode to the Ashlands' in the state of cumulative nervous tension to be expected, carrying the slender roll of blankets recovered with Rodger's saddle. She walked in unannounced, and first tried to find Rodge, calling his name up the stairs and through the empty rooms, without reply. She went then to the suite she knew to be Tyler Ashland's, knocked and gave her name through the closed door. Events and circumstances seemed to be herding her, a step at a time, into a course upon which she would never have been able to resolve.

Tyler Ashland had his boots off, and was slowly undressing, with a scared boy from the kitchen ineptly trying to help him. Not many would have been allowed to disturb him, in his present mood, but now he put on a dressing gown to receive Julie in his sitting room, and called to her to enter. In the last instant, on an impulse so unforeseen that it frightened her, she flicked out the blue sleeve that she had stuffed into the blankets for hiding, and let it dangle in view, as she had first seen. Then she went in, giving herself no time to ask what puppet strings had made her do that.

She crossed to her uncle, put the slim bedroom upon the library table beside which he stood, and delivered the kiss upon the cheek that was conventional between them. A sudden sick feeling that it was a Judas kiss she had given him impelled her to hide the blue sleeve, but it was too late.

"My dear," he acknowledged her, without expression.

"I've brought Rodger's bedroll home," she explained, "but I can't find him. It was lost in the woods when his horse ran away—you remember?—while you were taking the boat. Later, I sent his horse and saddle to the stables, but I thought I'd better keep this for him."

"Thank you. You may leave it with me, if you wish."

"I'm afraid it isn't exactly very nearly rolled. But I thought I ought to bring it exactly as we found it. I haven't looked into it, or anything."

Tyler Ashland now noticed that she had turned deathly pale. "Leave us," he said to the boy, who got out of there in a hurry. "I don't think you are being entirely frank with me," Tyler said gently. "What is it you suspect?"

"Nothing," she answered him, "I suspect nothing at all."

"The possession of a Yankee uniform is not necessarily, in itself, disgraceful. I, myself, until a very short time ago, expected to be wearing one."

"I know that, sir."

"As to why Rodger was carrying it to Boonville. . . . He may have hoped to be of service as a spy. It is not a service I regard as entirely honorable; although its entailment of the death penalty exonerates it, to a degree, in the eyes of some. However, Rodger may not have been aware of my views." He was speaking carefully, now, with the formality to be heard in courtrooms, where practitioners of the law never see, but only observe, never go, but always proceed.

"Of course, Uncle Ty."

That too ready "of course" was a mistake. "I see you are dissatisfied," he said.

"Why should I be dissatisfied, sir?"

"Perhaps because you might be wondering if Rodger had used this uniform before?"

"Sir?" Julie looked cornered, all but desperate; she had not been in control of the situation since she entered the room.

"Remember this," Tyler Ashland said. "Lately a good many thousands of Yankee uniforms have entered Missouri. It is hard to say that any particular one was worn at any particular place." He was certain now that she had some sort of definite information, and he was trying to get it out of her.

Julie's voice was trembling. She did not want to say what she was saying, yet somehow could not shut up.

"If you're thinking Rodge might have worn this uniform at Waynesville—"

"That is your suggestion, not mine."

"It can very easily be disproved. It would have to be a captain's uniform, first. One was there, so you know Rodge would not have been wearing one of lesser rank."

"How do you know this is not a captain's? Have you examined it?"

"I have already told you I did not!"

"Mind your tone," Tyler Ashland said.

The words were like a flick of a whip, and Julie steadied. When she spoke again her tone was quiet and cool, without fluster.

"I remind you that I am Julie Delorme. I am not on trial; I neither accuse nor stand accused. I came here in good faith to return your son's property, and I sung out for him before I came to you."

He was silent until he saw that she was about to excuse herself and withdraw. "I am sorry if I have spoken rudely," he said. "We both see something here that is in want of explaining. Certain undesired doubts require removal, for the same reasons that a bullet must be removed from a wound. I ask that you tell me what more you know."

"The captain at Waynesville got his shoulder board clipped by a bullet. If this tunic had been at Waynesville, it would have a new or mended right shoulder board."

"How do you know that?"

She cold not very well tell him that she had learned it from Trapper Daniels. Her sole reason for believing Trapper was that the detail had been meaningless when told, without purpose as an invention, and unlikely of recital unless it were true. "I thought everybody knew it," she improvised. "Wasn't it in Saloney Potter's testimony?"

"No. Or maybe . . . maybe it was. Perhaps I should only say I was not aware of it . . . until now."

Uncertainty had come into him, and suddenly she was sorry for him, he looked so old, and disheveled, and travel dusty. A tired old man. She said, "Will you excuse me, now, please? I have to see to—"

It was too late. She was cut off by a brisk knock, and Rodger Ashland came in without summons. For a moment he was stopped short by Julie's presence; and he saw, too, the rolled blankets upon the table, and the visible blue sleeve. His face did not change, but the too-correct precision that had come into Tyler Ashland's speech was also in his bow to Julie. All three were speaking and moving unnaturally, strangers to themselves and each other.

"I am interrupting," Rodger said; and he would have left the room.

"You are not. Now that you are here you will kindly remain," his father said. "Your cousin has brought in some of your equipment, lost the other day in the woods. The partially opened condition is that in which it was found. Nobody has looked into it, or disturbed it."

"Of course. Thank you, Julie. Were my carbine and my pistols recovered, do you know?"

Julie indicated that she did not know of their being found. "I'll leave you, now—I have to see about—"

"I ask that you stay," Tyler Ashland said to her.

"Sir," said Rodger, "I have come to ask your permission to depart."

"I don't recall having seen that blue jacket before," his father said, ignoring the request.

"You don't, sir? I suppose everyone has a blue jacket. And gold buttons, too, for that matter. I believe you have a set yourself."

"Bearing the coat of arms of the United States government?"

"I reject this line of questioning, sir," Rodger answered, without change of tone.

"That is your privilege. An accident has placed you in a peculiar light. I should think you would wish to clarify your position."

"Just what position, exactly?"

"You are carrying a Yankee uniform. The implication is that you have found use for it. The fact that you were carrying it to Boonville indicates with some certainty that you intended using it again. Yet its purposes remain unclear. Certain possible assumptions are unpleasant in the extreme."

"I'm sorry if you think so, sir."

"I will give you an example. You have said yourself that, in your belief, it was night riders, and not Yankee soldiers, who were wearing blue uniforms at the time and place of the Waynesville murders. I do not concede there to be the remotest possibility of your having been there. But I submit that your reticence is a sorry discourtesy in this instance."

"I haven't the faintest idea what it is you are asking me," Rodger said.

"By my information," Tyler said, "if you had worn that tunic at Waynesville, it would have to be the uniform of a captain, with a bullet-marked right shoulder board. I suggest that you vindicate my faith in you by showing it is nothing of the kind. For I remind you, we are not alone."

Julie cried out, "No—please, please—that's needless—"

"I'm afraid I must require it."

Rodger looked his father hard in the eye, while he very slowly turned a deep maroon; then just as slowly returned to his normal color. For a brief moment he turned his stare to

Julie. She met his eyes steadily, and though she was very pale, she gave no indication of the murderous anger that she saw there.

"I have asked your permission to leave your house," Rodger Ashland said. "I now propose to leave with or without it!"

Tyler Ashland held his voice low, but it was shaking with the effort. "You will get out of my house, and off my land, and you will not come back here while I live."

"I'll take my property," Rodger said, stepping forward to reach for the blanket roll.

"You have no property here," Tyler said, and swept the roll off the table and behind him, into a corner. "I propose to burn this wretched evidence. It can never tell me anything more than you have told me yourself. Now, get out!"

Rodger Ashland hesitated and a flicker of bewilderment showed through his anger. Perhaps he would never understand while he lived why his father, the hard-raiding leader of irregulars in the Border Wars, did not approve of what he had done. He turned his back and left the room.

"Bring me—tell—have somebody tell Captain Grover I must see him at once," Tyler Ashland said to Julie.

She made her escape.

✦ 41 ✦

CAPTAIN THOMAS F. (FOR FORTUNATUS) GROVER WAS A pleasant-faced and relaxed man in his early forties. He was a hemp planter in the middle range of importance, and his military title derived from his service in the Mexican War, for a short period of which he had held a brevet ranking. Quietly hearty, quietly friendly, he was well-liked by most of his class, and in consequence had served an unusual number of times as second in affairs conducted under the code duello; on two such occasions he had acted in behalf of Tyler Ashland. Yet, by his temperate habits and tolerant good humor, he had avoided participating as principal in even one.

He now allowed himself no sign of haste or impatience as he responded to Tyler Ashland's request. He had been intercepted in the act of taking the saddle, but he came to Tyler's sitting room without any indication that the delay was discommoding. He found Tyler slumped in his chair, staring blankly into the empty fireplace.

"I thank you for attending me," Tyler said, no more than glancing up; and fell silent.

Captain Grover was surprised by the uncommon phrasing, and by Tyler's failure to suggest he be seated; but he waited without remark.

"Pour yourself a brandy," Tyler said at last.

Grover went to the sideboard. "One for you?"

"I beg pardon? Oh. Nothing now . . ."

"You look as though you'd been thrown and sat on. By a tall horse. Can't say I blame you, though. It's about what's happened to us all." He brought a straight chair, and sat on its edge near Ashland, sipping his brandy.

"I taught him too much, and not enough," Tyler said.

"What?"

"All he has done, I myself have done through him. I brought him into the world. I made him what he is. The responsibility is solely my own."

"I don't follow," said Captain Grover.

"I'm sorry. I'm afraid I was talking to myself. Tom, I am going to have to kill my son."

"Ty, are you out of your head?"

"In a fair meeting, of course. . . ." He went on, coherently now, to explain to Tom Grover the crimes, and the Waynesville affair in particular, of which he believed Rodger Ashland to be guilty; culminating in what he considered to be his son's full wordless confession. He showed Captain Grover the crumpled blankets in the corner, which still contained the unexamined uniform—bullet-marked or not bullet-marked—which could clear or convict Rodger of involvement at Waynesville.

"You didn't even examine the evidence?" Grover demanded.

"Rodger was given the opportunity to present it. He did not."

"By Christ, Ty, I ought to fight you myself, in his defense!"

"Knowing him, I knew that the reason he did not clear himself was because he could not."

"Oh, for God's sake!" Disgusted, Grover went to the blanket roll in the corner, jerked it open, and shook out the blue tunic. Tyler Ashland did not turn his head as Grover examined the shoulder boards.

The right shoulder board had not been replaced or mended. The stroke of a grazing bullet had cut through it, straight across the middle, and there was a bloodstain, not extensive but unmistakable, on the fabric beneath.

Captain Grover stood undecided for some moments. Finally he wrapped the uniform in the blankets, tightly compact this time, and secured the straps that held it. He asked, "Do we know, with any certainty, where Rodger is now?"

Tyler Ashland believed he knew. He had been aware of the presence of Rodger's night riders at the cabin in the woods since first they came there.

"Suppose he's gone from there?"

"Your obligation will be ended. I realize that this must be irregular, in some respects, but circumstances force our hands. We will finish before sundown, or not at all."

"I believe I know you well enough," Grover said, "to feel sure that you'll shoot to kill, if that's what you walk out there to do. But what if he won't fire on you? Suppose he fires in the air? Code or no code, Tyler—that will amount to plain murder."

"I guarantee that he will kill me without the slightest compunction. If he can."

Grover mumbled something about supposed it could be looked on as an execution, if Ashland happened to be wrong. He considered for a little while longer, perhaps seeking an escape; he clearly had no liking for what he was being asked to do. But—

"All right," he said at last. "I'll act for you, Ty. If this is what you have to do."

✳ **42** ✳

SHEP AND TRAPPER DANIELS LAY IN THE EDGE OF THE WOODS, watching the ruined cabin across an open space of perhaps a hundred yards. This had been given over to a stand of second-growth chestnut, for a time, but Tyler Ashland liked chestnut for the open fires, and the numerous fireplaces in the Great House had punished the grove out of existence. Since then the area had been grubbed free of brush, but never seeded, so that only a ragged showing of knee-high weeds now stood where the trees had been. Beyond this the watchers were well fixed, able to see without being seen, while lounging comfortably—in so far as Trapper could find a comfortable position at all. They could even talk, though not much over a whisper.

From this advantage they had seen Rodger Ashland come here, his saddle packed for travel, but Shep had not let Trapper fire. The five riders who had been waiting for Rodger's orders in the cabin had still been there, then, and Shep didn't like the odds. Since then, three of them had left by a backwoods trail into the hills. Only Hobe and Yancey remained with Rodger; they were that much better off.

"You're gong to have to lance this shoulder again," Trapper said. His healed-over wound had abscessed deep inside, and though it had seemed greatly improved after Shep had opened it, the swelling had come back almost at once.

"Sure" Shep agreed. "We'll finish this today. Get you to someplace I can take care of you better."

"It was a big relief, the other time. Once the cutting-in was over."

"You sure stood it good. I don't know how you did it."

"They don't move around much in there, do they?" Trapper changed the subject, "Of course, so long as their horses are tied there at the side, we're all right. But what if Rodge don't start off until dark?"

"I'll walk over and call him out, I guess. He promised me a fight; maybe he'll stand by his word. I don't know. You'll have to cover me from here."

"I'll have to walk out with you. Get as close in as we can. I can't hit anything no more. Left-handed this way. Most especially in bad light."

"We'll see when the time comes."

Trapper let it go at that. More and more he let Shep make the decisions, without argument, and it made Shep feel that his brother was a whole lot farther down the hill than either one of them would admit. "This one last day," he promised again. "We'll get through it, Trapper."

"If only we do . . . I don't care so much what happens then." His determination to square the score with Rodge was all that was keeping him going. "I pretty near wish it would get dark soon. So we'd have to go in after them. And get this thing done, and past. I'm awful tired, Shep."

"I know." He would have left his brother in bed at the Bishop House, if there had been any way to make him stay there. "Just a little while now. A few more hours, at the very most."

But another thing happened first; for before Rodge showed himself again, they heard hoofs thudding softly in the cart track the woodcutters used. Tyler Ashland and Captain Grover appeared at the edge of the clearing and pulled up. One lone little Negro boy was trotting at Ashland's stirrup, to hold the horses.

"Now, what the hell here?" Shep said.

Captain Grover stepped down. The mahogany case that carried Ashland's dueling pistols was under his arm, but otherwise he was weaponless, as he walked alone across the open ground. Twenty paces from the cabin he stopped, and called Rodger Ashland's name. Rodger appeared at once. A heavy dragoon pistol was holstered at his belt, but of course he would not be expected to fight with that. He came directly, with neither haste nor hesitation, to where Grover stood; and they talked for perhaps half a minute, while Shep could not hear what was said. Then Grover signaled to Ashland, who had stayed in the saddle awaiting the outcome. Ashland dismounted, gave his horse to the little boy, and came forward on foot through the dusty weeds.

The two Ashlands and Captain Grover met in the middle of the field. Shep waited where he was, still puzzled as to what was happening here, while Grover gave brief formal instructions to the other two. But when Grover opened the pistol case, offering it first to Rodger Ashland, Shep knew without doubt what he was looking at. A curiously detached thought, with something of wonderment in it, went through some part of his mind. *These are the men the Yankees want to fight. How can they ever hope to win, against people like that? To beat the South they'd have to kill every last man, one at a time, and by hand....* He stood up and went out there.

"Now, hold your horses!" He shouted as he came near.

"What the devil do you mean by this?" Grover demanded as Shep came up.

"I have this man's pledged word to fight. I don't know anything about this affair you're setting up here. But I know my rights come first!"

"I represent Mr. Ashland. His rights here are my sole concern. You will either clear field, and at once, or I will fight you myself!"

"Very well," Shep said, meaning he was ready to fight Grover. Then he saw his error; he was throwing away all chance at the man he had come after, to kill a man with whom nobody had any quarrel at all. Kill him for being brave, and nothing more. He changed his meaning. "After you," he said. "I imagine he'll still be standing up when you're done with him. I'll fight him then."

"What you do then is no concern of mine. Now kindly move out of our way!" He was dissatisfied with the distance to which Shep first retired, and would not continue until Shep was placed well back toward the woods, and far to the side.

Then he added a final instruction, while the principals stood stony-faced.

Shep Daniels was angry, feeling balked, and cheated, but he was without recourse. He was hearing now the strange high, ringing note that seems to go with the presence of imminent death; a single unbroken note that increased and increased, generated by pressure of blood in the ears, in the brain, yet seeming to come from the sky, the earth, and the very air.

Grover had placed the principals back to back, the long barrels of the matched caplocks pointed straight up. He began to count "One—two—three—four—'" while the Ashlands stepped off in their opposite directions. Beyond, Shep saw that Yancey, then Hobe, came out of the ruined cabin, sliding along the wall toward the horses. They were not hurrying yet, and seemed only getting inconspicuously out of line, but their movements were wary and their rifles ready in their hands. Shep ran his hand over his carbine lock, and found it at cock, though he did not remember putting it there.

"—five—six—seven—eight—"

Tyler Ashland was stepping off to the count with a measured military pace, and there was a sense of fatalism in the way he moved. Without self-interest either way, Shep was suddenly convinced that the old man would never fire upon his son.

"—nine—ten—eleven—twelve— Turn!"

Rodger Ashland whirled and fired. His father turned sharply—was it to take the bullet in front?—but his pistol had not ben lowered as he pitched onto his face, his weapon discharging into the ground.

Rodger Ashland threw down the dueling pistol, pivoting toward Shep as he drew the heavy dragoon. Shep sat the carbine to his shoulder. Unhurriedly, almost deliberately, he aimed for the heart, yet as the dragoon pistol whipped up he was in time to fire. Perhaps he did not see the bullet strike, but his illusion was that he did; and he knew Rodger was dead as he fell.

Now Trapper's carbine cracked from the woods, and Shep glimpsed the aimed muzzle of Hobe's rifle in the instant that Hobe fell, and the rifle dropped unfired. Yancey fired once, his shout doubled by Trapper's second shot from the woods, but Yancey was not hit. He ran for the horses, jerked a tie rope free, and vaulted into the saddle. He had almost disappeared into the woodland trail when Trapper's carbine sounded once more, and brought him down.

Shep walked to where Ashland lay, turned on his back by Captain Grover. He looked half-dead, and mummified with age; but only his leg had been broken by Rodger's bullet, and he was not bleeding badly. He mumbled, "I missed my shot, I think."

"Sir," Captain Grover said, "your son is dead."

"I have no son," Tyler Ashland said. "I killed him slowly, many years ago."

Shep walked into the woods, and at first could not find Trapper, who had changed his position after his first shot, as he always did. Shep called his name, but got no answer; then almost stumbled over him in the brush. Trapper lay upon his carbine, one knee drawn up and cramped under him, and Shep saw by the position of the weapon that he had fired at least his final shot from his abscessed shoulder. He was breathing strangely, with an occasional great gulp for air, and his fingers clutched the turf. Yet he knew that Shep was there.

"Help me up," he said. "Cain't get my breath."

"Lie still." Shep knelt beside his brother, gingerly trying to find his hurt. No wound in the back, so Shep carefully turned him over. The ground was wet with blood where he had lain. Tearing open Trapper's shirt Shep found the bullet hole, still bleeding, but only slowly, now that he was on his back. It looked like an off-center heart shot, or very nearly one, just below the ribs, but it couldn't be that. Shep decided his brother had been shot while rolling over to change position after his first shot. It must have been the same shifting of ground after firing that he had learned in wild-hog hunting, long ago, and had used in the Black Mingo. But this time the bullet had caught him while he was momentarily on his back, head toward the enemy—a plunging shot, ranging downward through his vitals, and never coming out. Very few men had ever survived a wound like that, even with the best of surgery, but it had been done. Shep remembered an old man who in his youth had been shot sideways through the gut, so that he had a small scar at belt line on one side and a big blasted-out scar on the other; yet with all the internal damage there must have been, he had lived to be ninety-one years old.

But there was something worse.

"My leg's doubled under me," Trapper said.

Shep knew, then; for Trapper's legs were straight. The bullet had never come out because it was lodged in the spine. He made a pretense of moving Trapper's legs, and could tell that Trapper didn't feel his hands. "How's that?"

"That's all—all right now. . . ."

"Lie still, here," Shep said. "I'm going to send for the Doc."

"I ain't going any place," Trapper said.

No; he ain't going any place. Not ever again, without he's carried there. . . .

The sudden tears jumped to Shep's eyes again, as they had that time he had watched Trapper disappearing into the shadows of the swamp. It was so much the same, it was almost as if part of him had already known, back there in the Black Mingo, that they were at the beginning of the end.

He walked out to the middle of the dueling field, where Captain Grover was rigging a stretcher to carry Tyler Ashland off. The horse boy had scratched up an aged white-wooled Negro man from someplace, and they were about ready to carry Tyler Ashland away between them.

"Sir," Shep said to Captain Grover, "I ask your help. My brother is seriously hurt, there in the edge of the woods. It is quite possible you owe your life to the fight he made. I ask that when Mr. Ashland has been properly attended, you send the surgeon here."

"It will be a long time," Grover said. "There will have to be an amputation. It cannot be quickly done."

"In that case, will you send your horse boy to the Delorme House with a message? I am Shep Daniels. Please ask Miss Delorme if she will try to find help for my brother, out here. His wound is very bad."

Captain Grover looked at Shep strangely, but he said, "Yes, I will do that."

Shep went back to his brother, wondering what you did when a boy with a punctured stomach began crying for water.

Trapper lay perfectly still, his eyes closed, his face bloodless, saving every least ounce of life strength there was left to him. Shep thought he was unconscious, until Trapper asked plainly, "Where's Rodge?"

"Rodge is dead."

"Good."

Shep rolled up his jacket for a pillow, but Trapper's head lolled loose on his neck, and Shep was reminded that Trapper never used a pillow when he slept on his back. Might prop his head on his saddle, as they rested by their fire, but that was a manner of sitting up to talk. So he covered Trapper with the jacket instead. Nothing to do after that but sit cross-legged beside the hurt boy, fanning the flies away with a leafy branch for a fly whisk.

After a while two aged Negro women appeared, bringing an improvised stretcher. Shep thought at first that Julie might have sent them to bring in Trapper, but this was not their errand. They looked fearfully about them, without seeing Shep, then put down the stretcher beside Rodger Ashland's body while they went to look at the dead bushwhackers, which Shep could not see from where he was; all the time talking, and talking, in soft tones. "Do-o-o Jedus!" Shep heard one of them exclaim, but he made out nothing else. And finally they carried Rodger Ashland's body away.

A woods peewee was repeating its little clear, sweet song, now and then, somewhere deep in the cooler shades of the woodland, but nothing more varied the monotony of slowly passing time, for a long while. He supposed help of some kind would be sent to them eventually; yet he felt no strain of waiting, or suspense. Nothing but a stoic fatalism, as if all that was to be done in this place had been decided, and was a part of the past, changeless forever. He did not believe anything could be done for Trapper.

Then at last he heard a horse coming out the wood road. It was moving at a brisk rack, and he knew it was a Delorme horse, for Jim Sam had given Julie a couple of high-tailed Kentucky five-gaiters, while nobody else around there had any like that. Still, he didn't know who would be riding it—not for sure, anyway—until Julie came in view.

✷ 43 ✷

He stepped into sight from the bushes, so that she would know where they were, and waited there as she rode up. The horse blew thrumming snorts and kept shifting and swaying, disturbed by the ghost of gunpowder that still hung in the quiet air, and the smell of blood.

"How is he?" she asked.

He formed the answering words almost soundlessly, for fear Trapper might hear. "He's dying, I think."

"May I see him?" She was riding sidesaddle, in an ordinary dress, so now he lifted her down and tied her horse before he took her to where Trapper lay. She was looking different than he had ever seen her, in some ways more like the tomboy child he remembered from years ago; yet in other ways more entirely herself than she had ever been. She had combed her hair, but only tied it loosely at the back of her neck instead of taking time to put it up, so it hung free down her back, with wisps floating in straggles around her face where they didn't belong, unlike the careful arrangement he was used to seeing. Caleese had always whitened Julie's skin with the slightest stroked-on dusting of chalk powder, or something like that, and made her rub her cheeks with flannel (country girls used mullein leaves) to bring out a faint natural rosiness. These things had not been done, so that she looked more like a young woman made of common flesh, touched up a little with a moisture of perspiration, rather than an art work. And her dress—where had she dug up that? It was clean, but starchless and ordinary, with no stays worn under it; about the same thing Caylin Potter might have had. It was

Caleese, and not Julie, who had kept a façade of artificial perfection turned toward the world, and now Caleese was gone—forever, most likely.

And there was a sober absence of all sparkle. As she stood looking down at Trapper's gray face her eyes seemed very big, and dark, with violet shadows under them; and there were similar violet shadows at her temples, where a thready tracery of blue veins showed. It came to Shep that he ought to have done something about the dreadful great blood stain upon the grass beside Trapper, where Shep had turned him over; it was gumming and clotting in the afternoon heat, and drawing flies. He ought to have picked some grass to throw over it, or something. He was wondering if it was too late to do something like that when suddenly Julie's mouth twisted, she whimpered, and sat down close to Trapper, directly upon the blood stain itself.

He stared to stay, "Look out for the—"

But she shook her head. "It doesn't matter. A lot of things don't matter anymore." She spread her skirt a little more, to cover what part of the stain still showed.

"I guess they told you. . . ."

She nodded. "Captain Grover says you fired in self-defense."

"No—I went there to kill him. It was my whole intent. And he was your blood kin."

"His father denied him, and so do I. I'll never own to him as kin of mine while I live. But that doesn't signify, either. Four of us killed him, and not just you alone."

"Four? It was my bullet, Julie."

"All right. But without Trapper they were too many to one. You couldn't have got it done. And before that—his own father called him out; Uncle Ty doesn't want to believe yet that his own shot missed. And at the bottom of it—I was the one who killed him, Shep. For I opened his father's eyes."

"I don't understand. . . ."

"I didn't plan it, or mean to do it. But somehow the words came out of me, and it was done, with no way to turn back. And after that, Rodge was dead in about an hour. . . ."

They were silent for a time, listening to the metallic droning of the locusts in the trees, and to Trapper's troubled breathing. Shep didn't believe his brother was ever going to speak again. But now there followed a time when Trapper talked quite a bit, not strongly, or steadily, but using the outgo of his breath. Was it the last flare-up of vitality before death that people told about? It was spoken of in many ways, from a last opening of the eyes to whole hours of apparently great improvement, just before the end. No way to know what to expect, except that in itself it offered no form of hope. It was Julie who set it off, this time, without supposing that he could hear her.

"He's making a hard fight of it," she said. "He's very brave."

Trapper said faintly, unexpectedly, "It was Shep. He learned me. . . ."

Julie said softly to Shep, "He worships you, doesn't he? He always did."

"Nobody teaches anybody else to be brave," Shep said. "It's there or it ain't."

Trapper didn't answer that. He told Julie, "It was way back—the time Pap set his leg. And he never yipped. And later on I asked him—how he done it. I remember what he said—just as plain. He says—'Trapper,' he says, 'there wasn't nothing to worry about, Trapper. A thing only hurts about so much—and then it don't hurt no more than that.' "

He rested a minute; then his eyes turned to Shep. "I don't know how much," he said, "you remember about that night."

"Most of all," Shep said, "I remember Pap's face, as he set himself to pull; wishing every second he could take the hurt, instead of me. You know, I can't make up my mind to it that Pap's dead. I know it stands to reason. But I just can't believe, somehow, that he isn't alive, somewhere."

"He's dead, Shep. I've tried to tell you. But I always started to bawl . . .'"

There had been a young boy, Trapper told them, getting his story out in broke bits and pieces. This boy rode with one of Rodger Ashland's bands for a while, then wanted to quit, but they wouldn't let him. He made a run for it, and Trapper had helped him get away. "I could shoot a little ... in them days," he said wistfully, as if it had been a hundred years ago.

The boy had told him what had happened to Pap Daniels, whom the bushwhackers had talked about by name after he was dead. Pap had never gone back after more horses at all, not from Greenville nor any place other. What he had done was to make a lonely sniper's stand against the night riders, near the mouth of the Black Mingo Trace, to hold them back until his sons could get on through. He had gone back to kill bushwhackers, and he got him four or five, too, before they finally cut him off all sides, and finished him. . . .

It wasn't like Pap. All his life he had walked into the middle of feuds or anything else, but somehow he had always slid it off someway, so that he had never been in a real death fight, ever. Only, this one time he had fought with the chips down, and for a long time, so that the bushwhackers thought Shep, or Trapper, or maybe both, must be with him. That's what had made them so stubborn about catching up and doing away with the both, lest they had seen it all . . . . Trapper could not go on.

Julie picked up Trapper's hand, and pressed it to her cheek. "His hand's so cold," she said. "Just icy cold." She chafed Trapper's hand between her own, as if warming it could help him.

Trapper opened his eyes and saw her there, and he smiled. "Don't you let her go," he said to Shep. "Don't you ever let her go again."

Those were the last words he ever spoke.